Highwayman's Bite

Scandals With Bite Book 6

BROOKLYN ANN

To: Rob:

Don't let the vampires bite!

♥ Brooklyn Ann

Published by Broken Angels, an imprint by Brooklyn Smith

http://brooklynannauthor.com
contact@brooklynannauthor.com

Dedicated to my cousin, Annika Lilith Masten, a courageous and amazing woman.

And to my mom, Karen Ann. I still miss you.

Chapter One

Lancashire, England, 1825

Vivian Stratford peered out the carriage window and yawned, though sleep was impossible on this long journey. The full silver moon in the sky was so bright that the carriage lanterns were almost unnecessary. The rutted road to Blackpool was fully illuminated, a bright path to her impending isolation.

Vivian's father had packed her off to her reclusive uncle, who would keep her locked away until the scandal died down.

Madame Renard, Vivian's companion, made an indelicate snorting sound as she woke from her doze. "Have we arrived yet?"

Vivian shook her head. "No, but the moon is bright. Perhaps we can stop and have another lesson?"

Madame Renarde sighed and stroked her square jaw. "My joints are aching too badly for such rigorous exercise. Besides, it is not safe for women out in the dark."

"We are in the middle of nowhere," Vivian retorted a little sharper than intended. Immediately, she was contrite. "I am so sorry, Madame. I'm only weary of being trapped in this carriage. I want to stretch my legs and practice…"

Madame Renarde straightened her cap with a frown. "Your father told me to never allow you to touch a rapier again."

Vivian had expected as much, but hearing the confirmation still felt like a thrust to the heart. "Did he find out about you teaching me?" *Or worse, Madame's bigger secret?*

"No," Madame Renard said quickly. "And I will not stop teaching you. I know that fencing is your passion. Without passion, people wilt like flowers. But we must be careful, and I think it would be wise to keep our steel sheathed for a time. At least until we learn your uncle's habits, so we can discern a safe time and place to fence."

Yes, that sounded like the wisest course of action. Especially since it was Vivian's blade that landed her in this scandal-broth, which resulted in Father packing her off to her great-uncle's estate. But Vivian was veritably rabid with the need to have her sword in her hand. Those blissful moments of thrusts and parries, dancing on her feet with the ring of steel in her ears, were the only times she felt she had any control in her life.

The rest of the time, Vivian always had to submit to what someone else wanted of her. From her governess to her tutors, her dancing instructor, her father, and her suitors, she was always expected to comply, to play a part like a scripted actress that would end with her... *what?*

The unanswered question made her age-old panic slither over her like funeral crepe. While Vivian was aware that she was supposed to marry a suitable man with a good title and preferably a substantial income and bear him heirs, she couldn't stop from wondering, what else would there be? In all the stories of fair ladies and princesses, they ended when the heroine married her dashing hero. Why couldn't Vivian be more like a hero? Have adventures and defeat monsters just as Beowulf and Odysseus did in her favorite stories.

Her governess had told her such thoughts were unnatural. Her father only squinted and frowned. Most other ladies her age either shunned or mocked her for wanting more than landing a good match, even going so far as to say that with her small dowry and plain looks, she should be grateful for any match. In the face of such censure, Vivian learned to be silent about her unconventional thoughts and wordless sense of want for something more.

Only Madame Renarde understood Vivian's inner turmoil when she'd been hired shortly before Vivian's debut in Society three years ago.

"I know precisely what it is like to feel that the life Society expects of you is somehow wrong in a way that you cannot quite identify. Yet the notion haunts you like a shade." Madame Renarde once told her.

The paid companion had only been at Father's estate for two months before she'd come upon Vivian late at night out in the garden. Vivian had broken down in helpless tears without even knowing why. The French matron had pulled Vivian into her arms and coaxed the story out of her as Vivian rested her head on the companion's surprisingly broad shoulder.

"That is it, exactly," Vivian had said, wiping her eyes. "I only wish I knew what it was that I want."

"It will come to you." Madame Renarde stroked her hair. "Until you do, I advise that you find a hobby that gives you pleasure. Such can clear your mind and allow your deeper needs to come forth."

"I *do* have hobbies." Vivian had lifted her head from her companion's shoulder, slightly embarrassed that she'd been caught in such an emotional state. "I read, dance, and study various languages."

"Yes, and your dance steps are quite deft." The companion's gaze had turned speculative. "Wait here."

Vivian had sat on the marble bench, listening to the wind whispering through the leaves of the trees and rosebushes, her curiosity stretching the minutes to seem like hours. When Madame Renarde returned, Vivian blinked in astonishment to see two thin swords gleaming in the moonlight.

"You've brought rapiers?" she'd asked, wondering if she was dreaming. Vivian had never seen a woman with a sword, much less two.

"Would you like to learn how to fence?" Madame Renarde tossed one of the blades toward Vivian. The rapier streamed through the air in a gleaming arc and stabbed the grass beside Vivian like a javelin. She stared the quivering metal, fascinated by its delicate, deadly beauty. Slowly, she'd reached down and gripped the pommel, pulling the blade from the ground. A primal desire flowed through her being. The sword represented power. *She wanted it.*

"Yes," she'd whispered.

Madame Renarde executed a salute that was both elegant and theatric. "First you will learn the stances."

They'd trained almost every day. And sometimes, Madame Renarde would disguise Vivian and take her to witness fencing matches. Vivian longed to compete, but as a female, she'd never be permitted.

Madame Renarde was a master fencer, astonishingly quick and nimble for a woman in her forties. Vivian asked her how and where she learned, but it was two years before the woman trusted her enough with that story. And months more before she learned of her companion's ultimate secret.

A secret that her father must never uncover, or Vivian would lose her closest friend forever.

The memories cut off when the carriage jerked to a halt, throwing Vivian against the cushions, and making poor Madame Renarde fall to the floor. The horses shrieked and made the conveyance lurch again before a man's voice boomed, "Stand and deliver!"

"A highwayman," Vivian whispered, her pulse in her throat. She'd heard tales from her father of the times when the thieves ran rampant through England's country roads. But these days, highwaymen were rare.

Madame Renarde recovered first. She reached under the seat and withdrew her rapier, quick as the fox that was her namesake. Then she leapt up from her seat, positioning herself in front of Vivian.

When the carriage door was flung open, Renarde thrust her blade forward. Vivian heard a hiss of pain before a man came into view. The large slouch hat that he wore cast most of his face in shadow, but she could see an exquisite sculpted chin, mischievously arched lips—and the barrel of the pistol he pointed at them.

Madame Renarde sent the pistol flying out of the highwayman's grasp. Vivian expected him to flee right then and there, but instead, he brought his own blade to meet Madame Renarde's sword with a speed that made Vivian gasp.

The ring of steel was piercing in the closed space of the carriage.

The highwayman laughed. "I had not expected such a diverting encounter. You are quite good for an old man. I don't know why you hamper yourself with skirts."

Both Madame Renarde and Vivian sucked in sharp breaths. *How did he know?*

Madame Renarde had fooled everyone they'd encountered, including Vivian herself for several months. The shocking observation took the companion off guard, and her sword went clattering to the carriage floor.

"Don't you hurt her!" Vivian shouted and dove forward to meet the highwayman's blade with her own.

He moved back, visibly startled by her attack. Vivian continued to lunge, attacking him with fury of a magnitude that she'd never experienced. The highwayman deflected her blade with lazy parries, yet he continued to retreat.

Triumph swelled in Vivian's breast… until her feet touched the packed dirt road outside the carriage. He'd lured her out here so that he'd have more room to regain his offense. Sure enough, the highwayman danced at her and brought his arm across in a *Coup d'arrêt* attack. But it was a feint, she should have seen that. She barely got her blade back up in time.

"I see that you are a student of that Molly in the carriage," the highwayman said with a grin. His white teeth flashed in the moonlight. Something seemed off about those teeth, but she didn't have time to ponder it.

He moved into *reposte*, a counter attack that rivaled hers in speed and precision.

She matched his attack with the requisite parries, naming them in her head. *Tierce… quinte… septime.*

As they danced, and their rapiers clashed, Vivian realized two things. The first was that she could tell that he was holding himself back. He'd disarmed Madame Renarde with little effort, and yet Vivian was still holding strong. Yes, she was faster on her feet than the older woman, but Madame Renarde was quicker and more well-versed with her blade. Madame Renarde was a master who'd trained under someone even more impressive, yet this highwayman before her was equal, if not superior to her companion's skill. He moved beautifully, and Vivian could see that he was capable of more. She should be insulted that he was letting her continue the match. If not for her second realization.

She was enjoying herself.

As ludicrous as it was, her being outside in the middle of the English countryside in the cool September night, crossing swords with a highwayman bent on robbing her, should have been terrifying. Yet her blood sang in her veins, her face flushed with pleasant heat, and her heart pounded in exhilaration as they moved together, more exciting than any waltz.

"Flawless *passa-sotto*," he murmured as she dropped her hand to the soft grass and lowered her body to avoid his blade.

His praise warmed her all over. At last, a man appreciated her swordplay rather than scorning it. Vivian shook her head. Had she gone daffy? Why should she care what this thief thought of her? Furious that he was able to wreak such havoc on her emotions, Vivian redoubled her attack.

The highwayman grinned as if he read her thoughts. "I'm afraid I must cut this diversion short." In an executed move, he knocked the sword from her hand. "Out of respect for your defense of the Molly and the skill that he taught you, I will not rob your odd companion." Before Vivian could breathe a sigh of relief, he stepped forward and seized her arms. "But I cannot depart empty-handed."

He snatched the jeweled comb that held her hair neatly atop her head.

"How dare you!" she said as her brown tresses tumbled about her shoulders. "Give that back!"

"I have to take *something*." The highwayman chuckled. "I wager that fancy locket between those lovely breasts would fetch an even better price."

Vivian reared back, clutching the locket that had been her mother's and her grandmother's before her. The locket that held her mother's miniature. Desperation flooded her heart. "Please don't take it."

"I'll let you keep the trinket," the highwayman said, his gloved fingers lightly caressing the bare flesh of her upper arms. Gooseflesh rose up on her limbs, but surely it was only the chill night air. "In exchange for a kiss."

"I beg your pardon?" she whispered as her heart hammered against her ribs. She'd been kissed twice in her two Seasons and only one had been welcome. But she'd never had a man *ask* her for a kiss. Much less a highwayman who'd already taken her comb.

"A kiss from a beauty such as yourself to warm me in this cold, lonely night." The highwayman tilted his hat and favored her with a rakish grin. "That is the price I demand. That, or your locket."

Heat flooded Vivian's cheeks as she studied him. His eyes glittered in the moonlight, but the shadow of his hat made it impossible to discern their color. From what she could see of his nose, it was straight and pleasing. Her eyes traveled back down to his firm, masculine jaw, and the sharp curves of his lips. Her mouth went dry as she whispered, "Very well."

She rose up on her toes and lifted her chin to meet him. In time with her move, he lowered his head. Their lips pressed together like the meeting of their swords. His hands slid down to clasp her waist and she reached up to loop her arms about his neck. He deepened the kiss like a *Coulé,* sliding his lips over hers in a testing exploration as he'd done with his blade.

Vivian moaned and opened her mouth further, submitting to him even as she reveled in the taste of him and the forbidden sensations he wrought. This was no chaste peck on the lips like she'd received from an awkward suitor. This was passion made flesh.

Suddenly, he released her with a ragged gasp. "With kisses like that, I'd soon beggar myself. I will depart before I am tempted to ask for more." He saluted her with his sword. "Thank you for the diverting match and your sweet kiss. I will dream of you."

With a rakish tip of his hat, he disappeared into the shadows.

Chapter Two

Rhys Berwyn clutched the jeweled comb tight in his gloved hands, hoping a few of the young woman's mahogany tresses remained between the silver teeth. Although his haul from this robbery was shamefully meager—only the comb and a few pence and shillings from the driver—it was the most memorable encounter he'd had. Rhys had encountered armed carriage drivers and gentleman passengers countless times, but never had he met resistance in the form of a man disguised as a woman, nor an actual woman.

When he'd disarmed the Molly, the attack from the young beauty caught him off guard. Admiration brought a smile to Rhys's lips. It had been ages since anyone had unbalanced him so handily. The young lady was very good for a novice. Her *Coup d'arrêt* and *Raddoppio* were completely flawless. He hadn't been able to help himself from slowing himself down and dragging out the duel just to see what she was capable of.

He couldn't remember having a better time. For those few minutes when Rhys and the beauty danced with their swords, Rhys forgot all about his multitude of troubles, always being a hairsbreadth away from death, and the people who would suffer if he met his end before accomplishing his goal.

For those blissful moments, none of that mattered. The only things that existed were his feet on the grass, matching the beauty's step for step, the flush blooming in her full cheeks, the sparkle of excitement in her eyes, and then her kiss.

And oh, what a kiss. Though Rhys often claimed kisses from the beautiful women of whom he divested of coins and jewels, tonight's kiss had been so much more. Somehow, in that dark-haired beauty's embrace, he'd been transported to paradise.

And that was dangerous. He couldn't lose himself for a second, lest he risk getting caught. For if he were taken—

Rhys shook his head, unwilling to think about such dismal prospects. Before he reached the seaside cave where he hid during the day, he stopped and scented the air for any sign of pursuers.

When he was certain no one was lurking in wait, Rhys climbed down the cliff face and swung into the cave through an entrance that most would never find. The first few meters were treacherous, with up-thrusting rock and stalagmites. Then it smoothed to a sandy path.

At last, Rhys reached the door to his sanctuary, a door he'd carved himself to seal the tunnel, and outfitted with a heavy lock.

He unlocked the door, lit the lantern on a stone shelf and looked upon his meager furnishings with a degree of comfort. He'd worked hard over the decades, carving all these shelves, and constructing bunks for when other rogue vampires took refuge with him.

Placing the beauty's comb on the shelf containing his cache of stolen jewelry, Rhys then moved to a crevasse in the cave wall and withdrew the sack of coins he'd been accumulating. He reached in his pocket and added the shillings he'd taken from the beauty's coachman.

He tied the sack to his belt and left the cave. As he rushed to his next destination, several miles north and across a river, Rhys prayed he'd brought enough money.

The once prosperous farm sprawled before him. The stable roof was patched with crude wattle and daub. The hole in the barn roof had grown larger, the wind moaning through it as if mourning the slow death of the structure. An owl flew out of the hole, hooting as if reprimanding Rhys for his late arrival.

Rhys squared his shoulders and crossed the weed-choked field, where grain and barley had once turned the land gold. With no one to plow it, it had gone fallow.

He passed collapsed tenant cottages and ramshackle stables before he reached the main house. At least the roof was still intact, though the moss covering the shingles and the chipped paint on the walls gave the once noble structure a despairing appearance, like an aging courtesan.

Rhys fought off his melancholy and walked up the creaking steps, wondering how long the rotting wood would hold. He grasped the rusty knocker and rapped the solid oak door that would likely outlast the rest of the house.

A few moments later, he heard shuffling footsteps from inside the house, followed by the heavy clatter of metal as the locks were unfastened. The door opened just a crack and the hollow copper eyes of a woman in her early-thirties peered out. Suspicion and worry vanished as she recognized him.

"Rhys!" Emily opened the door and embraced him. "It has been too long since you've last come. I've been so worried."

He held one of his only remaining relatives and stroked her hair. "You should know by now that I'll always return."

"Don't lie to me, Rhys." She drew away and eyed him solemnly. "You could get caught any time. The newspaper says that there will be more patrols on the country roads."

"I will be all right. I know what I am doing." Though she was partly right. Although it wasn't the constables he had to worry about, it was others. In time, they could discover his activities and trap him.

Not wanting to think of all the potential and death looming over him, Rhys, pulled the sack of coins from his pocket and pressed it into Emily's work-roughened hands. "Has *he* been by yet?"

There was no need to specify who *he* was. The Viscount of Thornton loomed over them like a dark specter. Due to Emily's late husband's foolishness with money and love of gambling, Lord Thornton held the mortgage on the family farm. The husband had fallen behind on repayment long before he died, and Thornton was constantly sniffing about, trying to oust Emily and her children from the farm. Only Rhys's contributions staved him off.

Emily took the sack with a nod. "He says that unless I have paid the hundred and fifty pounds in full by the end of the month, my children and I have to leave."

"That black-hearted scoundrel! The month is nearly half gone!" Despair pooled in Rhys's belly. He'd never be able to steal that much money so quickly. "I'll think of something," he said, forcing himself to sound confident. "Use the money I gave you for food."

"I'd considered buying a calf." Emily sighed. "But it could not grow enough in a month to be worth the investment."

More footsteps clattered on the stairs as Emily's children raced down in their night shirts. "Cousin Rhys!" they shouted. "You've come back!"

Rhys embraced the boy and girl, amazed that even in little over a fortnight, they seemed to have grown. "Jacob, Alice, it is a joy to see you."

"Stay this time," five-year-old Alice pleaded. "You always leave."

Rhys shook his head. "I have to leave, Poppet. There is important work to be done." Such as coming up with a hundred and fifty pounds by month's end. "But I can stay for an hour or so."

Emily regarded her children with a weary look. "I'll make tea."

Once settled with his family at the polished maple dining table, the cloth long since sold, Emily told him about the farm. She and the children had managed to grow some herbs and vegetables and sell them at the market along with several bushels of apples from the orchard. They'd found a cache of coins her husband had hidden behind the barn after the cat had another litter of kittens. It had been enough to buy salted beef and fish to tide them over for winter and more importantly, an ox to pull the plow in the north field and seed to plant corn next Spring.

This news should have filled him with joy, but Lord Thornton had taken it away. Just as Emily, a young woman alone with small children, was bringing the farm back to life, the blackguard was going to foreclose it anyway.

Rhys did his best to conceal his grim disposition and focus on the children's smiles as he gave them sweets, and the comfort of the house, warmed by the fire he started. After tea, he rose from the table.

"I'm afraid I must go." Regret imbued his words.

"Must you?" Emily circled the table to meet him while the children echoed similar protests. "Surely it is safer for you if you stay here."

Rhys shook his head. "I cannot be traced to you." He took her arms and met her gaze. "I will find a way to either produce that money, or to persuade Thornton to give you more time."

"Be careful, Rhys," Emily whispered.

"Always."

Once outside, Rhys gathered firewood. From the look of the diminishing pile, he would have to return to the farm soon to chop more.

Then again, if Lord Thornton was going to take the farm, perhaps he shouldn't bother. The thought filled him with impotent fury. That nabob had plenty of land and money of his own. He didn't need any more.

Instead of heading straight back to his cave, Rhys dashed to the outskirts of Thornton's property. Making certain he stayed downwind, Rhys glared balefully at the stately manor house, with its elegant columns, covered veranda, and French doors. How could one have so much and others so few?

He didn't know what drew him here, putting himself in danger like this. If Thornton's guards caught wind of him, he'd be taken in an instant.

Then he heard the clatter of hooves and the roll of carriage wheels off in the distance. Who was this? Thornton wasn't one to have visitors.

When the conveyance drew closer, Rhys's jaw dropped as he recognized it. The beauty he'd robbed earlier in the evening was inside.

The front door of Thornton Manor opened, and his lordship stepped out to meet the carriage.

After the driver opened the door, Thornton handed the girl down.

Her voice was barely audible, but Rhys still heard one word as she addressed the viscount. "Uncle."

Rhys covered his gaping mouth to hide his gasp. The viscount had a niece? On the heels of his shock came a plan. He'd have leverage.

The fencing master disguised as a lady's companion exited the carriage next. From the abrupt stiffening of the viscount's shoulders, it appeared that Thornton couldn't tell what to make of the odd person either.

The mystery captivated Rhys like nothing else. What kind of woman travelled with a fencing master? And did her father know about the companion's identity? The disguise was very well done, as if the man had been playing the part for decades. But Rhys and Viscount Thornton had their own ways of seeing through such subterfuge, no matter how clever.

"Vivian," Thornton's voice carried in the wind. "Come with me to my study. There is something we must discuss in private."

Oh, how Rhys wished he could be privy to that discussion. But now the beauty had a name. *Vivian.*

Before he risked being seen, Rhys melted back into the shadows and quickly made his way back to his haven. His mind spun with all he learned. His plan would be the most dangerous endeavor of his long life, but worth it if all went right. But the danger could not be ignored. Not only was Aldric Cadell the Viscount of Thornton, he was also the Lord Vampire of Blackpool.

Rhys licked his fangs and shivered. And he'd come so close to feeding on Blackpool's niece. If he'd succumbed to temptation, the Lord Vampire would have had Rhys's scent, and all would be lost.

When he returned to the seaside cliffs concealing his cave, Rhys paused and scented the air once more for signs of vampires from either Preston or Southport. Yes, his hiding place was a no-man's land, but legitimized vampires often did not care about such scruples. To them, rogue vampires had no rights even for a moment's safety.

But if Rhys pursued the madcap plan forming in his mind, he'd forsake all rights to safety of any kind. He would be committing the worst of crimes under vampire law. All chances of eventually becoming a legitimate citizen would turn to ash.

The tired eyes of his cousin Emily—in truth she was his great-great-great grandniece—and the wan faces of her children flashed in his mind. If Rhys succeeded with his plan, his family would be saved. And that was all that mattered.

Once the safety of his kin was assured, Rhys no longer had a reason to live anymore.

Chapter Three

Aldric Cadell, Viscount of Thornton, and Lord Vampire of Blackpool, surveyed his great-great-great grand-niece with annoyance. When he'd been asked to take her in for a year to quell some inane scandal, he'd expected an awkward young miss who'd likely been launched too soon and didn't have a grasp on the rules yet. Or perhaps a vulnerable maid who'd fallen prey to a rake.

He'd not expected a steely-eyed vixen accompanied by a Molly for a companion. Did her father know that this Madame Renarde he'd written of was not what "she" seemed? Somehow, Aldric doubted it. Humans were easily fooled and had a poor sense of smell. Besides, the more significant question was whether Vivian was aware of her companion's secret.

After asking Vivian to see him about the matter in his study, Aldric looked to Vivian's father's carriage driver and the companion. Aldric addressed the driver first. "I will have my stable boy rub down the horses and Jeffries, my footman, can provide you with victuals, a bath, and a room for the night before you depart." He then turned to Madame Renarde. "As for you, Madame, my butler, Ames, will escort you to the drawing room and provide refreshment while you await my niece."

Renarde bobbed a curtsy, unable to see discern any suspicion. "Yes, my lord."

Aldric blinked. Though the companion's voice was indeed on the deep side, it still managed to sound womanly. Like the voice of a sweet grandmother. He also noted the protective glint in the companion's eyes as Aldric took Vivian's arm and led her away. Whatever this person's purpose, Renarde at least definitely cared for his niece's well-being.

Once Vivian was seated in front of the desk in his study, Aldric poured them some wine from his cabinet.

Placing a glass before his niece, he sat and took a drink of his own. "How was your journey?"

She took a ladylike sip and set her glass on the desk. "Quite dull, until we were stopped by a highwayman."

Aldric choked on his wine. "I beg your pardon?" he managed between coughs.

"We were stopped by a highwayman. He stole my comb and all the driver's money, but otherwise left us unharmed." A blush crept up her cheeks and down her slim neck. A neck that was still adorned with a gold chain and a locket. Something a thief would have had off her throat in a thrice.

She wasn't telling him everything about the encounter. Aldric studied her closer and saw that indeed, without the comb, her dark hair tumbled about her shoulders. But it was in such disarray, like she'd been out in the wind. And she smelled of dry sweat. On a cool autumn evening such as this, the carriage could not have been that warm.

"I will want to know more of your encounter with this blackguard. Where you were, and what happened to make him depart so suddenly before report the incident to the constable." Aldric eyed her sternly. "But for now, there are other things I am curious about. Your father tells me you had a bit of a scandal in London, yes?"

Vivian nodded. "I challenged Lord Summerly to a duel."

Aldric was thankful that he hadn't taken another sip of wine, else he would have spewed it across his desk. "You did *what*? Why in the name of heaven would you think to engage a man in pistols at dawn?"

His niece calmly sipped her wine. "Not pistols. Rapiers. And I had perfectly good reason for doing so. Summerly propositioned that I should be his mistress and put his hands upon my person. That impugned my honor, so I thought I was well in my rights to defend myself."

She had a point. Reluctant admiration welled in his chest. *However*... "While I agree that this cad did indeed besmirch you with his proposal, it is not proper for a woman to duel, much less defend herself. That is a gentleman's duty."

"If I had told any gentleman that Summerland had absconded with me and held me alone in the Cavendish's conservatory, I would have been blamed and still been ruined. At least this way, I was able to assure everyone that I was the virtuous party." Vivian lifted her chin, daring him to challenge her.

Once more, her logic was sound. She would have been saddled with blame and scandal no matter which way the dice fell. Still, what kind of woman would even think of fighting a gentleman with a rapier. "Do you even know how to fence?"

"I do." Pride rang in his niece's voice.

"Who taught you?" he asked, though he already suspected.

He watched the multitude of thoughts skitter across her face. First the temptation to lie, then resignation for the truth. "Madame Renarde."

Oh yes, her companion. Yet another topic that must be addressed immediately. "Are you aware that Madame Renarde is really a Monsieur?"

Her eyes widened, not in surprise at the fact, but at his knowledge. "How did you know?"

"I have a good eye for seeing through deceptions." He leaned forward and lowered his voice. "Does your father know what your companion is hiding under those skirts?"

Vivian shook her head so violently that locks of her hair slapped her cheeks. "Please don't tell him. I do not wish to lose my only friend."

"If you can assure me that Renarde's intentions are honorable, I may consider keeping your secret." Aldric said grudgingly. Her talk of having no other friends also concerned him. "Though I must say, I do not countenance deception. Is this person truly from France?"

Vivian finished her wine with an unladylike gulp and took a deep breath to gather her courage. "Madame Renarde escaped during the revolution. There is no home for her in France any longer, so she is loyal to England and only wants to live out the rest of her days doing honest work."

"Honest work?" Aldric snorted and refilled her glass. Though this… person was not an enemy of his country, he was still suspicious. The situation was so queer that he had trouble wrapping his head around it. "A man pretending to be a lady's companion? Why do you insist on calling him 'she?'"

"Because she has the heart and spirit of a woman," Vivian said fiercely. "All her life, she felt that there was a mistake in her birth. When she first put on ladies' clothing, she felt right."

"And you believe… her?" He had trouble with the pronoun.

"Yes." Vivian took another sip of her wine and leaned forward, her teeth bared in a sneer. "Women have no rights under the law. We are chattel, doomed to be imprisoned and manipulated by male whims. We have no recourse if a man wrongs us, as you are observing this moment with my presence here. We are subject to the most suffocating rules of how we are to behave. I cannot imagine a man willingly choosing such a life.

So Madame Renarde must indeed be female in spirit to thrive in a woman's lot in life."

From her impassioned speech, it was clear that Vivian told the truth. Whether or not this Renarde was honest remained to be seen. Aldric sighed. "Very well, I shall keep quiet about the matter for now."

Gratitude welled in her large grey eyes. "Thank you, Uncle."

"We'll talk more later. Let us see you and your companion settled in your rooms." Aldric rose from his seat and escorted his niece back downstairs to the drawing room, where Renarde was sipping a cup of tea and warming herself by the nearby fire.

Immediately, the companion rose and curtsied. "My lord, it is a pleasure to make your acquaintance." If Renarde was aware of Aldric's suspicions, 'she' did not let on.

"Madame Renarde," Aldric said with a slight bow. The companion's voice and body language were feminine indeed. If not for his preternatural senses, he may have been fooled as well. At least Renarde had been honest with Vivian… as far as he could discern.

Now he addressed both his niece and her companion. "Welcome to Thornton Manor. Although the house is isolated, I do hope you'll find it to be cozy. I'm afraid my illness prevents me from being about much during the day, but the servants should see to your every need."

Just like his previous descendants who'd visited him over the centuries, Vivian blinked at his declaration. However, he also detected a glimmer or relief in her eyes. From her talk of male tyranny, he wondered if her father was a cruel man.

Once settled beside his niece, Aldric poured her a cup of tea. "How was London? I haven't been there in over a year, and I am eager for news."

For the next hour, they spoke of the goings-on in Town, the balls, operas, weddings, children born, and the weather. Aldric studied Renarde, watching for signs of disingenuousness, yet all he could discern was that this companion genuinely appeared to care for Vivian. And that may be sufficient for Aldric to refrain from telling Vivian's father about Renarde's secret.

Maybe.

When his guests were visibly concealing yawns of exhaustion from their journey, Aldric had the servants heat tubs of water for baths, and bade them good night.

He was tempted to ask more about their encounter with the highwayman, but decided it could wait. For now, it was enough that his niece had arrived safely.

Instead, he left the house to seek his meal for the night and ponder on this firebrand niece of his.

This one was as free-spirited as his sister had been. From the scandal Vivian caused and her unconventional friendship with her companion, Aldric suspected that she'd cause a fair bout of mischief before she left his home.

All the more reason to ensure she did not remain here long. Although he did enjoy providing a haven for his mortal family from time to time, he could not risk having his own secrets discovered.

The scandal about her attempted duel was far more serious than he'd anticipated. Very few gentlemen would countenance having such a willful, rebellious wife. Furthermore, she was untitled, and her dowry would have been nonexistent had he not contributed a generous sum. Still, the pot would need to be sweetened further.

Perhaps if he deeded her some land, a match with her would be more appealing to a worthy suitor. Aldric had properties throughout England as well as one in Spain and another in France as vampires had to move every half century or so before the local humans noticed they did not age. But he did not wish to part with those. He did hold mortgages to a few farms, however, and he was intending on foreclosing on the Berwyn land. The widow of the wastrel who'd tricked Aldric into loaning with no ability to repay had been putting forth a valiant, yet pitiful effort to pay Aldric off, but even a halfwit could see that there was no chance of her closing the debt in her lifetime.

Aldric sympathized with the woman, he truly did. As it was, he'd allowed her to give him her meager payments and care for her children, giving her time to find a new husband to perhaps take over the loan, or for her to give up and find some relatives to stay with or a situation in service.

And yet the stubborn wench clung to her failing farm and Aldric eventually lost patience and demanded full payment at months' end. Then he would seize the farm. The fields, orchard, and buildings were in dreadful shape, but land was land. Perhaps it could go to Vivian as part of her dowry.

He rose from his desk and rubbed his temples, between providing for his wayward niece and dealing with the widow's mortgage, he'd have no peace in the foreseeable future until both were resolved.

Chapter Four

Vivian yawned again as she made her way downstairs for breakfast. She'd barely gotten a decent wink of sleep last night. Her body was still jarred from the long carriage ride, her mind worried endlessly about how she and her uncle would get on, and her heart pounded from memories of the highwayman's indecent kiss.

If she'd known kissing could be so spellbinding, she very well could have been ruined in a more traditional manner. Not that she would have allowed Lord Summerly or even any other gentleman of her acquaintance to get so far. None of them captivated her like the mysterious thief had. If Vivian closed her eyes, she could still see the rakish glint of his eyes, his flashing smile, and hear his decadent, low laughter.

Frowning, she paused on the stairwell and took a few deep breaths to calm her inappropriate thoughts. Was she mad? The man had held up her father's carriage, pointed a gun at her, and robbed her and her father's coachman. She shouldn't be simpering after him like he was one of King Arthur's knights.

Madame Renarde was already seated at the table with a heaping plate of morning victuals. "Good morning, *Cherie*. Did you sleep well?"

"Not really." Vivian smiled at her friend's ever hearty appetite as she took her plate and served herself a few pieces of bacon, a sausage, and a scone. "Did you?"

"Like the dead." Madame Renarde spread jam on one of her pieces of toast. "The carriage was so dreadfully uncomfortable that I could never nod off properly since we left London. And the inns on the way were little better."

Vivian couldn't disagree with that sentiment. The bedchamber her uncle had given her was more luxurious and comfortable than her own at home, yet she'd tossed and turned all the same.

Blast that man! She didn't even know his name, and if God was good, she'd never see the scoundrel again.

She needed to put him out of her mind. There were more important matters facing her. Such as her uncle's knowledge of Madame Renarde's identity. Both he and the highwayman had known right away when countless others had taken Vivian's companion at face value. What had tipped them off?

Vivian nibbled on a piece of bacon and surreptitiously studied her companion. Her chin was free of stubble. Her neck was covered with the lace collar of her modest dress, so no

Adam's Apple could be discerned, though from what Vivian had seen, it wasn't very prominent anyway. Madame Renarde's corset gave the impression of a bosom, especially as she was on the plump side and though her jaw was square, she'd met biological women with more masculine features.

"Is something wrong?" Madame Renarde asked. Her blue eyes were wide with concern.

Should she tell her friend that her uncle knew her secret? Vivian weighed the idea carefully. On one hand, it would be courteous to give Madame Renarde a warning in case her uncle wrote Father, for she would be sacked immediately if that happened. On the other hand, Uncle had seemed to be very understanding of the situation and willing to consider keeping the secret. Vivian didn't want to worry her friend needlessly if all would be well. She decided to hold her silence and observe Uncle's interactions with Madame Renarde to see which way the wind blew.

Vivian shook her head and voiced another concern. "I am only worried how I will get on here. Uncle is known to be eccentric and reclusive, and though I am not a picture of normalcy either, I do not know if he will like me. He interrogated me quite rigorously about the scandal I caused."

"Did he seem angry?" Her companion signaled the footman to clear their plates.

"I couldn't tell." She shrugged as she rose from the table. "He is more difficult to read than Father."

Madame Renarde nodded. "Yes, he was quite enigmatic. Do you suppose he'll be down for breakfast soon?"

Vivian shook her head. "He said his illness keeps him from being about during the day. He will be down for supper, though."

"That poor man." Madame Renarde sounded genuinely sympathetic, but then she smiled. "That could work in our favor for our exercises. Shall we explore the estate?"

Vivian grinned. A good bout of fencing was just what she needed. Perhaps it would banish the memories of her last match. "That sounds lovely."

Arm in arm, they walked through the rooms of the main floor, but didn't venture upstairs so as not to disturb Vivian's sleeping uncle. Madame Renarde was delighted with the game room, complete with a billiards table and dartboard. Vivian preferred the library, with its walls of books, massive fireplace, and cozy chairs. The ballroom was the most neglected, its scratched floor and aged décor making it apparent that Lord Thornton did not entertain often. Vivian was somewhat relieved. She was never comfortable when hordes of people invaded her home in London.

Quite hypocritical since she didn't mind invading others' homes for balls and musicales, but Vivian never claimed to justify her sentiments.

They then walked the grounds outside. Vivian lifted her face to the warm sunshine, a rarity in England in the Autumn. If she'd still been in London, she would have been forced to shield her face with a parasol or bonnet. Perhaps being exiled wouldn't be so bad.

Lord Thornton's gardens were simple almost to the point of being crude compared to others Vivian had seen. The rose bushes were a wild thicket of buds and thorns, the shrubs were shaggy, and there was very little in the way of other flowers.

However, between the thick wall and the tall shrubbery, the place would be perfect for her and Madame Renarde to practice their fencing. Vivian saw the same idea reflected in her companion's twinkling eyes and satisfied smile.

"Shall we fetch our rapiers?"

They practiced for two hours, blades ringing in the peaceful afternoon.

"You are getting to be quite proficient." Madame Renarde saluted Vivian with her blade. "No wonder you were able to hold your own against that brigand."

Heat crept up Vivian's cheeks. Drat. Why did Madame Renarde have to remind her of *him*? "He was holding himself back intentionally because I amused him."

"Perhaps," her companion said agreeably. "I think more because you are comely, and he liked you. From the look of that kiss, it is fortunate that we likely will never encounter him again."

Vivian gasped. "You saw that?"

"I saw everything." Madame Renarde's blue eyes sparkled with mischief. "I recovered my sword quick enough and was about to return to the fight, but I saw that you were doing quite well on your own. There was no need for me to interfere until he disarmed you. But then the sheer cheek of him asking for a kiss compelled me to remain behind and see how that played out. A most riveting diversion, I confess."

"You're supposed to protect my virtue," Vivian said with a laugh.

"Eh, in France, kisses are not seen as the hazards they are in this country." Her companion gave a shrug that was decidedly French. "Besides, I had his pistol pointed at him the entire time. If he'd tried for more than your lips, I would have put a ball in his head."

Vivian shuddered at the gruesome image even as she beamed in admiration. Back when she was a *Monsieur*, Renarde had been a soldier. She would have indeed been capable of killing the highwayman if she'd had the inclination. Thank heavens Vivian had Renarde with her rather than a dour dragon of a companion who would have likely fainted at the sight of a highwayman and left Vivian with no knowledge or capability of defending herself.

She embraced her companion with a laugh. "Oh, how I love you, dear friend."

"And I love you, *Cherie*," Madame Renarde kissed her cheek. "You have a pure heart, to accept me as I am. I do not have to hide from you. Do you have any notion as to how rare that is?"

Vivian shook her head, though she had an inkling. After all, Madame Renarde was the only person she who understood and accepted Vivian's oddities. "I wish more people would at least tolerate those that do not fit the common mold of society. I wish society wouldn't try to break down individuality and would instead welcome people in all varieties so long as they were good. Like nature gifts us with wildflowers of all colors, yet in our gardens, the roses are one hue."

Madame Renarde nodded thoughtfully before rising from the bench. "Come, we should take our swords inside and change before His Lordship comes downstairs for the night."

When Lord Thornton did come down for supper, Vivian was warmed at his genuine kindness and sincere efforts to get to know her and Madame Renarde better. Conversations with her father at meals had been stilted and dull, but in Thornton Manor, the lively talk went on for hours. Uncle had long been known to be a recluse, but perhaps he hungered for news of the outside world.

It was only when her uncle left the table to embark on a solitary walk when she noticed that he'd barely eaten.

And that was only the first of many oddities she observed about him. It seemed that nighttime walks were a routine for Uncle that he followed religiously. With his illness keeping him from going out during the day, she could understand that he'd want a bit of fresh air, but his absolute insistence on going alone struck her as queer. Most people of her acquaintance preferred company when they took a stroll.

Another strange thing was the fact that Lord Thornton had very few servants, and most were elderly at that. There was only one butler, Fitz, the housekeeper, Mrs. Potts, and one footman, Jeffries, who also doubled as a driver. The chambermaid also assisted the cook. There was no valet, and Madame Renarde had to act as Vivian's ladies' maid. Vivian knew the skeleton staff was not due to Uncle having a lack of funds, for it was well known that he was a wealthy man. Perhaps he just did not bother to have so many people about caring for one man. After all, the estate was in capital shape. Villagers came in three times a year to dust the manor from top to bottom, and a crew of gardeners tended the grounds once a month.

Despite Uncle Aldric's eccentricities, Vivian quickly became quite fond of him. They played chess together in the game room and he even taught her how to play billiards. He recommended excellent novels from the library and they spent many delightful hours discussing them.

After only a week at Thornton Manor, Vivian realized she was happier here than she had been in London. The neighbors came calling too early for the nocturnal schedule they'd adopted, but out in the country, things were not as rigid as in Town, so the visitors forgave Vivian's yawns and some even vowed to come by later.

The closest neighbors, the Carringtons, brought Vivian and Madame Renarde on a carriage ride through the village of Blackpool. Vivian breathed in the salty sea air, cleaner and brisker than the London air and admired the sight of the waves lapping the stony shore of the coast. Beautiful cottages lined the straight streets, and elaborate hotels stood near the beaches for all who visited to indulge in sea bathing.

The best aspect of staying with her uncle came when he once more abruptly called her to his study.

He poured them glasses of wine and did not prevaricate. "I am told that you and Renarde fence in the afternoons."

Vivian's glass paused on its way to her mouth. Would he forbid it? Would he tell her father? "We do," she answered warily.

"So you were not jesting when you intended to duel that rake in London," Lord Thornton inquired in an unreadable tone. His eyes narrowed. "And where did Renarde learn to fence?"

Vivian wondered if his insistence on leaving off the Madame when referring to her companion meant he had her confused with a lady's maid, who was to be addressed by surname only, or if Uncle was merely unwilling to refer to Madame Renarde with a female address. "She was a student of the *Chevalier*."

To her disbelief, her stoic uncle laughed. "I should have guessed."

Le Chevalier was a French spy who was exiled to England after declaring to the king that he wished to live out the rest of his days as a woman. She'd been a notorious figure in Britain until the end of her days. She'd even defeated Monsieur de Saint-George in a match while wearing full skirts and petticoats. Vivian had been fascinated when Madame Renarde spoke of her old friend.

"So Renarde still fences and taught you." Aldric took a small sip of his own wine, wishing he could drink like a mortal man. This night, he needed more fortification. "How did that come about?"

"She found me in the garden weeping. I felt the confines of my life pressing upon my soul most dreadfully. She thought a new hobby would lift my spirits. And it did. With a sword in my hand, I feel some semblance of control over my fate."

"Yes, life can be difficult for women." Uncle sighed and trailed his finger around the rim of his glass. "Although I hear your skills are impressive, I feel it is much too dangerous for you to be playing with swords in skirts and with your face unprotected.

Vivian's heart sank. Closing her eyes, she waited to hear him claim her favorite pursuit to be verboten.

"So," he continued, "We shall have to see you equipped with proper garb and masks before you are harmed under my care."

For a moment, she stared at him, flabbergasted at his words. "Oh, Uncle," she breathed, heart too full of hope to dare believe. "Do you truly mean it?"

"A merchant is supposed to arrive tonight with everything you require to practice in safety." He was unable to continue, for Vivian launched herself out of her chair and hurled herself into his arms. He patted her back awkwardly and cleared his throat.

"We should probably head down to supper before your companion starves. She has quite the appetite."

Vivian grinned and drew back. "That she does."

Supper began amiably, with Vivian and Madame Renarde expressing their delight at the prospect of receiving proper fencing equipment. Lord Thornton even discussed the possibility of finding skilled gentlemen who would be willing to participate in matches.

But then, Uncle brought the cheer of the evening crashing to a halt. "Speaking of matches." He cleared his throat. "We've been invited to the Galveston's ball on Friday. I will not be able to attend as I have an engagement I cannot put off."

Vivian's shoulders relaxed in relief, though she didn't know why. She enjoyed dancing and sipping champagne.

"However," Uncle continued, "I think you and Madame Renarde should go. Your father had been trying to find a husband for you and I see no reason for the search to end simply because you are here. There are plenty of eligible gentlemen in Lancashire."

He wanted to marry her off? Vivian's vision darkened and narrowed as dizziness made her head feel as if it were caught in a storm-tossed sea. She'd thought she'd have at least half a years' reprieve, if not more. Panic made her stays feel over-tight as her heart thudded against her ribs.

Uncle Aldric's dark eyes narrowed as he frowned at her over his hardly-touched dessert of blackberries in clotted cream. "Vivian, is something amiss?"

How could she explain this terror that swarmed through her soul when she had no means of explaining its source? Quickly, her mind struggled for a means to prevaricate. "It is just… with my scandal, I am uncertain that attending a ball so soon would be the wisest course."

Aldric's countenance softened, and he reached across the table and patted her hand. "I understand your concern, but allow me to reassure you that things are different in the country. Many gentlemen here do not care for the bustle of the Season. And there are likely gentlemen who would not care a whit about your so-called scandal. I daresay, some may even admire you for having the backbone to stand up for your own honor." He withdrew with a look of slight surprise, as if he were unaccustomed to affection. His reassuring smile deepened. "And if there are any qualms, they can easily be assuaged if I increase your dowry. Your father has a respectable sum set aside, but I think some land would hold more appeal."

Fitz, the butler, interrupted the talk of marriage and dowries by announcing the arrival of the merchant. For a few blissful hours, Vivian forgot about her marriage prospects and delighted in her new fencing costume and mask as Uncle watched her duel with Madame Renarde in the ballroom.

The tight, though protected, knickers gave her freedom of motion that she'd never imagined, and the padded vest granted a sense of security and confidence to attack and defend without holding anything back. Uncle also surprised Vivian and her companion with new practice swords, *foyles*, that had small ball tips to avoid one being hurt. Madame Renarde's swords lacked those tips, so they always had to hold back on their thrusts.

Vivian smiled at her uncle before saluting Madame Renarde. This new practice sword felt perfect and well-balanced in her grip, but she still preferred the real, unsharpened rapier that she'd wielded against the highwayman. It had given her power.

Now, as she sparred with her companion, she fantasized about a rematch.

Chapter Five

Rhys stood on a large rocky outcrop overlooking Thornton Manor. Even with his preternatural vision, he had to squint to see the forms of Vivian and her companion practicing with their rapiers. This time, there were no skirts to encumber them, for both wore fencing uniforms of white breeches and jackets with protective padding. With the meshed masks that covered their faces, only Vivian's slim form made her identifiable.

She moved with such grace and precision that Rhys's chest tightened with awe at her beauty. The outdoor lanterns placed around the lawn made hers and her companion's shadows dance like mythical beings, further emphasizing the perfection of the scene.

Rhys caressed the hilt of his own blade at his hip, wishing to spar with her again. He hadn't felt so alive, so… stimulated, in decades. And if he were being completely honest, he would very much enjoy kissing her again.

Alas, that could not be. Not with the plan he had in mind.

Forcing the memory of Vivian's soft lips from his mind, he returned his attention back to her deft movements. If Rhys was still human, she may have posed a challenge to him.

Her teacher had trained her well, and for an aging man—woman, this Madame Renarde was impressive in her prowess. Renarde wasn't the first male Rhys had encountered that preferred to live as woman. It was an odd proclivity that Rhys would never understand, but he wasn't one to judge how others chose to lead their lives.

Rhys was only curious as to how Vivian's father had come to hire such an eccentric person to be her lady's companion. Or did her father know that the companion was more than she seemed? Somehow, he didn't think so. When not fencing, Renarde's appearance and movements gave the appearance of a genteel matron.

Yet Vivian's uncle knew and must not have any qualms. From all Rhys had heard, the Lord Vampire of Blackpool was a stern and implacable ruler over his small territory and even smaller populace. Only twenty vampires lived in this small borough. Which made it easier for Rhys to avoid them. From the week he'd been watching the manor, he already knew when Blackpool's second in command would come 'round to patrol the Thornton estate and when Blackpool himself did his own inspection of the perimeter.

As long as Rhys stayed away during those times, he was able to remain undetected and spy on Lord Thornton and his niece.

In the last few nights, he learned much. Unlike many other mortal descendants who came to stay with the Lord of Blackpool from time to time, Lord Thornton seemed to genuinely adore Vivian. Aside from accepting Vivian's unorthodox companion and not telling her father, Lord Thornton also permitted her to fence. Through the windows, Rhys observed them often talking together in the study, reading together in the library, or playing chess in the game room. Rhys had even seen the cold and stringent Lord Vampire embrace her. That meant that Blackpool now had a weakness to exploit.

And exploit it Rhys would.

Vivian and Renarde saluted each other with their rapiers and removed their masks. Rhys sighed in appreciation as Vivian shook out the rich, dark tumbles of her hair. He still remembered how soft those tresses felt between his fingers.

With heavy regret, Rhys watched them walk back towards the manor. He could have watched Vivian for hours. When they instead sat on a wrought iron bench on the rear terrace, he smiled in relief.

Their voices carried on the wind, but Rhys moved closer to hear better. This was what he was supposed to be skulking around for. Information.

Madame Renarde regarded Vivian with a concerned frown. "You seem out of sorts tonight, *Cherie*. Is something amiss?"

Vivian's despondent sigh made Rhys move forward, as if he could comfort her. "I confess that I am not at all looking forward to the Galveston ball."

"Why not?" Madame Renard placed her hand over Vivian's. "You love dancing."

"I know I do, but…" Vivian trailed off with a shrug. "For one thing, I have been enjoying the peaceful quiet in the country far more than I'd anticipated. For another, I'd assumed that Father sent me here to keep me hidden away until the scandal is forgotten."

Rhys's eyebrows rose. *Scandal?* What scandal? He shoved back his curiosity and the surge of jealousy in wondering if it involved a man, and returned his attention to the conversation.

"…and so I thought the husband hunting would be put to the side for the time being," Vivian was saying. "But Uncle said that he intends for me to try and find a suitable match while I'm with him."

"That is reasonable of him," Renarde said. "Some of the respectable families here may not have heard of the scandal. After all, the Waverlys and the Brightons didn't seem to know about it when they paid us a call yesterday. And I am sorry to say this, but time is of the essence. This was your third season and you are growing close to the age of spinsterhood."

"I do not care," Vivian said coldly. "Spinsterhood doesn't sound so terrible."

Renarde's eyes widened. "Are you saying you do not wish to wed?"

Slowly, Vivian nodded. "I don't think I do. I've been thinking of it ever since Father sent us here. In fact, I think that was why I recklessly ruined my reputation."

"Why do you not wish to marry?" The companion prodded gently. "I'd thought you'd enjoyed conversing and dancing with gentlemen when we were in London."

"Sometimes I did," Vivian said. "But most of the time, I was uncomfortable when they looked at me like I was someone, maybe something else. None truly saw me. And when I think of marriage, I am filled with such terror that I almost feel ill with it. The idea makes me afraid, though I do not know why."

"Do you fear the marriage bed?" Madame Renarde asked softly.

"A little," Vivian answered with a tight shrug. "But not any more than the average maiden. At least I don't think."

Rhys's face heated with guilt. This was a very intimate conversation and one that he did not need to hear for his purposes. Except, perhaps that she was still a maid. Unreasonable pleasure filled him at the knowledge, and not because it was useful.

"I've told you what happens between men and women, but I can elaborate further," Renarde said. "And reassure you that most women enjoy it."

"I am not so green that I do not know that some find pleasure in the act." Vivian looked down at her lap as if embarrassed. "If that were not the case, married women would not carry on with affairs. Perhaps you can enlighten me further another time. Right now, I wish to think of a way to dissuade Uncle from seeking to get me leg-shackled."

Renarde shook her head. "Part of my responsibility is to see you make a good match, and though I care about you too much to pressure you into doing what you do not wish to do, I feel I must understand the situation more, so that I can better help you find happiness." The companion leaned forward, and Rhys had to strain to hear the next question. "Are you perhaps romantically interested in women?"

"Goodness, no!" Vivian laughed lightly, but with no disgust or malice. "My second cousin, Elizabeth, once tried to show me the ways of Sappho and I had no interest. I did recently hear that she has taken up residence with the widowed Lady Mortimer and they are very happy together."

"Splendid for them." Renarde beamed and clasped her hands together. "I didn't think that was your inclination, especially after observing your response to the highwayman's kiss, but one never knows unless one asks. Now that we've established that you have no physical objection to marriage, we can explore what lies in your heart and mind."

Masculine pride swelled in Rhys's chest. Vivian *had* responded to his kiss. He hoped she would never forget. In case she did, he would give her one more before he never saw her again.

The pleasure of that thought was doused with another. He'd had no idea that Madame Renarde had left the carriage and watched him duel with Vivian, much less that she'd seen Rhys kissed her. That unnerved him. No one, human or vampire had caught him unawares before. A darker realization filled him. And Renarde must have had Rhys's gun, for he'd dropped it in the carriage.

He could not afford to have Vivian distract him like that. Not with everything that was at stake.

"Yes," he heard Vivian say, "That kiss will haunt my dreams for the rest of my days."

Damn it.

"But," she continued, "Men like that cannot be found in Society. And besides, what are passionate kisses worth when you're consigned to a lifetime of thing-hood?"

Madame Renarde's brows rose to her hairline. Or was that a wig? "Thing-hood?"

Vivian nodded. "Yes. Wives in Society are basically things to their husbands, expected to look attractive on their arms, bear an heir and a spare, and host balls."

"You would be in charge of the household," Madame Renarde countered. "There is power there."

"That is true, and I do not mind that aspect. After all, I've done it for Father." Vivian fell silent a moment, stroking her chin before she turned back to her companion. "Perhaps I could stay with Uncle Aldric forever and care for him. I like it here."

Rhys shook his head. There was no chance for that. Although the Lord of Blackpool often allowed his mortal descendants to stay with him, he never allowed them to remain long, lest they discover what he was. No wonder Lord Thornton was so eager to have his niece married off. Still, after only having Vivian with him for a week, the viscount seemed to be in a rush.

Unfortunately for Lord Thornton, his match-making plans would have to wait.

"Well," Madame Renarde said as she rose from the bench, "I do not see how attending the Summerly ball will harm your chances of remaining in Blackpool. In fact, you may make a friend or two."

"You're right." Vivian rose as well and held her fencing mask to her chest. "It is not as if I'll receive an offer after one ball anyway."

The rear door of the house opened, and Lord Thornton emerged to join them. He paused a moment and scented the air. Rhys froze and thanked the heavens that he was downwind.

"Good evening, Vivian," Thornton said with what sounded like genuine affection.

Rhys wasn't fooled, though. If the cad was so eager to get rid of his niece, he clearly didn't care for her much.

Sure enough, the point was proven as Blackpool continued. "I hope you are not too disappointed that I am unable to escort you to the ball."

Rhys saw that she was disappointed by the pained hunch of her shoulers before she straightened them. "Of course not. Madame Renarde and I shall have a wonderful time despite your absence."

Blackpool shuffled awkwardly on the flagstones, at least looking shame-faced. "I am sorry, Vivian." Suddenly, he paused and sniffed the air.

Rhys slipped away before he was detected.

As he trekked to the village to hunt, he gnashed his fangs in irritation. Here Rhys was, trying to save his only living relations that the Lord of Blackpool was trying to force from their homes. All the while, His Lordship was talking about some superfluous ball where he would auction his niece off to the highest bidder.

Vivian's words echoed in his mind. *"...when I think of marriage, I am filled with such terror that I almost feel ill with it."*

But Lord Thornton didn't care. Rather than allowing one of his only relations to remain with him awhile and care for him and then give her enough money to live out her life as she chose, Lord Thornton was in a rush to rid himself of her shortly after she arrived. How could anyone be so cold-hearted?

Shortly after feeding from a merchant outside a pub, Rhys scented the approach of some of Blackpool's vampires. Two of them, from the smell. If necessary, Rhys could probably take them in a fight.

He flattened himself against the wall of a narrow alley and listened to their conversation as they passed.

"What do you suppose tomorrow's Gathering will be about?" the first asked.

"Probably the usual listening to mundane petitions, inquiries on rogue sightings, and a possible acknowledgement for our service," the second said, sounding bored. "Though he may deign to mention the niece he has visiting him. Warn us to keep our distance and all that rot."

"Oh, I'd forgotten." The voices faded as the pair made their way out of the village. "I do not understand why he continues to bother with his descendants like that. Nothing good can come of it."

"Makes him quite open to weakness, if you ask me."

A bitter smile curved Rhys's lips as Blackpool's vampires passed out of earshot. No, he hadn't asked that vampire, but Rhys had already discerned the Lord of Blackpool's weakness. And he fully intended to exploit it.

Once he determined that there were no other Blackpool vampires in the area, Rhys ducked out the alley and left the village in the opposite direction the others had went. As he walked, he thought about what he'd heard.

There was to be a Gathering tomorrow night. Tomorrow, while the Blackpool vampires were there, Rhys would gather all the supplies he required for his plan. Normally, Gatherings put Rhys in a cheerful mood, for it was the only time that he was free to roam a territory without the fear of being caught and arrested as a rogue vampire. This time, however, his mind was preoccupied with its struggle between his plotting and his unhealthy fascination with Vivian. The Gathering must be the reason why the Lord of Blackpool would not accompany his niece to the ball.

Rhys remembered the hurt in Vivian's eyes when he'd told her that she and her companion would have to go alone to this ball she didn't even wish to attend, and his anger increased with every step. Lord Thornton didn't deserve such a vibrant, talented young woman in his life.

And Vivian didn't deserve to be handed off like an unwanted burden.

His fury ignited to a blaze when he paid a visit to his cousin.

"He was here again," Emily said the moment she admitted Rhys into the farmhouse. From the sight of her fearful eyes and wringing hands, she did not need to say who *he* was.

Worry churned his insides. "But he was only here a week ago! Is he taunting you?"

"He said he has plans for the property, but that I may remain in hopes that the new owner will give me a position as a housekeeper." Emily looked down at her threadbare slippers, avoiding his gaze. Was there a note of consideration in her tone? Did she think of accepting such a degrading offer?

"But it's not the end of the month yet!" Rhys shouted and shrugged in apology when Emily frowned at the stairs. He would have hell to pay if he woke the children.

"Does it really matter?" Emily said bitterly. "It's not as if I'll have the money by then. At least Lord Thornton is being merciful in not throwing me and my children off the land straightaway. Perhaps I will have gainful employment before winter."

Rhys closed his eyes against a haze of red. "*Mercy.*" He chuckled drily. "The whoreson is wealthy enough that he could have allowed you to make payments and keep the family farm."

"No man would be so generous," she scoffed. "Even with your contributions, the payments would take longer than my lifetime to recompense."

"That is about to change." Rhys spoke through gritted teeth. "This is Berwyn land and I intend for it to remain Berwyn land until the end of the world. Do not speak of surrendering it to Thornton and working as his servant. I have a plan."

"What?" Emily began, but he held up a hand to silence her.

"It is best if you know nothing. I must go now. I will return as soon as I am able." With that, he donned his slouch hat and headed out the door without a backward glance.

He would have to act sooner than he'd planned. However, thanks to Blackpool's Gathering tomorrow, he could carry off his scheme that night.

Chapter Six

Vivian tried not to be sullen as she and Madame Renarde were handed up into the Thornton carriage. She even managed a smile when Uncle bent to kiss her cheek. But the truth was, she did not at all feel like dancing and being introduced to countless new people and socializing with the few she'd already met. All she wanted was to curl up in the cozy overstuffed chair in the library and finish the novel she'd started this afternoon.

Lord Thornton's hooded eyes seemed to pierce through her façade of gaiety and he frowned as he held the carriage door. "I am sorry I am unable to escort you. If my business concludes soon enough, I promise to come to the ball and perhaps have a dance with you before I fetch you home."

"I would like that very much." Vivian would indeed feel better about this ordeal if he'd be able to accompany her for at least part of it. Something about him made her feel safe and accepted.

He inclined his head with a soft smile. "Try not to break any hearts. Or cause another scandal."

The door shut before she could respond. Perhaps that was for the best.

As the carriage began to roll, Vivian leaned against the velvet squabs and fought back a wince as her back muscles spasmed. She'd been a little too vigorous with her swordplay last night and was paying the price. Her calves and thighs throbbed as well. Not at all a good constitution for dancing.

She peered out the carriage window, watching the light of the three-quarter moon paint the rolling hills and pastures in gilt silver. Perhaps she and Madame Renarde could find a nice balcony with some matrons and avoid the dancing.

Suddenly, the horses screamed, and the carriage lurched.

"What on earth?" Vivian reached for the leather strap to keep her balance.

But her silk gloves were too slippery to secure her grip. The carriage slammed to a halt, throwing Vivian onto the floor. Madame Renarde groaned in pain as her head struck the carriage wall.

"Are you all right?" Vivian asked, scrambling up from the floor.

"*Oui, Cherie*," Madame Renarde replied and continued in French as she tended to do when she was out of sorts. "Did we crash, or did something spook the horses?"

"I don't know," Vivian replied in French. It hadn't felt like a crash, but then again, she'd never been in a carriage that collided with another, so how would she know? She took a deep breath to slow her rapid pulse. "I'm going to check on the driver."

Vivian opened the window and leaned out to look at the driver's perch. "Jeffries?" she called, switching back to English. "Are you hurt?"

The footman did not respond. Heart in her throat, Vivian opened the door and stepped out of the carriage. Madame Renarde would be behind her in moments to scold, but Vivian would be contrite later. She needed to know if the poor man was all right.

"Jeffries?" she repeated, keeping one hand on the side of the carriage. Her boots sank slightly in the soft earth. The autumn rains had made the road muddy, but it shouldn't be severe enough to bog down a carriage.

A horrifying thought leapt into her mind. What if the footman's heart gave out? What if he was—She rounded the carriage and the driver's perch came into view. The lanterns flickered, illuminating the footman's profile in sickly yellow light. Jeffries lay back in the seat, his head thrown back.

Vivian's breath froze in her lungs, ice in the October night air.

He was dead.

A harsh, snarling noise pierced the graveyard silence. A sharp whimper escaped her lips. Then she saw Jeffries's chest move up and down. The snarl rumbled in his throat.

Vivian gasped with relief. He was only asleep.

The realization drew her brows together in a frown of perplexed irritation. Was *that* why the horses had stopped? Jeffries was old, but far from his dotage. It was difficult to believe he'd doze off on a drive. She rose up on her tiptoes to sniff the man for the scent of spirits, and stiffened as one of the horses whickered.

Something didn't sound right. Vivian turned and gasped.

The horses were no longer attached to the carriage!

Instead, they stood on the other side of the conveyance. Something large was draped over one of the geldings. Vivian went still.

Someone else was here. And they were stealing the horses. As she crept back to the carriage door, her mind raced and put it together. The thief must have put out the driver with chloroform or some sedating drug. And then he must have pulled the reins and unfastened the horses.

But how had he carried off such a brazen stunt so quickly? Vivian struggled to puzzle it out. There must be more than one thief.

Madame Renarde was still in the carriage. Worry twisted Vivian's belly into a tight knot. Neither of them had their swords. But perhaps the footman still had his pistol. Indecision froze her in place. Should she check the driver for a weapon? Or go back to Madame Renarde and hope they could steal away unmolested?

Closing her eyes, she fought to keep her head clear. Her companion must come first. Perhaps Madame Renarde had seen the thieves and had hidden from them. Maybe that was why she hadn't followed her out of the carriage in the first place.

As Vivian grasped the door handle, she vowed that she'd never go anywhere without a weapon again. Propriety be damned. After all, the last time she'd had a blade in her hand, she'd fought off a highwayman. A rush of dizzy heat flushed her face as she remembered their duel and his kiss.

Then the dreamy recollection was doused with a cold thought. What if it was *him*?

Immediately she dismissed the speculation. If the rake had wanted to steal horses, he would have done so when they were far from the village. All that thief had been interested in was money and jewels…and a kiss

She needed to stop thinking about that rogue, Vivian thought as she slowly pulled the carriage door open. She needed to make sure Madame Renarde was all right.

The carriage was empty. The door on the other side hung open. Vivian's heart leapt into her throat. Did Madame Renarde escape? Or had the thieves abducted her?

Crouching beside the carriage, she strained to listen for an indication as to where the thieves were. She heard one of the horses snort. Shouldn't they be off by now? What if they were lying in wait for her?

Vivian crept back around to the driver's perch. Jeffries continued to snore. She tried to shake him awake, but he didn't respond. What sort of substance could put a man in such a deep slumber? Fear flickered in her heart like a dark flame. Whoever had done this was dangerous.

A horse whickered again. Vivian peered closer at the load on the gelding's back. Her jaw dropped as she recognized the shape. It was Madame Renarde! Somehow, the thieves had knocked her unconscious and were going to abduct her!

Vivian had to rescue her. Slowly, she reached inside the sleeping footman's jacket until her hand closed over the butt of his pistol.

With her back pressed against the carriage, Vivian crept closer to the horses. There was no sound or sight of the thieves, that grew more unnerving, the closer she got. The skin between her shoulder blades trickled with sweat as she felt like they were watching her from somewhere.

When she reached Madame Renarde, relief doused a measure of her terror as she saw that her friend still breathed. Though it had to be difficult for her, lying on her stomach over the horse's back. Vivian cringed in sympathy. Her companion's stays had to be digging into her ribs.

With the gun held against her hip, Vivian pondered how she could go about her rescue. If Madame Renarde was drugged like Jeffries, Vivian would be unable to wake her.

And she certainly couldn't carry her. Her friend was fairly large-boned.

Vivian peered around the carriage. Still no thieves in sight. What if she could just lead the horse away? Perhaps, if they hid in the grove of trees to the east, the thieves would leave with the other horse and Vivian and Madame Renarde could ride to safety.

Dismay weighted Vivian's shoulders. The grove looked further away on second glance. And she felt so exposed on this stretch of the road, far from the next estate and even further from the village.

Grasping the horse's bridle, she started toward the trees.

A low, silken voice spoke behind her, achingly familiar. "Going somewhere?"

Vivian turned around and gasped. "You!"

The highwayman stepped closer to her with a wry grin. He bowed with a flourish. "How lovely to see you again, Miss Stratford."

Unease clenched her belly. How did he know her name? They most certainly hadn't been properly introduced the night he'd tried to rob her carriage.

"Have you been following me?" she asked between her teeth. Revulsion filled her at the thought.

"Not intentionally," he answered. "It's your uncle I've been watching. But you will prove to be very useful to me."

Vivian frowned in disgust at the prospect of being used for anything. Wistful disappointment threatened to distract her from the matter at hand. He was just like all the other men she'd known. Only seeing women as means to serve their own ends. She straightened her shoulders and favored him with her most practiced, icy stare. "You're going to try to abduct me?"

His laughter sent shivers down her spine. "Try? No. I *am* going to abduct you." That wicked grin broadened as he moved toward her, now only seven paces from her. "But do not worry, I won't hurt—"

Vivian pulled the pistol's trigger and let out a cry of surprise as the gun tried to leap from her hand. Her wrist throbbed with the shock of the recoil and her ears rang from the explosive roar. She blinked and looked back at the highwayman.

He stood, staring at her in slack-jawed astonishment. "You *shot* me!"

She blinked again. If she had, why was he still standing? Then she saw a dark spot on the arm of his coat, glistening wetly in the moonlight. She'd clipped his forearm. Fear rippled through her being as his eyes seemed to glow with unholy coppery light. What if she'd angered him so much that he'd kill her?

Vivian turned to run, but the highwayman seized her wrist and yanked the gun out of her hand. She sucked in a startled breath. How had he moved so quickly?

He tossed the pistol into the bushes near the horses. For a moment, she raised her brows at the action. The only bullet had been spent, so the weapon was useless.

Then he jerked her into his arms. The feel of his hard body, pressed indecently against hers, forced the breath from her body. She'd never been in such intimate contact with a man before. Not even Lord Summerly had gotten so close when he'd offered his indecent proposal. The highwayman hissed through his teeth, and for a moment she thought that he was just as affected by this improper embrace as she was. Then she remembered that she'd shot him.

Vivian struggled to maintain her composure and not swoon at the overwhelming sensation of intimacy. "Are you going to drug me like you did with Jeffries and Madame Renarde?"

He gripped her shoulders and lowered his head, so they were face to face. For a moment, Vivian thought he was going to kiss her again, and to her dismay, part of her wanted to feel his lips on hers once more. She stared into his sherry-colored eyes, and the sculpted planes and angles of his face, savagely beautiful in the swaying light of the carriage lanterns.

Vivian realized that she could see him better now, because this time he wore no hat. His russet hair was longer than any gentleman would keep it, aside from her uncle. But Uncle kept his black locks neatly tied back in a queue. The highwayman's tresses fell across his face, making him look wild and uncivilized.

Something about the sight stirred her body, much like the memory of his kiss.

Then he spoke, his voice low and rich, like her morning chocolate. "No, Miss Stratford, I will not drug you."

With his uninjured arm, he reached up and brushed his knuckles across her cheek. "Sleep," he whispered.

Her limbs melted, and he caught her before she collapsed into a puddle at his feet. Unconsciousness cast her into a void of shadows.

Chapter Seven

Rhys cradled Vivian in his lap as he led the horses through the rolling hills of the countryside, taking care to avoid the roads. She was smaller than she'd seemed when she'd faced him down with that pistol, her dark eyes blazing with unholy wrath. He shook his head with wonder. She'd been so brave both times she'd faced him. So unlike the cringing, aristocratic females he'd been robbing for the past six years.

His admiration dampened at the throb of pain in his arm. He needed to feed to heal, but he also couldn't allow the wound to close over the lead ball. Rhys had suffered cutting himself open to dig out a slug once and never wanted to repeat the experience. The problem was that he would have to ride all the way to his hidden lair in a weakened state before being able to deal with his injury.

And then he would have to feed as soon as possible. Unbidden, his tongue raked across his fangs with the compelling urge to feed on the tempting woman in his lap.

"No," he whispered to himself. Leaving Vivian untouched was a crucial aspect of his plan.

However, that meant he may have to feed on Renarde if he failed to come across another human before dawn. Guilt niggled him. It was bad form to feed on those under a vampire's care. But with his wound, Rhys might have no choice.

By the time he passed out of Blackpool's borders, dizziness threatened to topple him and the precious burden he carried from his horse. Once more, he cursed the slow, mortal way of travelling. Taking deep, steady breaths, Rhys covered the long, plodding miles as fast as he dared, staying near the coast to keep the ride as smooth as possible.

At last, he reached the no man's land, where his hidden cave lay. The horses protested the dangerous, rocky path until Rhys had to stop and tie them to the cliff-side. He left the sleeping ladies' companion draped over her horse while he swung Vivian into his arms and carried her down to the mouth of the cave. Once he had her settled in one of the cots he kept prepared for guests, he went back and collected Madame Renarde before leading the horses down one by one. He would have preferred to turn them loose, but didn't want an honest citizen to find them and report them found in the area. Besides, Vivian may like to do some riding while Rhys awaited Blackpool's response to his demands.

He wouldn't begrudge the lady fresh air and exercise in her captivity even though he'd have to double his vigilance at those times, lest she try to escape. And he was certain she would indeed try more than once.

That in mind, he bound her ankles with a strip of linen and did the same with Renarde.

With the horses tethered outside, cropping the grass, and his hostages secured, Rhys sat on the cot opposite from the sleeping women.

A twinge of remorse chewed at his heart as he looked down at Vivian's composed face. A whisper of a smile shaped her lips, contentment personified.

She would hate him for this. He wondered why he should care. After all, Vivian was the kin of his second most hated enemy. He didn't spare a thought as to what Renarde would think of him.

Rhys sighed. He may as well get it over with. Fixing his gaze on the women, he summoned his will. "Awaken," he commanded.

Both women opened their eyes at once. Vivian gasped and Madame Renarde let loose a shrill shriek. Rhys blinked at the feminine sounds. Though expected, he was still unaccustomed to hearing such noises in his sanctuary.

Vivian recovered first. Her silvery-grey eyes narrowed on him with loathing.

"You blackguard!" she spat and launched herself at him, not realizing her ankles were bound. Immediately, she tripped.

Rhys caught her and sucked in a breath as her breasts pressed against his chest. The warmth of her body and the pounding of her heart in his sensitive ears brought forth his raging bloodthirst. He tore his gaze from the vein in her pale neck, but his torment took a new turn as his gaze landed on the tops of Vivian's breasts, spilling over her blue satin ball gown. He then became aware that his hips were flush with her lower body.

His cock stirred with lust.

The slap came unexpected, her palm crashing into his cheek with a sharp crack. "How dare you drug us and take us to this place!"

Rhys held his grip on her shoulders, but moved her back before his arousal made itself known.

Renarde finally spoke, her voice ringing out with imperious outrage. "Unhand her at once, you animal!"

The eccentric companion was closer to the truth than she knew. Rhys glanced up at her, biting back a smile at the sight of her reddened face as she wrestled with her restraints. "Madame, I suggest that you remain still, lest you further tighten the knots." He kept his tone civil and turned back to Vivian. "As for you, Miss Stratford, surely I do not have to point out that you are at my mercy. As such, your stay here will be far more comfortable if you do not strike me again."

She glared up at him mutinously as he pressed down on her shoulders, easing her back onto her cot. "What do you want from me?" she said through clenched teeth.

Rhys laughed, masking his regret at destroying any goodwill towards him. "A woman who comes straight to the point. I appreciate that." He sat back on his cot and reached for a wooden box on the shelf beside his bed. The bullet wound in his arm burned in agony with the movement.

Concern furrowed Vivian's brow for a moment before her eyes hardened once more. Rhys concealed his delight that she had cared for a second. "Your prestigious uncle is determined to toss my relations out of the home that's been their rightful place for centuries."

Vivian drew back, clearly not expecting this revelation. "He wouldn't do such a thing. He is generous with his tenants."

"That may be," Rhys allowed. "But my cousin is not a tenant. She owns her own small farm and has been paying the mortgage faithfully."

Madame Renarde spoke suddenly. "Is that why you rob people? To fund your cousin's payments?"

Understanding filled Vivian's large eyes, along with another hint of compassion. However, there were some things he wanted his captives to know, and other things he did not.

Arching his brow, he cast a sneering glare at Renarde. "Do not talk of my life's path and I'll do the courtesy of not discussing yours."

The companion flinched, bright flags of color blooming in her plump cheeks.

Vivian was not so easily cowed. "Perhaps my uncle has the moral fortitude to not accept payments that were ill-gotten."

"He doesn't know where the money comes from. Besides, plenty of the money is honest, from the crops." That wasn't precisely honest, but Rhys was past caring. "The point is, Black—" he stopped and corrected himself. "—Lord Thornton, should allow my cousin to remain on her land and continue to make the payments."

"How dare you call my uncle a blackguard!" Vivian said waspishly.

Rhys hadn't meant to say any such thing, however, he leapt on the explanation for his slip of the tongue. "And what would you call a man who would willfully toss an innocent woman and her two children out in the cold?"

Vivian huffed and crossed her arms over her chest. "Are they paying less than what was agreed upon?"

"Yes," he admitted with reluctance. "However, he is wealthy enough to not depend on my cousin's payments, and he has all the time in the world to wait for her to give him the full balance." And Vivian would faint if she knew just how much time her uncle had.

Renarde spoke again. "She shouldn't have mortgaged her farm if she was unable to make the full payments."

"Her wastrel husband took out the loan." Rhys wondered why he bothered justifying himself to these women. "He died, leaving my sweet cousin nothing but a mountain of debt."

Vivian made a sympathetic sound before forcing a stern expression. "I am sorry to hear of your cousin's misfortunes, but what does this have to do with me and my companion?"

"I think I know," Madame Renarde said before Rhys could answer. She fixed him with a level stare. "You're holding Miss Stratford for ransom."

Rhys nodded. "I am."

"Ransom?" Vivian looked shocked, and yet somehow relieved. "Do you mean that if my uncle gives the deed back to your cousin's farm, you'll let me go?"

"In a manner of speaking. He will give me the money owed on the mortgage," Rhys explained. "And my cousin can pay him and be held blameless in all this."

Vivian nodded, whether in agreement with his strategy or simply comprehension of his reasoning, he could not tell. Then a line formed between her brows as she frowned. "But why did you take Madame Renarde as well? You could have left her with Jeffries and they could have returned together to my uncle's home safely."

Renarde made a disapproving sniff. "I would have refused. It is my duty to watch over you and ensure your safety."

"Precisely." Rhys favored Renarde with a respectful nod before turning back to Vivian. "As well as to vouch for your chastity when you are returned to Lord Thornton." An ache formed in his heart at the words. He hadn't expected to mourn the loss of the opportunity to make love to her as much as he was now.

He shook his head. What kind of a fool was he? Even if she hadn't been the great-grand-niece of the Lord Vampire of Blackpool, there would have been no hope for a carnal relationship between them anyway. First because she was a mortal and he was a vampire, second, because she was of gentle birth while he was a criminal. And even if those things could be overcome, it was doubtful their paths would have crossed again, had he not needed to kidnap her for ransom.

"You fool," Renarde hissed as if she'd been reading his thoughts. "Miss Stratford is already ruined. You've destroyed her reputation the moment you brought her here. My testimony of her purity will mean little to nothing as she's already spent company in the presence of a criminal."

In most circumstances, the companion would be right. "On the contrary, Madame," Rhys said. "I know Lord Thornton better than you might think. He will have ways of keeping this situation secret. All of his peers will believe Miss Stratford went to visit other kin, or even returned to her father in London, if that is what he must say to convince them." He glanced back at Vivian, directing his words to her as well. "However, I have the feeling he would care very much if someone of my ilk were to spoil his niece's innocence."

Vivian's face flushed a deep crimson at the topic of her maidenhood. Rhys sympathized, yet one must be pragmatic in these sorts of circumstances.

Renarde nodded, yet her countenance was still rife with doubt. "And what makes you think His Lordship will believe my testimony?"

"He will believe you," Rhys assured her. "Lord Thornton has ways of discerning truth from lies."

"He does," Vivian said softly, her cheeks still pink. "You sound as if you know him."

"I've yet to make his acquaintance," Rhys said cautiously. And he wished to keep it that way, as he wanted to keep his head on his shoulders. "However, I do know quite a lot about him."

Madame Renarde waved an impatient hand. "Let us say you are correct in your assumption and Lord Thornton would indeed believe me if I told him that my charge remained untouched during her captivity. That would be most ideal. However, there is still a large problem."

"And that is?" Rhys inquired.

"I do not believe you will be able to keep your hands off of Miss Stratford. I saw the way you kissed her after you robbed our carriage."

Rhys drew back at the discomfiting reminder. He'd been so engrossed in that captivating kiss that he'd been completely oblivious to witnesses. He hadn't lost his head over a maiden since his mortal days. A feeling of unease settled deep in his bones. Yes, he found Vivian to be breathtakingly beautiful and he admired her courage and spirit, but he hadn't really factored those observations into his scheme.

He'd thought taking her companion would keep Vivian's presence in his cave as proper as possible under the circumstances. But Rhys was a vampire, and if he wanted to keep Renarde out of the way to steal kisses, it would be as easy as plucking a rose from another's garden.

Faced with that fact, Rhys had to ask himself, *could* he resist the temptation to touch his hostage?

He glanced at the object of his fascination and was scorched by her wrathful glare.

Well, that solved the issue. She loathed him now. And he would never touch a woman who did not desire his caress.

But if Vivian's icy resolve thawed?

That would be a different matter entirely.

Chapter Eight

Vivian held her breath, waiting in unbearable anticipation, as the highwayman hesitated to answer Madame Renarde's question.

Would he kiss her again? Or, heaven forbid, force himself on her? She remembered the hunger of his kiss the night they'd met. She'd matched him with equal fervor that shocked her to the core. She remembered the dark desires he'd awakened with his embrace.

At last, her captor met her eyes with an intensity that burned.

He shook his head in a firm negative. "I do not bring my attentions where they are not wanted." He raised his head and regarded Madame Renarde with a wry smile. "Furthermore, although I'm a highwayman, I do have some semblance of honor."

"Honor?" Vivian concealed her relief at his words with feigned scorn. "You drugged our carriage driver, stole the horses, and abducted us to extort money from my uncle! Forgive me if I do not take your vow to not assault me as proof that you're a gentleman." An inane thought flitted through her mind and she voiced it on impulse. "We haven't even been introduced!"

The highwayman clapped his hand over his mouth and roared with laughter.

Vivian realized how absurd she'd sounded and nearly joined him in his chuckles. Fighting back giggles, she forced a level tone and attempted to bring back reason. "I'm glad I was able to amuse you," she said drily, "but what I meant to say was… shouldn't my companion and I have the right to know the name of our jailer?"

The highwayman regarded her with that rakish grin before he rose from his cot and bowed with a flourish. "Rhys, at your service."

"Vivian Stratford, at your mercy," she retorted drily, noting that he did not give his surname.

Rhys grinned. "Touché."

She inclined her head and turned to her companion. "And this is Madame Renarde."

He extended his hand to shake, then suddenly, he grabbed his arm and hissed in pain. Oh Lord, Vivian had forgotten that she'd shot him. After all, he was quite lively for a wounded man.

"Ladies, forgive me," he said through gritted teeth. "I must attend to this ball in my arm before we continue this lovely chat." With that, he opened the box he'd placed on the cot earlier.

Vivian stared in horror at the array of torturous surgical instruments. He sounded so calm about the grisly matter. Rhys then took out a little brown bottle that she'd seen in many noble households. Laudanum. Was that what he'd drugged her and the others with?

Doubt immediately imbued her. She'd had laudanum before, when she'd sprained her knee from a tumble down the stairs. The substance had made her feel foggy, but it hadn't made her fall asleep. And if he'd given her that same drug, surely she'd be muzzy-headed. Instead, Vivian felt more awake and alert than she'd been in her entire life.

Rhys took a large swig from the bottle, as if it were a dram of whiskey.

Tentative hope bloomed in her chest. If he were drugged, perhaps she and Madame Renarde could escape. She glanced up at her companion and saw that Madame Renarde had the same thought.

Rhys quashed their notion before they could even plan. Even worse, he did not slur from the drug. "Don't entertain the thought of attempting to depart while I'm occupied. I've installed a door in the cave's tunnel and it locks from the inside. Feel free to have a look."

Heat flooded Vivian's face. How could he read her so easily? All the same, she was curious at the concept of a door within a cave, but the idea of fruitlessly poking at the barrier to freedom under Rhys's knowing smirk was beyond humiliating.

She slumped back against the cave wall, full of impotent anger. "Well, I hope your wound becomes infected and you grow too weak to prevent us from searching for the key!"

His eyes widened in shock at her malicious words. Then he regained his devil-may-care composure. "If my wound festers, that means I shall most likely die. And it would be your fault as you're the one who shot me. Are you quite certain you can handle having my death on your conscience?"

Vivian's shoulders sank. The answer was a resounding no. However, she refused to give him that satisfaction. "Oh, just dig out the ball and bandage your arm and we'll let God decide what trials I can endure."

His eyes blazed with something akin to admiration. "And so I shall." The confidence in his voice should have sounded foolish, yet it did not. Rhys withdrew a pair of scissors and bent to his task.

Vivian watched with morbid fascination as Rhys first cut away his sleeve until the wound was revealed in all its gruesome glory. Dark brown flecks of blood were spattered along his muscular forearm. She cringed to see such beauty damaged.

The bullet hole was a red ruin, clotted and revolting. Yet Vivian continued to watch, even when he dug the pliers into his flesh, searching for the ball. She had done this to him. It seemed cowardly to look away.

Fresh blood spurted and ran down his arm, and Rhys had to pause to staunch it with the fabric of the sleeve he'd cut off. His cocksure smile had vanished, lines of pain creasing the skin around his copper eyes.

Reluctant pity swelled Vivian's heart at his obvious suffering. An apology nearly crept from her throat, but she bit it back. This wouldn't have happened if he had not kidnapped her.

For a moment, the sight became too much, and she looked back up at Madame Renarde, who also watched the operation with an alarming pallor to her countenance. Yet there was a look of familiarity in the companion's blue eyes. As if she'd seen bullets pried out of people's bodies before. From what Madame Renarde had told Vivian about her past, it was likely that she had.

Her curiosity high, Vivian turned back to watch Rhys. He still hadn't freed the bullet, and fresh blood oozed all over his arm. He groaned in agony as he wiggled the pliers from another angle. She could no longer cling to her belief that she'd been right to shoot him. Her heart ached with guilt and sympathy at his pain.

I'm sorry, she wanted to say, but the words lodged in the lump in her throat.

Finally, hissing through his teeth, Rhys pulled out a bloody lead ball and dropped it into a small metal tray with a clang. After he cleaned the wound with a cloth dipped in water from the basin, she thought he'd bandage his arm next, but instead, he took another pull on the bottle of laudanum and set the pliers aside, only to take a pair of tweezers from the box.

As he dug into the wound again, Vivian must have made some sort of noise, for Rhys paused and looked up at her. "If you are feeling squeamish, you should turn away. I do not want you casting up your accounts on my floor."

She shook her head. "I am not so delicate."

He arched an eyebrow. "Are you admiring your handiwork then?"

"No," she said quickly. "I only…"

"Want to see that I come through all right?" he asked in a mocking tone. "Are you concerned for my fate now?"

Yes. She changed the subject. "Why are you still prodding your wound?"

He frowned at her evasion. "I am removing bits of fabric before my skin heals over them."

She nodded in understanding. "That sounds practical." Though surely that hole wasn't going to mend overnight. Then she looked closer and blinked. For some reason, it appeared smaller. But that couldn't be. Surely her worry had only made the wound look worse than it truly was.

Rhys picked at the hole more, depositing bits of wool in the tray that held the bullet. At last, he cleaned his wound one more time before wrapping the bandage around his arm. A measure of tension eased between Vivian's shoulders. She hadn't known she'd been so concerned.

Her fists clenched in her lap. She should be more concerned with escaping. Her teeth clenched in mute frustration as she observed that, despite having consumed enough laudanum to put down a horse, Rhys appeared to be perfectly alert, albeit quite pale.

He cleaned up his surgical instruments and changed into a fresh shirt from a trunk in the corner of the cave. Vivian bit back a gasp at the glimpses of his bare back and chest, and the planes of muscles kissed by the light of the lanterns. The view made her stomach flutter in the most alarming manner.

"Are you ladies hungry?" he asked in a courteous tone, as if he were their host and not their jailer.

Vivian wanted to refuse food on principle, but Madame Renarde spoke up. "Victuals would be most welcome, as you so rudely deprived us of the meal we would have received at the ball."

Rhys nodded. "I am sorry about that." He delved deeper into the cave and she heard a cabinet door opening. It was so dark back there. She wondered how he could see.

He emerged with a basket of scones and two plates. "I also have bread, cheese, and eggs. And I can put the kettle on for tea, unless you prefer wine."

Vivian accepted her plate with a nod of thanks. "Cheese would be quite nice."

"And wine," Madame Renarde added. "The whole decanter."

Rhys and Vivian laughed at the same time. The mingled sound made heat flush to her face. She broke off her laughter and took a scone from the basket.

After Rhys brought out the cheese and wine, he started a fire in a cunning hole carved into the cave floor and topped by an iron grate. As the heat from the first flickers of flame reached her, Vivian realized how chilly the cave was. Strange, she hadn't noticed until now.

She also hadn't noticed that she was ravenous until she'd devoured her scone and reached for a second one. Guiltily, she glanced up at Madame Renarde to see if her companion had observed her unladylike bites.

But Madame Renarde was occupied with pouring a second glass of wine.

She turned her attention back to Rhys. "Are you not going to eat?"

He shook his head. "I dined earlier." Once he had the fire going, he sat back on the cot opposite hers. "Tomorrow, I'll secure a hot meal for you. And if I can acquire some ice, I can better stock the larder."

"Thank you," she said, with her ingrained manners.

Madame Renarde eschewed any pleasantries. "It is good that you wish to keep us well fed, but don't expect that to ingratiate us to you."

Rhys inclined his head respectfully. "Madam, I had no such lofty expectations. I wish for this ordeal to go as smoothly as possible."

"How can you call it an ordeal?" Vivian shot him a glare. "We're the ones being held prisoner."

He sighed. "Yes, and as the one holding you, I now have two women to look after and contend with until Lord Thornton gives me the money."

A tremor ran through her limbs at his talk of holding her. Vivian shrugged off the distracting sensation. "And how long do you think that will take?"

"Hopefully no longer than a night or two," Rhys said. "In the meantime, I will try to make things as comfortable for the both of you as possible."

Despite herself, Vivian was touched by his attention to their comfort. Madame Renarde also appeared to soften towards him.

Her companion poured Vivian a second glass of wine and then a third for herself. She leaned forward and tilted her head to the side as she studied Rhys. "On our first encounter, you called me an old man. Now you address me as Madam. What brought about the change in manners?"

"At first I thought you were a Molly, or enacting a deception to take advantage of your charge. I apologize for that swift judgement." Rhys sounded genuinely contrite. "After observing you and your interactions with Miss Stratford, I realize you are like other individuals I met, who feel as if they were born in the wrong form. I can't claim to understand such a thing, but if you wish to live as a female, I have no qualms with addressing you as such."

Both Vivian and Madame Renarde gaped at him in astonishment. People like Madame Renarde were generally regarded with amusement, scorn, and virulent loathing. Vivian had heard from Madame Renarde that sometimes if one's secret was discovered they were brutally beaten to death at worst, and publicly humiliated and driven out of town at best.

Vivian couldn't imagine facing such prejudice, though she knew very well how one was regarded when they did not conform to their expected role in society.

Rhys's acceptance of Madame Renarde's chosen way of life was nothing short of a miracle. Not even Uncle Aldric was as tolerant.

He was accepting of her too, Vivian remembered. He'd expressed genuine admiration for her love of fencing, with not even a hint of judgement. She hid a frown with a sip of wine. It was very difficult to hate such a man.

And him being so unbearably handsome did not help matters in the slightest.

Madame Renarde interrupted Vivian's dangerous path of thought. "I thank you for your courtesy. It is a pity that we hadn't met under *friendly* circumstances." Her stress on the word reminded Vivian that no matter how charming this rakish highwayman was, he was *not* their friend at all.

"I quite agree," Rhys said and drank the rest of the wine straight from the bottle. "But I do hope we can at least be civil." He rose and took their glasses back to the dark part of the cave, then did the same with their plates. "Now, as it is past dawn, I hope you do not object to my suggestion that we retire. Kidnapping is exhausting business."

Madame Renarde covered her mouth and yawned. "That does sound agreeable. However, I cannot approve of Miss Stratford sleeping so close to you. I think we should switch."

"I am sorry you feel that way," Rhys said mildly, though there was a thread of steel in his voice. "Miss Stratford is my primary hostage and I intend to keep her close." Then his lips curved in a smile of pure wickedness. "I could have her closer, if I wanted. The cots on the bottom can move, unlike yours, which is suspended from the wall."

"You wouldn't!" Madame Renarde hissed with outrage.

Rhys's eyes narrowed. "Keep trying to dictate my arrangements and you will find out."

Vivian sucked in a breath as her heart hammered against her ribs. The thought of sleeping across from him was alarming enough, but for him to slide her cot against his? It would be sharing a bed with him! "What about my privacy?"

Rhys gave her a look of consideration. "If you look above, there are curtains that pull down. There are also chamber pots beneath the bunks."

"Splendid," Madame Renarde said and reached up to untie the roll suspended from the ceiling.

When the curtains came down, Vivian saw that they were made of thin slats of bamboo and had beautiful paintings of tigers on their tawny surfaces. She'd seen them in homes where the

Chinoise trend had been embraced. Utterly beautiful, and more importantly, their captor would be unable to see through them. "These are lovely," she said. "Did they come from China?"

"India." Rhys's voice penetrated the thin barrier. "Before you undress, I do have a trunk of various clothing that may be more comfortable."

A travelling trunk slid beneath the curtain. Vivian found a dress that may fit her for tomorrow, as well as a man's night shirt that would be comfortable for sleeping. At first, she wondered how he'd come by the clothing, then realized that he probably stole the trunk from one of the carriages he robbed.

Madame Renarde found a second night shirt with a nod of satisfaction. As she helped Vivian out of her ball gown and unlaced her stays, Vivian couldn't stop glancing at the bamboo curtain. Even though Rhys couldn't see her, she could feel his presence behind the barrier as she undressed. A most unnerving sensation.

Even worse, she could see his boots hit the stone floor and hear a rustle of fabric indicating that he too was undressing. Some imp within speculated as to what Rhys would look like without his trousers. Then heat crept to her cheeks as she wondered if he was thinking the same about her lacking skirts. This was far too intimate.

Her discomfort eased as the lanterns were doused and she was tucked under the covers of her narrow cot. Madame Renarde was snoring almost immediately, drowsy from the stress of the night's events and three glasses of wine. Sleep took longer for Vivian.

It seemed she'd barely slept when Vivian opened her eyes to see Rhys leaning over the top bunk, where Madame Renarde was snoring away. She sat up with a gasp. What was he doing to her friend?

Suddenly, Rhys bent down and met Vivian's gaze. His eyes glowed amber flame and a trickle of blood trailed from the corner of his mouth. "Go back to sleep, Miss Stratford," he commanded.

Vivian sank back down on her thin pallet and didn't awaken until Madame Renarde shook her shoulder, telling her that tea had been made.

Her companion looked calm and unharmed as she helped Vivian dress. When she emerged behind the curtain, Rhys gave her a polite nod as he fried eggs in a pan heated on his clever grate above the fire.

The scene was so amicable, albeit awkward, that Vivian blinked at the memory of what she'd seen from her bed.

It had to have been a dream.

Chapter Nine

This was the worst night of Aldric's life. The Gathering had dragged on until midnight because one of his vampires had argued Aldric's decision to accept a petition allowing a new vampire into Blackpool simply because he thought there were too many females. The current female vampires of Blackpool loudly voiced their opinion on that sentiment until Aldric ordered the meeting adjourned.

He'd rushed to Galveston Hall, his apologies and excuses memorized as he anticipated Vivian's hurt at his tardiness. He'd hoped the dancing was still going on, so he could at least fulfill that promise.

But when he'd arrived, the hostess, Lady Galveston had blinked at him with owlish eyes and informed him that Miss Stratford had not attended the ball at all.

Before Lady Galveston could begin poking into the situation, doubtless to feed the village's dearth of gossip, Aldric bade her farewell and returned to his home, wondering what had

91

possessed his niece to order the carriage turned around and return home. It smacked of disobedience, even though he hadn't precisely commanded her to attend.

Aldric was angered at her defection as well as the ill manners to not make an appearance after the invitation had been accepted. Yet he also wondered if perhaps he should have had a talk with her and gotten to the bottom of her obvious lack of enthusiasm for the event. What if someone had gossiped about her scandal in London and she'd been afraid of being shunned? Or what if there had been a deeper reason?

Self-recrimination weighted his shoulders as he'd plodded up the drive to his manor. Perhaps he should not have been in such a hurry to find a husband for Vivian. She'd only been here for less than a fortnight. Yes, his secret had to be secured at all costs, but the poor girl was surely distraught over being uprooted from her life in London to live with a relation who had been all but a stranger to her. And he had agreed to shelter her. Only then did Aldric realize that should mean more than his roof.

With scoldings and apologies swirling through his head, Aldric strode into the house, only to discover that Vivian and Madame Renarde had not returned home.

That was when real fear crawled over his flesh. A fear that penetrated him with stinging tendrils and curled around his heart when he retraced her route and found the empty carriage. The horses were gone, the driver as well, and there was no sight of his niece or her companion.

For a moment Aldric wondered if his own footman had done something sinister, but he immediately dismissed the notion. Jeffries was the sort to smuggle wounded birds into his quarters to heal them and he was always kind and courteous to every female he encountered.

"Not Jeffries," Aldric whispered as he inspected the carriage. "Yet something sinister is indeed afoot."

To his everlasting relief, there was no scent of blood. Hopefully that meant the women and his servant were unharmed.

Then he saw a folded piece of parchment resting on the velvet seat cushion. Aldric opened it easily, for it wasn't even sealed with a blob of wax, much less a crest.

With a deepening frown, he read the missive.

Lord Thornton,

I apologize for the loss of your horses and the inconvenience have caused, but sadly, it is necessary.

I have taken Miss Stratford and Madame Renarde under my hospitality. The former is a tempting morsel, but the latter is with me to testify that I behaved as a gentleman so long as my instructions are followed.

If you want to see your niece alive again, bring two hundred pounds in coin to the Saint Nicholas parish cemetery in

Wrea Green, and place it atop the granite stone with the name of 'Gerald Burlingame' tomorrow one hour before midnight.

I will then send you a letter giving you a time and location to collect Miss Stratford and Madame Renarde.

The letter was expectedly unsigned. Aldric had just shoved it into his pocket when he heard a rustle from the brush lining the rutted country road.

"My lord!" Jeffries shouted. "Thank God you're here. I've been searching all over for Miss Stratford and Madam Renarde. I could not find them, and I don't know what else to do!"

Aldric resisted the urge to seize the footman by the shoulders and demand Jeffries to tell him everything that happened. For one thing, the ransom letter already painted the picture, for another, the poor old man looked like death warmed over. His hands shook as if he suffered from palsy and he swayed on his feet.

Forcing a gentle tone, Aldric patted Jeffries's shoulder. "For now, let us return home and get you a nice hot meal and a fortifying glass of port. Then you can tell me everything that transpired tonight."

"What about the carriage?" Jeffries cast a worried glance at the abandoned conveyance.

"I'll send Fitz and the stable boy with horses to collect it."

They walked to the nearest house, owned by the Waverlys, who were more than pleased to take them to Thornton Manor.

Aldric lied and told them that his niece was well and only missed the ball due to a headache. If it got out that Vivian had been abducted by a man, her reputation would be blackened beyond redemption.

After Jeffries had changed out of his filthy livery and eaten a hearty meal, Aldric poured them each a glass of port and tried to keep his voice level. "Now, I know you must be tired, Jeffries, but I need you to tell me everything about the man or men who abducted Miss Stratford and Madame Renarde."

"I can't remember anything!" The footman's lower lip trembled. "Somehow I... fell asleep. When I awoke, the women and the horses were gone."

Aldric stroked his chin and voiced his worst speculation. "Do you think someone struck you and knocked you unconscious?"

Jeffries shook his head. "I don't have any lumps on my noggin."

"Then you must have been drugged," Aldric said with a frown. That would mean that the abductor could have gained access to his kitchen. He'd have to ask the others if they too had fallen asleep. Then again, at this late hour, such a thing would be natural. As much as he tried to keep his servants on a nocturnal schedule, human nature had them often turning in after midnight. Besides, his original thought may have been premature. "Did you go anywhere today before it was time for you to drive the women to the ball?"

Jeffries nodded. "I popped into the pub for a spell." He held up his hands as if to ward off any forthcoming recriminations. "But I only had one pint. I swear I wasn't foxed."

"I did not say you were," Aldric said, though perhaps Jeffries had indeed imbibed more than he confessed. "I was merely speculating when you could have been drugged. Unless… there haven't been any strange visitors to the house, have there?"

"No, my lord," the footman answered quickly. "It must have happened at the pub, as you suspected." He shuddered. "That means the villain must have been right beside me. Poisoned my drink. I could have died!"

"I am glad you did not," Aldric said, hoping Jeffries would calm down enough to be useful. "Do you remember who was at the pub?"

"Just our cook, the butcher, Olson, the vicar, and a few farmers." Jeffries took a deep drink of his port. "I thought I recognized everyone."

Aldric hid his disappointment. Whoever had done this had been clever. And for all he knew, it could have been any of those people who'd taken his niece. After all, Jeffries may know them, but Aldric did not. And he'd granted more than one farmer a loan after a bad harvest. Three were in arrears, including the Berwyn widow.

"What can you tell me about when you woke up to find the women gone?"

Jeffries sipped his port and told of how he'd jolted awake in the driver's perch to find the horses gone and his pistol vanished from his pocket. He'd found the gun discarded in the grass. It had been fired.

Aldric flinched at that news. What if the kidnapper had lied and Madame Renarde or Vivian had been harmed after all?

He relaxed slightly when Jeffries then clarified that he hadn't seen any blood in the grass.

With nothing else to be learned, Aldric dismissed Jeffries with a sigh. "Thank you for all that you've told me. You may retire for the rest of the evening."

Jeffries bowed. "Thank you, my lord."

The moment the footman left, Aldric reread the ransom letter. Some despicable criminal had dared abduct his niece to bilk money out of him? He clearly had no notion of what sort of man Aldric was.

He crumpled the letter in his fist and poured a second tot of brandy. He should have postponed the damned Gathering and escorted his niece to the ball.

For but a second, he considered leaving the money in the demanded location just to see his niece home safely. After all, it would be easy for him to part with two hundred pounds. He had accumulated several thousand over his long life. May as well give the whoreson a sum that had become pithy to Aldric and have his niece home safe.

However, his pride rankled at the notion. Aldric was a four-hundred-year old vampire. An immortal. Furthermore, he was the Lord Vampire of Blackpool. This village was his domain, under his command. To allow a mere human outlaw to best him was anathema to him.

No, he wouldn't quietly pay the ransom. Instead, Aldric would track down the cad and demonstrate what happened to those who dared toy with the Lord of Blackpool. And Vivian and Madame Renarde would still be returned home safe.

A surge of momentary guilt wriggled in his belly at the thought of leaving his niece with her captor longer than it would take to deliver a sack of coins. Aldric suppressed it with the justification that the man had written that he'd also taken Madame Renarde to vouch that Miss Stratford would remain untouched. Since Vivian was a hostage, her value was in remaining in good health. That meant that she should be fed, sheltered, and treated gently.

At any rate, it shouldn't take Aldric long to track her down. The first places he would try would be the farmers who owed him money. Between his preternatural abilities and his knowledge of everything that went on in his territory, he should have his niece back under his roof the following evening, before the sun rose.

Thinking of the sun, Aldric frowned as he realized that was his largest disadvantage in this entire affair. He wouldn't be able to search for Vivian until dusk tomorrow.

However, that was only a minor inconvenience, he assured himself and pulled a sheet of vellum out of his desk drawer. It irked him to waste such valuable writing material on a bloody outlaw, but he had to make an impression.

Aldric dipped his quill in the ink blotter and wrote a letter of his own.

Chapter Ten

Rhys crouched behind the trunk of an ancient oak that spread its wide branches over the eastern corner of the ancient parish graveyard. He reached in his pocket and carefully opened his pocket watch at an angle that would not reflect the moonlight.

A quarter past eleven. Blackpool was late. Or rather, that was what the Lord Vampire likely wanted him to think when in fact, Blackpool was likely circling the area, searching for him.

Just then, a tall, stately figure strode into the graveyard. Authority and power radiated from the man. The Lord Vampire of Blackpool had arrived.

Rhys's breath tightened in his lungs as Blackpool approached a moldy headstone with the name "Burlingame" carved into its rectangular stone face. The Lord vampire looked around the cemetery one more time before reaching in his pocket and placing a leather pouch atop the grave.

This was the most dangerous part. If the wind changed direction or if Rhys moved at the wrong moment, Blackpool would sense his presence. And the longer it took for the second half of his plan to commence, the greater the risk of discovery.

Speaking of the second part, Blackpool wasn't the only party who was tardy.

That sodden fool had better follow through with his task, or Rhys would give him a thrashing. Just as his knees began to cramp, Rhys heard the distant sound of whistling approaching the graves.

Blackpool stiffened. As expected, he heard it too.

The whistling grew louder as both vampires tensed. The moment Rhys's hired decoy strolled into sight, the Lord Vampire of Blackpool was upon him. He seized the drunken sailor, lifting him by his shoulders until his feet dangled in the air.

"Where is she?" Blackpool snarled, baring his fangs.

Rhys blinked at the brazen reveal. That was a foolish error of judgement right there. He would have expected better of a Lord Vampire.

Sam, a man Rhys had bribed in a pub just this evening, squirmed in terror. "I don't know who you're talking about! I only came to visit my grandmother's grave. She raised me since I was a boy."

Very good, Sam, Rhys thought. *Play the innocent bystander.* There was a chance that Blackpool would feed on the man and learn the truth, but even if he did, Rhys had been disguised with a false bushy red beard when he'd paid the man a dear sum simply to pretend to visit a grave at this late hour.

Rhys didn't wait to see if the ruse would be uncovered. While Blackpool continued to interrogate Sam, Rhys dashed to the gravestone with preternatural swiftness and seized the leather bag. He ran on past the other headstones and out of the cemetery, not daring to look over his shoulder.

Only when he was miles away did Rhys stop and enter a pub in a village halfway to the No Man's Land. Technically, he was still in danger as this was under the Lord of Lytham's domain, but Rhys had learned that His Lordship turned a blind eye to rogue vampires passing through so long as they did not cause trouble.

The barkeep regarded him with a look of irritation, for strangers who arrived at such a late hour were often looking for trouble. Rhys ordered the cheapest ale available with hunched shoulders and a lowered tone to put the man at ease. And once he took his cup and slunk away quietly to a table in the far corner, the barkeep relaxed and turned his attention back to the men playing cards near the fireplace.

Rhys sipped the ale, surprisingly good for the price and rough location, and withdrew the leather sack that Blackpool had left on the grave.

Something didn't feel right about the bag. When he opened the sack, he immediately saw why. Rather than two hundred pounds of coins, Blackpool had stuffed the bag with chunks of coal. Rhys blinked in astonishment. Did the Viscount of Thornton truly not give a whit for his own blood? He hadn't anticipated that. What would he do with Vivian and Madame Renarde in that case?

The bag crinkled in his clenched fist. Rhys sneezed from the coal dust as he reached inside and drew out an envelope, sealed with a blot of wax bearing the Thornton crest. He tore it open and found a folded letter written on vellum, far sturdier than the foolscap Rhys used.

The letter however, was quite a bit briefer than the one Rhys had penned.

It read:

"You have chosen to extort the wrong man. I will find you, and I will kill you."

Rhys stared at the angry, slanted words in stunned silence. What was he to do now? He couldn't call Blackpool's bluff and kill the women. The very idea filled him with revulsion. But was he supposed to keep them prisoner forever? That wouldn't do either.

Perhaps Rhys had been too jovial in the ransom letter and not given the impression that he was serious about this business. He would have to get another message to Lord Thornton. One that would convince the vampire that Rhys was not to be trifled with.

But what would he say? Rhys took another deep drink of ale and left the pub. He needed to walk, to think. Then he realized that if he would be holding his captives longer, they could use a hot meal. He went back inside and ordered two meat pies, which he wrapped in handkerchiefs and tucked in the pockets of his greatcoat.

He also fed on the barkeep before departing. He really didn't care to take the blood of those who provided a service to him, as such was considered bad manners in vampire society, but Rhys didn't have time to hunt, and he certainly did not want to feed on Madame Renarde again. Aside from the taboo of feeding from guests, Rhys couldn't banish the memory of the blazing accusation in Vivian's eyes when she'd suddenly sat up in her bunk and caught him drinking her companion's blood.

He'd willed Vivian to fall back asleep, but from the suspicious looks she'd cast in his direction this afternoon, Rhys suspected some part of her retained the memory. That wouldn't be so much of a concern if he was returning her to Blackpool before dawn as originally planned, but now that her stay was being extended, the risk of Vivian or Madame Renarde discovering Rhys's secret had multiplied ten-fold.

An idea flickered in the back of his mind, as teasing as it was daring. But no, Rhys would save that option for a last resort.

When he reached his cave in the no-man's land, Vivian and Madame Renarde rose from their seats on Vivian's bunk, bent heads snapping up guiltily.

Rhys bit back a smirk. He wondered what they had been plotting in his absence. Though keeping a pair of women prisoner was an inconvenience, it did certainly abate the prospect of boredom.

"I've brought luncheon," he told them with a broad smile and withdrew the meat pies.

Vivian turned her nose up and opened her mouth to issue what would doubtless be an imperious refusal, but then her stomach growled loudly, echoing in the cave.

She took the proffered bundle with a mutinous frown.

Rhys waited for his prisoners to finish their meal before delivering the unfortunate news. "I've received a reply from Lord Thornton."

Vivian gasped and Madame Renarde fixed a suspicious stare at Rhys, already mistrusting his tone.

"Did he give you the money?" Vivian asked.

Rhys shook his head and handed her Blackpool's note. Her shoulders slumped as she read the curt message and passed it to her companion. Madame Renarde's scowl was fearsome to behold. "This is his writing. Bloody foolish male pride."

"Yes, pride." Rhys latched onto the explanation. "I do hope that was his reasoning rather than cold disregard for your safety. Either way, it appears that I have made a grave error in my approach to this situation."

Vivian's dark hair rippled over her shoulders with her vigorous nod. "Indeed, you have. You may rectify it by releasing us at once."

Rhys chuckled at her boldness and allowed his gaze to rove over her luxurious hair. Her tresses weren't the usual dun-color that was prominent with many English women, but rather a rich, dark shade, that reminded him of coffee from the Americas.

"No, my error was that I mistakenly gave your uncle the impression that I am a jovial man and far too soft to contemplate harming a gently born maiden. And indeed, I shall rectify that immediately." He reached in his pocket and withdrew his hunting knife.

Vivian gasped as he lunged at her.

Chapter Eleven

A scream built in Vivian's throat as Rhys came at her with the knife. But before she was able to let it out, he already withdrew. Her gaze lit on the blade, its sharp steel surface reflecting the light of the lanterns.

No blood.

Still, she tentatively reached up to touch her neck and feel for the cut she'd anticipated.

Rhys held up a lock of her hair. "I will include this in my next missive."

Madame Renarde snorted in derision. "Now you prove that you are so ruthless that you will damage her coiffure. So terrifying! What shall you do then? Tell His Lordship that next time it will be a finger?"

Vivian turned to her companion in horror. "Jeanette! Do not give him ideas!"

Rhys laughed. "I think your wise companion was calling my bluff and pointing out that I lack the stomach for such brutality. Jeanette, is it? A lovely name."

"You will address me as Madame Renarde." Her companion's stern gaze swept between Vivian and Rhys. "Both of you."

Vivian bowed her head in contrition. Madame Renarde may be her dearest friend, but she was old-fashioned and a stickler for formality. Then the implications of her companion's exchange with their captor sank in. Though she was greatly relieved that he didn't wish to inflict any violence upon them, she couldn't help but wonder what sort of fool would admit to his own hostages that he lacked the nerve to pose a threat? He must be a poor kidnapper indeed.

But she kept that sentiment to herself. "And when will you deliver this letter to my uncle?"

"I will send it with tomorrow's post, which will unfortunately take a few days to reach your uncle, so that means that you will be enjoying my hospitality longer than I anticipated." Rhys shrugged as if in apology.

Madame Renarde sniffed in disgust. "Hospitality is not at all the word I'd use to describe the dreadful conditions you are subjecting us to." Her righteous indignation was ruined with an indelicate sneeze.

"Bless you," Rhys and Vivian echoed in tandem.

Vivian found that she did not share her companion's outrage at this awkward state of affairs. Instead, she'd somehow come to regard her time in this cave as a sort of adventure, though she'd never dare admit to something that had to be morally wrong. To atone for her traitorous thoughts, she forced a defiant tone. "And what will you do if my uncle still refuses to pay the ransom?"

Rhys leaned forward and curled his long fingers around her shoulders. "You had better pray that he sees reason. Just because I do not wish to sever your finger does not mean that I am incapable of doing other things that would horrify your uncle and that you would doubtless find unpleasant."

Vivian shivered under his piercing gaze. And yet, not out of fear. He wouldn't hurt her. He'd already made that clear.

Madame Renarde coughed. "And I suppose you'll start by driving us mad from boredom."

Rhys laughed. "Actually, I intended to keep you occupied. For example, I will permit one of you at a time to ride one of the horses along the beach, so you may have fresh air and exercise."

"That could be dangerous in the dark," Madame Renarde said. "What if the horse turns an ankle?"

"That is a risk you may choose to take or decline," Rhys admitted. "But that is your only option, for you cannot go out during the day."

"Why not?" Vivian asked.

"I don't want you to be seen." Rhys avoided her gaze, as if there was more to it that he didn't wish to divulge. "You are hostages, after all. I do not think you could refrain from calling for help, and then I would be forced to dispatch some poor, hapless fisherman as a result."

Vivian sighed. She couldn't picture him killing anyone, much less a fisherman, but thought it wise not to point that out. "Very well. I would like to ride now."

Rhys grinned and replaced his slouch hat on his head and extended his arm to escort her. He locked Madame Renarde inside the cave when the companion tried to follow.

"That wasn't very kind of you," Vivian admonished him. "Surely Madame Renarde could at least walk along the beach while we ride."

"And risk her wandering off to the nearest village?" Rhys shook his head as he led her up a narrow trail that seemed to be carved into the cliff face. "I think not. She is as eccentric as she is wily. Was her birth name Jean?"

Vivian nodded, taken aback by the abrupt inquiry. "Yes, but don't you dare address her by that name. When she became Jeanette, her peers mocked her by insisting on calling her Jean, and they lived to regret it. She is one of the finest fencers I've ever seen."

"Ah, so she taught you swordplay?" Rhys took her hand to help her up a particularly steep incline.

"Yes." They reached the top of the cliff and saw the horses, both of which were tied to a squat pine tree and cropping the grass. Vivian was pleased that they were positioned in the lee of the stone face, so they weren't battered by the wind.

Then a surprising realization struck her. Rhys didn't have a horse of his own.

And if he didn't have a horse, that meant that he robbed carriages afoot. Vivian thought back to the night they'd met. He had indeed been on foot when he'd robbed her carriage. Reflecting on it, that seemed very strange to her. How was he able to get away so fast? Furthermore, how did he travel the countryside and return to his home so swiftly?

It was yet another mystery about this infuriating man.

Her thoughts broke off as Rhys's hands encircled her waist and he lifted her as if she weighed nothing. She sucked in a surprised breath, momentarily wondering if he'd lured her outside to ravage her. But then he set her on the horse. The heat of his palms remained even after he released her.

It took an endless moment for her to recover from his touch. Only then did she realize that he seemed remarkably unaffected for one who'd been shot in the arm.

With no sidesaddle, Vivian had to adjust her skirts and throw her leg on the other side of the horse. Rhys regarded her with a nod of approval. "Did Madame Renarde teach you to ride astride?"

Vivian nodded. "It is of her opinion that all ladies should learn, and that riding side saddle is foolish and dangerous."

"I quite agree," Rhys said as he mounted the other horse. "I wonder what possessed society to require women to ride in such a silly manner in the first place."

"I suspect that it is to make it more difficult for us to best a man in a race," Vivian said. "But Madame Renarde told me the reason is even more ludicrous."

"And what reason is that?" he inquired as they cantered along.

Vivian blushed. She'd nearly blurted something so indecent it was unthinkable. What magic did he weave that made her so comfortable talking to him? "I... ah, shouldn't speak of such things."

Rhys drew his horse closer to hers and regarded her with a smile that was sin incarnate. "I wager I can guess. Some people believe that the rocking of the horse against your cunny will make you aroused."

Flames seemed to engulf her face as that dreadfully naughty word repeated itself in her mind. Worst of all, even though she'd never experienced any sort of carnal sensations on horseback, she certainly had felt something in that place when Rhys had kissed her. Vivian lifted her chin, fighting for composure. "You really shouldn't speak in such a crude manner in a lady's presence."

"Pish-tosh." Rhys used the mocking inflection of an aristocrat. "Madame Renarde taught you to fence and how to ride astride. You cannot tell me she didn't teach you vulgar words."

Vivian huffed in outrage. "She most certainly did not!"

"Then I shall be happy to be of service in that regard." Rhys favored her with a rakish smile. "I have accumulated quite a salty vocabulary from my many travels."

"And who is to say I have any wish to learn how to curse?" Vivian retorted, though in truth, she could not help but be curious.

Rhys shrugged. "You'll never know when it could come in handy. Besides, at the least, it could alleviate your boredom since I lack embroidery hoops and thread."

"I dislike needlework anyway," Vivian admitted, drawing her horse to a trot.

For the rest of the ride, Rhys taught her countless new words for various parts of human anatomy, making her blush deepen with each one.

By the time they returned to the cliffside and tied up the horses, Vivian realized she'd been too engaged in the lessons to take note of her surroundings. Perhaps that was his intent all along.

Yet Rhys didn't possess the smug look of a man who'd outwitted a helpless woman. Instead, his eyes glittered with boyish humor. "Go on, say it."

Vivian was overcome with helpless giggles. "I can't."

"Of course, you can. Imagine you're saying it to one of those stuff-shirt nobs who seem to think the world should lick their boots." Rhys dismounted from his horse and tied it to the tree before helping Vivian down.

Vivian remembered Lord Summerly's lecherous stare and the feel of his fat fingers pinching her bodice. Because she'd dared to challenge him and defend her honor, she was ruined, while he was free to corner other innocent young women and compromise them. That old fury boiled in her heart as she snarled, "Go fuck yourself in the arse with your own pizzle."

"Very good." Rhys beamed at her with pride. "We'll make a sailor out of you yet."

When they returned to the cave, Madame Renarde cast Vivian an anxious look that was easily read. Did Rhys try to force himself on her? Vivian answered with a minute shake of her head and raised her arms slightly to demonstrate that she was still in one piece.

Rhys addressed Madame Renarde. "Would you care to ride for a spell?"

The companion nodded primly and turned to Vivian. "I found a shelf of books and magazines and newspapers over in that part of the cave." She pointed.

Vivian's heart lifted. Until now she hadn't realized how much she'd dreaded being cooped up in the cave with nothing to do. Reading a good story would transport her from the prison. Then she grasped the significance of something Madame Renarde had said. *Newspapers*. That meant that she may be able to discern where they were.

The scheme quickly came to nothing, as she realized that the papers were from various places that were too far from each other to indicate a locale, along with others she'd never heard of. Where in heaven's name was Much Hoole?

Reading through the paper didn't give any clues, aside from the fact that Much Hoole was a small village and likely isolated from any large towns. Most of the news consisted of dull topics such as the weather and state of local farmers' crops, but she found a serial story that was quite eccentric and entertaining.

The main character was a chipper constable trying to solve a murder in a secluded village called "Two Hills." Constable Cooper Daleson took his tea "black as a smugglers moon" and stopped into Norman's Inn for a cherry tart every morning. The denizens of the Two Hills were equally queer. An old woman who carried a tree limb everywhere and claimed it spoke to her, and another woman who constantly disguised herself and made mischief quickly became Vivian's favorites.

By the time Rhys and Madame Renarde returned, she'd found every issue of the Much-Hoole papers and sorted them in order so she could read the story from the beginning.

"Ah," Rhys said. "You've found the 'Two Hills' serial. I am still flummoxed as to where the tale is going, but I cannot stop reading it."

Vivian nodded. "It's utterly bizarre, yet completely fascinating."

Madame Renarde covered a cough with her handkerchief. "Although I am intrigued, perhaps we should have something to eat."

Rhys obliged them with cheese, bread, and fruit. "I have some errands to complete. I apologize, but I must leave you locked inside." He took the envelope containing the lock of Vivian's hair and his reply to her uncle and left the cave.

The moment he departed, Madame Renarde blew her nose and fixed Vivian with a probing stare. "He didn't do anything inappropriate while you were alone with him, did he?"

Vivian shook her head. "The only time he touched me was to help me on and off the horse."

"He helped me as well," Madame Renarde said. "Very gentlemanly of him. Also, he's incredibly strong. I am *not* a slender woman, yet he didn't even strain."

At first Vivian was only surprised that Rhys had assisted Madame Renarde. At both her father's townhouse and her uncle's estate, the footmen usually hesitated to offer her assistance in mounting a horse or even a hand to a carriage, and Madame Renarde simply ignored their reluctance and went without. Such was common for ladies' maids and companions who were on the stout side, and Madame Renarde had the double inconvenience of being...different. Though her secret remained intact, Vivian wondered if they could sense that Madame Renarde was not an average woman. For Rhys to know and be so gallant was unbearably touching.

Then Vivian's musing ceased as she thought of another implication within her companion's statement. "He is indeed strong. Did you see that he doesn't have his own horse?"

Madame Renarde nodded. "I'd wondered how he was able to rob carriages and get away without one. And how he took those trunks." She muttered something in French too low for Vivian to hear and then suppressed another cough with her handkerchief. "Perhaps he steals the horses from all of the people he robs and just releases them when they've served their purpose."

"That must be the explanation," Vivian said, and rose from her cot to fill the tea kettle with one of the jugs of water Rhys kept. Nothing else would make any sense. Yes, she did picture the highwayman running with heavy trunks on his shoulders as easily as if they were loaves of bread, but that had to be because she was going mad from being imprisoned by an outlaw. A handsome, charming outlaw, but a criminal all the same. Just because they were his prisoners and under his control did not mean she needed to give him more power in her imagination. "Do you suppose we should look for a way to escape while he is gone?"

Madame Renarde shook her head. "I've already looked. The cave has no other exit and the door is impenetrable. He has this cave sealed better than some prisons I've seen."

At any other time, Vivian would have asked her to elaborate on said prisons, but current circumstances captivated her attention. She set the kettle on the grate above the fire. "Then where does that occasional breeze come from?"

"I'll show you." Madame Renarde took one of the lanterns and led her to the back of the cave. She then turned a corner into a space Vivian hadn't noticed when she'd been in this section looking at newspapers.

"My goodness," Vivian breathed as they walked into a narrow shaft. Unlike the slate gray rock of what she'd been referring to as the "living area," this part of the cave was infused with veins of quartz and some other glittering crystal. Long pointed columns of rock hung from the ceiling like deadly icicles. Despite the danger, the sight was beautiful.

Madame Renarde lifted the lantern and pointed. "There is an opening in the top of the cave. Can you see the stars? That's why the cave doesn't fill with smoke from the fire."

Vivian nodded. The hole was too high up for them to climb, and even then, it appeared to be too narrow for a person to fit through. She rubbed the back of her neck. It had gotten sore from craning it. She saw that cunning little shelves had been carved into the walls of this part of the cave as well. Little wooden figures lined the stone surfaces, gathering dust.

"Look at these," she said and lifted a wooden cat that was so expertly carved that it looked like it could nuzzle her and purr at any moment. "Do you think he carved these?"

Madame Renarde inspected an owl, humming in appreciation. "He should sell them."

"He truly should." Vivian agreed. "Since we can't escape, perhaps we should persuade him to turn to honest work."

"That's a lovely thought, but this man is too stubborn to see reason." The companion smiled sadly. "He is hell-bent on coercing that money from your uncle."

"I cannot believe that Uncle refused to pay him." A fresh hurt pierced her heart. "Do you suppose he does not care for me?"

Madame Renarde shook her head. "No, *Cherie*. He adores you. It is only that he suffers from the same unyielding pride as Rhys. He is used to having his way and thinks that this highwayman is a feeble enemy, easily defeated."

The tea kettle whistled, and they returned to the living area of the cave. While the tea steeped, Vivian cursed this male pride that caused her to be held like a bone before slavering hounds. "And do you think Uncle will find us?"

Madame Renarde frowned as she poured their tea into heavy clay mugs that were more fitting for ale. "No, *Cherie*, I do not. This Rhys is as clever as he is determined. From the look of these shelves and figures he's carved, and the door he built for this cave, I can see that he has been here for a long time and survived in comfort while countless authorities are already doubtless hunting for him. Your uncle is cunning, but he is still an aristocrat, accustomed to a life of comfort and ease. That hinders his imagination."

Vivian blew on her tea to cool it. "I have a feeling we shall be here a long while then."

"As do I." Madame Renarde said. "We may as well make the best of it. At least he has sugar."

They sipped their tea in pensive silence.

She wanted to hate him, but she couldn't. His noble reason for abducting them, coupled with the fact that he truly did not want to hurt them wore away at any animosity she could muster. He was like Robin Hood, stealing from the rich to give to the poor, only even more endearing since he stole to keep his own family from being thrown out of their home.

What was Rhys's family like? Vivian couldn't help pondering the question. Did they know he was a highwayman? Did they worry when he was away from them? Was that where he was now?

As if summoned by her thoughts, the round oak door swung open and Rhys strode in, bearing a large stuffed sack over one shoulder and a bundle of firewood on the other. Heavens, he was strong indeed. Vivian became possessed by a mad urge to grasp his bicep and feel those muscles capable of bearing such weight.

She looked down at her tea to hide her blush.

Rhys set down the firewood and sat on the cot opposite her. "I come bearing victuals," he said merrily and opened the sack.

As he brought out bread, crocks of butter, cream, cheese, and small barrels of salt meat, fish, honey, and even some sweets, Vivian looked at him in wonder. Villains in novels did not keep their victims in cozy places and provide them every comfort possible. They threw their prisoners in dark, damp dungeons and fed them gruel. Villains did not joke with their captives and take them riding, or teach them how to swear like a dockworker. They did not reveal that they were too soft to be cruel.

Rhys grinned at her and reached into the sack like someone presenting a gift on Christmas morning. "And finally, I was able to procure the latest issues of the Much Hoole paper, so we can read more 'Two Hills' stories."

Vivian couldn't fight an answering smile. Villains were not kind.

But if Rhys was not a villain, what was he?

Chapter Twelve

Only three nights had passed since Aldric sent his fiery retort to the kidnapper's demands. Now he'd come to regret it.

He'd scoured all of Blackpool and every surrounding town and borough and hadn't found a trace of his missing niece or her companion.

The kidnapper was far cleverer than Aldric had anticipated. None of the farmers had any knowledge of the situation in their minds as he'd crept into their rooms and fed on their blood and memories.

The Horne widow at Berwyn Farm had given him a stab of remorse, as her thoughts were consumed with how she'd break the news to her children that they were to be evicted. Nightmares taunted Aldric's day rest. What if the criminal had given up on the chance of ransom money and slit Vivian's throat and tossed her into the sea?

Had Aldric's pride and anger killed his niece?

Things were not supposed to have gone the way they had. The whistling drunk should have been the kidnapper, but the scent of the man had been all wrong, along with the lack of recognition in his eyes.

And while Aldric had been occupied questioning the drunk, the man he was after managed to seize the note Aldric had written and flee the area.

The question was, did the kidnapper arrange for the drunk to wander in and keep Aldric occupied, or had he merely taken advantage of the situation? Aldric should have fed from the man and read his thoughts to see if he'd been complicit, but he'd been so enraged by the fact that the kidnapper had swept right under his nose and back out again that he'd instead chased after the criminal in a fruitless pursuit.

By the time he returned to the cemetery, the drunk had wandered off.

Next time—if there was a next time—Aldric wouldn't let himself be taken in like that.

When the butler delivered his mail, Aldric's breath caught as his gaze lit on an envelope with no return address.

Apparently, the next time had arrived.

Aldric tore open the envelope like a man possessed. Inside was a folded square of foolscap and a lock of Vivian's hair. Disregarding the note, he seized the severed bit of dark tresses and brought it to his nose. Aside from his niece's scent, all Aldric could detect was a thick reek of wood smoke, a slight tang of salty sea air, and the vague essence of leather.

Blast it! The whoreson had worn gloves.

However, that evidence gave him pause. Had the kidnapper known that he had to conceal his scent, or had he simply been cold? The smoke smell indicated that he was either holding his captives outdoors, or in close quarters, perhaps a small cottage.

Aldric inhaled the lock of hair once more, straining his preternatural senses for more clues. There was a decided lack of fear sweat, which at least reassured him that Vivian and her companion were unharmed. He also thought he detected something unidentifiable, yet familiar, but that was likely wishful thinking.

With a sigh of disappointment, Aldric unfolded the letter.

Bury the money beneath the stone angel in the Wigleigh Priory cemetery in Mythop at noon on Saturday. Or next time, I'll send you her finger.

"You'll do no such thing," Aldric muttered. If Vivian's captor had any inclinations to violence, the scent of terror would be soaked in both her hair and the paper. He sniffed the foolscap and detected the same permeating smoke, cheap ink, leather, and again something familiar that he wished he could place.

Of course, there was no way for Aldric to do what the kidnapper wished anyway. The noon sunlight would scorch him to a crisp. It was the one advantage that humans had over Aldric's kind. But why cemeteries in isolated villages? At first Aldric had assumed Vivian was being held somewhere near Wrea Green, the first place he'd been directed to go with the money. But he'd scoured the area and found no scent of Vivian.

Aldric rose from his desk with a sigh and left his study. He'd wanted to keep this disastrous mess quiet, but it was now maddeningly apparent that this was a problem he could not resolve on his own. He descended the stairs and went out the front door with a quick nod to his butler, who regarded his departure with indifference. His servants were quite accustomed to the viscount's unusual comings and goings.

His first stop was the home of his second in command. Alas, Bonnie was not home. He found her at Gordon's Pub, sipping ale and laughing at a group of sailors telling bawdy jokes. Her mirthful grin vanished the moment she spotted Aldric and she excused herself and took her ale to a table in the corner.

Aldric sat across from her and spoke low. "My niece has been abducted."

Bonnie's eyes widened. "I thought she was visiting a friend in Manchester."

"If the truth gets out, her reputation will be ruined, and no man will marry her." The explanation sounded so petty when he voiced it aloud.

"Ah." Bonnie nodded, though there was a note of disapproval in her tone. "I forget that blue-blooded females have to be sheltered from the world to be worthy of a man's attention."

Aldric rubbed his temples and tried to conceal his irritation. He did not have time to debate society's treatment of women, even if he did agree with Bonnie's opinions most of the time. Why else would she be his second in command? But now he needed to devote his attention to finding the cad who held Vivian in his filthy grasp. He reached in his pocket and withdrew the first ransom letter. "I found this in my carriage five nights ago. The bloody fiend somehow drugged my coachman and stole the horses and my niece and her companion."

"That sounds like the operation of more than one man." Bonnie read the letter with a frown. "Why didn't you just give him the money?"

"Because I am not about to let a foolish mortal turn a profit by crossing me." Aldric hid his surprise at the assumption that he was only dealing with one man. He'd been so blind with rage that the logistics of the actual abduction hadn't been processed. "If our people hear of it, they'll lose all respect for me. Besides," he continued with increasing confidence. "With you and a few other good vampires, we should easily be able to track him down and make him pay."

"Would you like me to call a Gathering?" Bonnie asked. "With the whole network on the hunt, we should locate your niece in a trice."

"No." Aldric was not ready to let all his vampires hear that a human had stolen Vivian out from under his nose. "I wish for this matter to remain between us. I will write a writ of passage and I want you to travel the surrounding territories to the south and see if you can sniff her out while I do the same north." He handed her the lock of Vivian's hair. "This is her scent."

Bonnie took the dark lock of hair and bowed. "Yes, my lord."

When she departed, Aldric buried his face in his hands. Was he a fool to leave Vivian and her companion at the mercy of their kidnapper? What if he was wrong and the man or men would resort to violence? Would he truly receive his niece's severed finger next time?

He ran his hands through his unfashionably long hair and clenched his jaw. No, he had no choice but to embark on this course. For what he'd told Bonnie was the unvarnished truth.

If other vampires thought Aldric was weak, someone would move on him soon and try to take over his territory. As it was, he'd heard rumblings of disapproval from some about Aldric allying with the interim Lord Vampire of London and becoming involved in his civil war three years ago.

But in the end, Aldric felt he'd made the right decision in bringing his pitiful small force to aid England's most powerful vampire. Blackpool may be a small territory, but hopefully the courage and strength of his people would be remembered.

Furthermore, the Lord of London had returned the favor in many ways, the least of which being ensuring Vivian's safety throughout her three failed London Seasons—a feat that Aldric himself had failed.

On his way home, Aldric's imagination tormenting him of visions of Vivian's fear and suffering.

"My poor dear," he whispered. "I will bring you home safe and not rush in marrying you off. Instead I will find you a husband that will be kind and gentle to you, for you've surely suffered enough."

Chapter Thirteen

The past three nights had been a revelation for Rhys. For the first time in decades, being consumed by this mission to save Berwyn Farm while at the same time evading legitimized vampires who hunted rogues for sport did not consume his waking existence. Those things still weighed heavily on his mind, of course, but now he'd also found laughter, companionship, and intellectual stimulation.

After he hunted in the evenings, Rhys would take Vivian and Madame Renarde outside to the beach to walk or ride. Vivian delighted in collecting seashells and Rhys taught her and her companion to skip rocks.

They also practiced fencing with sticks they'd snapped off a tree. Rhys later straightened them with his carving knife. He spent many hours leaning against a rock, watching Madame Renarde teach Vivian new steps and maneuvers. Renarde's knowledge impressed him. Rhys himself had learned in his mortal days as a privateer. The captain was insistent on every member of the crew knowing their way around a blade. That had saved his life and countless others.

After he'd become a vampire, he'd honed his skill by sparring with other vampires who could fence, his preternatural abilities opening him up to new and innovative techniques. Thinking of transformations, Rhys wondered if Renarde had learned to fence before or after she'd made the decision to live as a woman. Likely before, as most men were against teaching a woman swordplay.

He'd tried to glean information about the eccentric companion's past, but Renarde remained close-mouthed and always redirected the conversation back to him. For his safety as well as theirs, Rhys couldn't talk about his past. He did reveal that he'd once been a privateer, leaving out that it had been back in the late 1600's.

"Ah," Renarde had said, "That's why you've done such efficient work on securing this cave. You've designed it like a ship."

Vivian had favored him with a heart-stopping smile. "You're remarkable with carving things. The animals are beautiful. Did you cut all these shelves too?"

"Yes." The compliment had warmed him all over. "As a— an outlaw, I am forced to spend long hours in this cave. I had to find something to occupy the long hours. You may choose one, if you like... both of you," he added at the companion's sharp look.

Madame Renarde shook her head. "A lady is not permitted to accept gifts from a gentleman unless she is to marry him."

He'd laughed. "I am no gentleman."

Vivian had bounded to the shelves where he kept the wooden figures. "I hardly think the rules apply in our circumstances."

She'd selected a hawk he'd carved, its wings spread, and its beak open as if to emit a defiant screech.

"What made you choose that one?" he'd inquired, surprised that she hadn't preferred the puppy or the hummingbird.

"It looks so free and fearless," she'd said with a musing smile as she'd stroked the talons. "No one could keep it locked away."

Madame Renarde offered no explanation for the sculpture she chose aside from, "I like owls."

Between the walks outside and practice with swordplay, they'd occupied themselves reading through the stories of "Two Hills." Some supernatural elements had appeared in the serial, with Constable Daleson dreaming of otherworldly beings. Madame Renarde opined that they were only dreams, while Vivian speculated that they were demons, and Rhys was convinced that they were fey creatures from Underhill.

That led to a long discussion of the legends of the fairy folk across the world. Vivian only knew what Shakespeare had referenced, while Rhys shared the Welsh tales he'd heard growing up. Madame Renarde knew both French and Irish stories.

He'd been so enraptured with spending time with Vivian and Madame Renarde that he'd nearly forgotten that they were supposed to be his captives.

Madame Renarde gave him a cold reminder one night when he'd finished playing a game of Speculation with Vivian. Their heads had been bent over the cards, inches away from one another and they'd been exchanging humorous banter. Rhys was just thinking of offering to play another round so he could keep conversing with her when Madame Renarde cleared her throat.

"Rhys, I would like to have a word with you in private." The companion's tone indicated that she wouldn't brook any refusal.

Rhys nodded and led her outside.

"You're attracted to Miss Stratford," Madame Renarde said coolly, pacing in front of the cave.

Rhys jolted, suddenly feeling like a child caught with his hand in the cookie jar. "She is a beautiful woman," he admitted. "Charming and intelligent as well."

"She is," Madame Renarde allowed, then muffled a cough. "However, if you care about her, you will not act on your attraction."

"I believe we've had this conversation before." Rhys feigned tired indifference. "I have no designs on her maidenhood, though perhaps Lord Thornton may be more concerned if I give that impression." He held up a hand as the companion opened her mouth to protest. "I have decided not to go that route."

Madame Renarde did not appear to be reassured. "And what if Miss Stratford forgets her position and welcomes your advances?"

A pang of longing struck Rhys at the suggestion. Not in the loins as he'd expected—though there was definitely a stirring there—but in the heart. And what did Madame Renarde mean by Vivian forgetting her position? Was she referring to Vivian being a captive, or simply her status as a blue-blood?

His shoulders slumped. Either way, Rhys's standing as an outlaw eliminating him of being worthy of Vivian's affections. And that didn't even take into account the fact that he was a vampire and she a human.

"If she expresses any sort of girlish interest in me, I will quickly dissuade her," Rhys promised. Though there was nothing girlish about Vivian. She'd taken to what was doubtless a terrifying situation with a courage and pragmatism he rarely saw, even in men. She was straightforward in all matters and determination radiated from her every word and deed. How could he not admire her?

Madame Renarde interrupted his reverie. "I find that difficult to believe. Not that I don't think you'll try, as you seem honest about your intentions to remain within the bounds of propriety, however, I will speak plainly. You are a handsome young man, dashing and charming, and placing an impressionable young woman in what she could constitute as a grand adventure. Moreover, Vivian is stubborn. I do not see how you can withstand temptation and dissuade her if she sets her cap for you."

"Do not fret, Madame," Rhys said, heading back to the cave. "I have my ways." In truth, all he would have to do was bare his fangs at Vivian and then reluctant affection would no longer reflect in her large brown eyes, but fear.

Yet aside from the myriad disastrous results such a reveal could bring, he did not want Vivian to be afraid of him. The prospect stung more than he'd imagine.

***

Vivian replaced the cards in the deck while Madame Renarde and Rhys had their private conversation. Irritation niggled in her belly at being left out. What could they be discussing? She was certain it had something to do with her.

When her captor and companion returned, their rush to distract her confirmed her suspicions.

Rhys cleared his throat. "I propose we spend more time on the beach tonight. A fairly warm breeze is blowing, but I smell a storm approaching. We should enjoy the fresh air while we can."

They once more ventured out. Vivian tried to pull Madame Renarde aside to ask what she'd discussed with Rhys, but her companion instead fetched the carved sticks they'd been using as practice swords and offered to spar.

Rhys occupied himself with digging for cockles and clams. The process looked so interesting that Vivian kept watching him instead of focusing on her fencing match, and thus was trounced thoroughly.

By then, she forgot all about the covert conversation and instead became captivated with the process of identifying the little puckers in the sand that indicated the presence of delicious shellfish and digging them out with a cunning stick that Rhys found for her.

"I wish you'd allow us to come out and do this during the day," she complained as her stick missed a clam and it buried itself deeper in the sand. "It's devilishly hard to see in the moonlight."

"I am sorry, Miss Stratford, but it's a necessity that cannot be helped." Disappointment rang in his voice, as if he too longed to cavort in the sun.

Madame Renarde nodded at him in what looked like approval. Was it because he addressed her properly, instead of scandalously using her Christian name as he was wont to do?

It had to be. Surely her companion despised being cooped up all day just as much as Vivian did.

As they took the shellfish back into the cave and shucked them, Vivian wondered if the risk of them being spotted was truly as substantial as Rhys claimed. Somehow, she doubted it. They seemed quite isolated.

But maybe they weren't.

Just as they were eating a creamy stew made with the clams and cockles, Rhys suddenly froze with his spoon halfway to his mouth, raised his head, and sniffed the air. Before Vivian could ask him about that strange action, his eyes flared with dangerous light, seeming to glow in the firelight.

He rose from his seat and bolted out of the cave.

"Mon Dieu!" Madame Renarde exclaimed. "What was that about?"

"I don't know." Vivian set her bowl aside. "But I would like to find out."

Madame Renarde followed her to the oak door sealing the tunnel. To their amazement, Rhys had forgotten to lock the door behind him. Just as Vivian was about to open it, they froze as they heard voices. Vivian crouched and pressed her ear to the door and Madame Renarde followed suit above her.

"What do you mean, we cannot take shelter here for the day?" an unfamiliar male voice said, sounding peeved. "You've always welcomed us before."

"I'm sorry." Rhys sounded sincere. "But I'm currently involved in an extremely dangerous situation. If I let you inside, you could be at risk."

Another voice spoke, this one female. "We've been running from Warrington's people all night and we're exhausted. We'll be discreet about whatever new trouble you've gotten yourself wrapped up in. We always are."

"I know that, Lucy." Envy roiled in Vivian's belly at Rhys's affectionate tone. "But trust me when I say that my latest venture puts all my past escapades in the shade."

The other man spoke up. "I think he's right, Lucy. Can you smell that chowder? And other things? It seems he already has company. The kind we do not involve ourselves with."

Vivian glanced up at Madame Renarde and whispered, "Should we open the door and call for help?"

"*Non.*" Madame Renarde shook her head. "These sound like outlaws just like him. There's no telling what they'd do to us."

She was likely right. Especially with the nature of the conversation and the fact that these people had taken shelter with Rhys before. Who were they running from in Warrington? Were they highwaymen too? Was there perhaps some sort of highwayman's guild? Vivian had heard of flash houses in London where pick-pockets formed such an alliance, but she'd always thought that highwaymen acted alone.

With a sigh, she pressed her ear back to the door. She missed Lucy's response to her companion's statement that they should move on, but she must have acquiesced, for Rhys was now offering suggestions.

"You've already overcome your biggest danger. Warrington is a long way from here and his people don't stray far from their bounds. There's another cave about five miles north of here, but you'll have to go in deep to avoid the tide. And there's sustenance to be had at a monastery, twelve miles east of there. If you hurry, you can catch the monks when they rise for Matins."

"Catholics!" the male echoed. "I didn't know any of them were around here these days."

"Oh, Andrew," Lucy said, "Are you afraid we'll catch their heresy? We're not good Anglicans anymore. Besides, those papists seem to be as fond of blood as we are."

Vivian gasped. Fond of blood? No, she most definitely did not want to open this door and meet these people. Just because she liked fencing did not mean she approved of violence.

Rhys chuckled at the macabre remark. "They were too poor for old Henry to bother with when he dissolved most of the other monasteries. And their isolation has kept them safe for centuries."

"Thank you for the direction," Andrew said. "North it is. Perhaps our paths will cross again, if you survive this latest escapade."

Their voices faded and Vivian and Madame Renarde moved back to the fire and returned their attention to their stew. By silent agreement, they pretended to have heard nothing when Rhys returned.

Still, he gave them a knowing look, but didn't say anything.

After they finished their late supper, Rhys took a cauldron and fetched water for Vivian's bath. His stew was barely touched. As she frowned at the strangeness of his mouse-like appetite, she also marveled at the ease in which he was able to carry the heavy vessel of water. His wound didn't appear to plague him at all.

He went back outside as she bathed, and when he returned, his hair was plastered to his head with water and the air vent in the cave howled like a banshee.

"The storm has come," he said just as thunder rumbled like a dragon's roar. "It's quite a fearsome squall, but we should be safe and snug in here.

They listened to the storm rage while Madame Renarde brushed Vivian's hair and Rhys smoked the remaining clams and cockles they'd gathered. Then, to Vivian's disbelief, he went back out in the storm.

Vivian wanted to wait up for him, but Madame Renarde declared that they should go to bed. She reluctantly complied and only because her companion looked haggard and exhausted. Vivian worried that Madame Renarde was falling ill, with all the coughing and sneezing she'd been doing for the past few nights. Tonight seemed worse. Hopefully some rest would have her well again.

As Vivian lay in her bunk, trying to sleep, she pondered the mystery that was Rhys. What sorts of outlaws called him friend? How had he been aware of their approach so soon? He'd seemed to smell them, but surely he wouldn't be able to do such a thing. His friends mentioned smelling the chowder as well. Vivian hadn't thought the stew was so pungent.

And then there was his small appetite. How could a man remain so strong while eating so little? And was his wound plaguing him at all? She hadn't seen him so much as flinch since the night he'd dug out the bullet.

When Rhys returned, she had her answer. She watched his silhouette move past the privacy screen and to the bathing tub she'd used earlier. She could see the tub if she craned her neck toward the head of her bunk.

At first, she thought Rhys was simply taking the tub out to dump the water, but to her astonishment, he began to undress. He pried off his boots, then shrugged out of his sodden coat. Her lips parted as he peeled off his sodden shirt. The muscles in his back seemed to ripple in the firelight. Heat flared in her face as his trousers came off next, revealing a backside that looked carved from marble.

Her admiration at his stunning physique halted as he turned just enough so she could see his muscular forearm. She gasped. His wound was gone. There wasn't even a scar, just smooth male skin.

Rhys turned his head at her gasp and raised a brow in rebuke for her watching him. Her face flamed as she ducked down in her bunk and pulled the covers over her head.

Yet sleep didn't come for hours. Not with the sound of water splashing as he bathed, naked less than three yards away from her. And not with what she'd seen of his body, and his arm.

How could he be healed? That should be impossible!

Vivian's lips curved in a rueful smile. How many times had a similar thought crossed her mind? Rhys and the impossible seemed to be old chums.

Chapter Fourteen

Rhys awoke to the sound of coughing. Not the gentle clearing of a throat, or the embellished affectation Madame Renarde had employed when trying to make a point, but a deep, racking explosion that echoed through the cave walls.

"Are you quite all right, Madame Renarde?" he inquired softly.

The ladies' companion lit the lantern beside her bunk and blew her nose with a honk. "It's the damp," she explained. "I've never been able to abide it long."

Rhys peered at her closely. With her first coughs and sneezes, he'd suspected she was attempting to feign illness so that he may release her, but from the look of the woman's pale visage and watery eyes, that was not the case. Fine stubble also sprouted over her face, betraying the body in which she was born.

"Lord Thornton ought to have received my letter today," he said in reassurance. But that didn't feel like sufficient comfort. "I have a jar of honey that should ease the cough. And I can prepare a hot bath and give you use of my razor if you care to shave."

Madame Renarde gave him a look that made his throat tighten. "You're a good man, Rhys…" she trailed off, hoping he would slip and give his surname, then shrugged when he did not. "Too good to be a criminal. Why did you not engage in honest employment rather than theft and kidnapping?"

"Aside from the fact that theft is more profitable, and thus more effective in helping my family, it is a complicated situation." Rhys shrugged and took a large cauldron from its place. He could have taken the whole bathing tub, which he did when he was alone, but that would look suspicious. "I'll fill this with seawater for your bath."

"May I accompany you?" a voice asked.

He glanced at Vivian's cot. She was awake and buttoning her boots. A surge of pleasure flickered through him at the prospect of her company. "Of course."

Madame Renarde began to object, but another coughing fit took over. Selfishly, Rhys took Vivian's hand and led her out of the cave.

"I'm worried about that cough," she said, bending to pick up a seashell.

Rhys nodded. "I'm going to put honey in her tea and encourage her to rest. I'll see about finding some soup for supper as well."

"And if she doesn't get better?" she looked up at him imploringly.

He stopped and watched the waves crash against the shore. "Then I shall take her back to your uncle."

"But not me?" Her hand touched his sleeve, a pleading whisper.

He shook his head, refusing to weaken. "Not you. I need that money, Vivian."

"I know." She sighed. "You may not believe me, but I do sympathize for your family, I truly do."

"Thank you." It seemed no one did these days, and her words meant more than he'd anticipated. "I will know on Sunday if your uncle pays the ransom." He bent at a curve of shale that formed a shallow pool and dipped the cauldron in the water. "I hope he does."

"As do I." Vivian followed as he carried the cauldron back into the cave. "I wonder what Uncle has made of my absence?"

"He likely fabricated a tale to preserve your reputation." Rhys wanted to reassure her further, but the words stuck in his throat as they were once more back in the presence of her chaperone. Instead, he shrugged and set the cauldron on the grate and added more wood to the fire. "I know enough about Viscount Thornton to be confident that he will ensure that you are beyond reproach when this is over."

Madame Renarde regarded him with narrowed eyes. "And how are you certain of that? Ladies have been disowned for less."

Rhys crossed his arms over his chest. "You had best pray to the heavens that you never learn what I know of Lord Thornton." But as he issued the threat, he realized that perhaps it was Lord Thornton who should be praying.

He could use that as leverage, but he wouldn't, not unless he needed to. Revealing the existence of vampires to a mortal was punishable by death.

Then again, Rhys was already a rogue vampire, who invaded other territories and had abducted a Lord Vampire's kin. He already had a death sentence hanging over his head and had for some time, what was another?

While Madame Renarde bathed, Vivian and Rhys walked along the beach once more. He observed her pensive frown as she sifted through shells buried in the sand. "How did you come to learn secrets about my uncle? Do you know each other?"

He noticed that she did not bother asking what the secrets were. Clever woman. He answered carefully. "As I told you before, I have not made his acquaintance, but he is well known in certain circles I frequent." Though they'd exchanged letters one time, when Rhys had petitioned to become a Blackpool vampire and Lord Thornton had rejected his request.

Vivian's eyes widened. "Is he a criminal then?"

"Forcing a woman and her two children from their home should be a crime," Rhys said. "But no, he hasn't broken any... English laws that I know of." This conversation was veering toward dangerous territory. He changed the subject. "Why are you afraid of marriage?"

A seashell dropped from her fingers as she froze. "I beg your pardon?"

"I heard you speaking with Madame Renarde about it the night before I took you."

Her fists clenched at her sides and her chin jerked up as she looked at him with blazing fury. "You were spying on me?"

He took a step back and held up his hands in mock surrender. "I needed to gather information about your comings and goings so I could execute my plan."

"Ah, so you spied and eavesdropped to best know when to kidnap me." Vivian faced him with her hands on her hips and a derisive curl of her lips. "You know, that does not redeem you in the slightest."

Rhys shrugged off the guilt that threatened to engulf him. "What can I say? I am the villain in this situation." He circled around her in a way that he hoped looked menacing. He needed to remind her who was in charge. "Answer my question. I thought all blue-blooded maids dreamed of nothing but landing a man with a lofty title and running a noble household. Why not you? You're certainly beautiful enough to take your pick."

Roses bloomed in her cheeks at his acknowledgement of her beauty. "I do not see how it is any business of yours what I want or don't want for my future."

His voice was cold and clipped. "It is my business because if you are planning on being a spinster, the matter of your chastity holds less weight as a bargaining chip."

She flinched as if he'd struck her and crossed her arms over her chest as if to shield herself from his advances.

Rhys cursed and backed away. "No, I am not plotting to ravage you. I only seek to find the most expedient manner of making your uncle pay my ransom."

Her face reddened further. "I am not about to aid you in making myself a tool for your benefit." She paused and added through clenched teeth, "Or my uncle's."

She was hurt, he realized. He'd done that to her and so had Blackpool. Her words that he'd overheard twisted in his heart like a blade. *"...I am filled with such terror that I almost feel ill with it.... Consigned to a lifetime of thing-hood."*

Thing-hood. Rhys was beginning to grasp what Vivian meant by that. He and Blackpool were indeed using her as a pawn in a game, giving no consideration for her thoughts or feelings.

The realization made him feel terrible. Alas, it was not to be helped. Not if he wanted to keep Emily and her children out of the poorhouse.

Perhaps there was a way to atone for his callousness. "What if I allowed you a chance at gaining your freedom?"

Her eyes narrowed in suspicion. "What do you mean?"

"I suggest we duel. If you draw first blood, I'll release you."

She frowned, but there was a glint of hopeful joy in her eyes. "Is this some sort of trick?"

He shook his head. "No. I just think we spar better with swords than words."

"And you're confident that you'll win." Her lips curved in a reluctant smile.

"I am." Skilled as she was, Vivian was still a mortal and could not match his speed.

"Then why bother giving me the chance?" Oh, but despite her argument, naked longing emanated from her, with those sparkling eyes and her fingers curling in readiness to hold a sword.

Rhys gestured for her to follow him back to the cave. "Because then at least you'll have some agency in the matter. Despite the circumstances and my intentions with you, I do regard you as more than a game piece."

"You're allowing me, your prisoner, to fight you with a sword just to prove you regard me as a human being?" Vivian shook her head and chuckled. "I think you may be the worst villain ever."

Though he was gratified to see her spirits raised, his pride stung. Without thinking, he seized her shoulders and pulled her against him.

Her mockery could not stand. He needed to remind her who was in control.

He lowered his face until their lips almost met. "Would you prefer me to be more villainous? I could always dispense with the blades and ravage you after all."

She sucked in a breath, her large brown eyes searching his to see if he was serious. He'd meant to frighten her, but from the way she leaned into him and her tongue wet her lower lip, he may have failed in that goal.

Her hands moved up and splayed against his chest. A low growl rumbled in his throat as his lips almost claimed hers.

Then Vivian shoved him away with such sudden force that he nearly fell on his arse. "I'll happily duel with you," she bit out and strode into the cave.

Rhys followed in a daze and unlocked the door he'd carved to keep the cave sealed from both intruders and the sun.

For the last five nights, he'd held commendable restraint in keeping his distance from her, even when Madame Renarde's eagle eye was not upon him. He'd nearly convinced himself that the kiss they'd shared was forgotten. Now he'd undone it all in grabbing her and pulling her into his embrace.

A terrible mistake, for her scent made hunger roar through his being like a flash-fire. But it wasn't primarily hunger for her blood, it was lust. Rhys couldn't remember the last time he'd desired sex before blood. It wasn't that he lacked virility, plenty of women, both vampire and human, could attest to that. But as a vampire, the blood craving was always at the forefront. For

Vivian to disrupt his priorities... it left him deeply unnerved. Was it because she was forbidden fruit? Or was it something else?

No matter, he couldn't lose that sort of control again. He wasn't the sort of monster who forced himself on women.

Then his guilty conscience reminded him of the kisses he'd stolen whenever he robbed a particularly beautiful lady.

He wouldn't steal another kiss from Vivian again. He'd only take what she'd give willingly. The memory of her licking her lips and yielding against him filled him with agonizing temptation.

No, he couldn't let their relationship become intimate, no matter how much he ached to have her naked in his arms. Not only because she would indeed be ruined afterward, no matter whether she chose spinsterhood or not, but because he could fall in love with her and that would kill him because they could never be together.

Even if she was willing to join him in nocturnal damnation and immortality, Rhys would never consign her to his life. He was a rogue vampire, hunted and despised. If he were to Change Vivian, she would be one too.

Those thoughts cooled his mad passion enough for him to regain composure and look unruffled as Madame Renarde studied him with her usual suspicion.

Now dressed in a rich emerald brocade gown that must have come from the trunk he'd stolen from a stocky countess, the companion appeared as if she outranked Vivian, whose dark blue gown was drab in comparison, probably belonging to a maid.

Despite the lack of bright plumage, Vivian fairly sparkled with youth and excitement. "Rhys and I have come to a bargain that may win us our freedom."

Madame Renarde blinked in surprise. "And what bargain is that?"

"We shall duel, and if I draw first blood, he will let us go home." She bent and touched the toes of her boots, stretching in preparation.

The companion's brows rose to the hairline of her wig as she turned to Rhys with an arch smile. "You must be quite confident in your victory. I hope that will be your downfall, for you don't know who taught her."

"I presumed it was you," he said, suddenly confused.

Madame Renarde's smile broadened. "Ah, but you do not know who taught me."

Rhys fought off a twinge of unease at her smug tone and reached beneath his shirt for the chain that held the key to his sword case. Who *had* taught such an eccentric person the art of fencing?

They marched back outside and walked to the beach, brilliantly illuminated under the light of the full moon.

Rhys and Vivian took their places on the sand with the requisite seven paces from each other and stood *en garde*.

Madame Renarde sat on a rock between them to overlook the match, ready to call out the slightest violation.

As Vivian raised her blade to salute her opponent, the companion spoke.

"Know this, Rhys." Madame Renarde regarded him imperiously from her place on the rock. "If you cut her face, or wound her, I will carve out your heart."

Rhys inclined his head. "And if that should happen, I will gladly allow you."

The companion did not seem convinced, for it seemed that he and Vivian remained in position for an eternity before she called out, *"Pret!" Ready!* And finally, *"Allez!" Fence!*

Vivian nearly took him off guard with a *Patinando*, a step forward with an *appel*—a quick beat on the ground from her rear foot at the same time as the front foot landed, coupled with a compound *riposte*. A brilliant preliminary attack. Rhys had to concentrate to parry in time at a human speed.

Exhilaration flooded his being as their blades slashed and kissed. Vivian was a brilliant fencer, far superior to many men he'd dueled.

Yet the experience felt different than sparring or fighting with a man. With them, there was a fierce competitive edge, a desire to best them, sometimes to humiliate or even hurt them. With Vivian, the duel felt like a dance, each of them moving in coordinated splendor.

Their bodies moved closer with each thrust and parry, withdrawing, then meeting again. Rhys was captivated with the rosy flush in Vivian's cheeks, her parted lips, the dark, vibrant cloud of her hair as it flared out with each time she danced away from his blade. Her silvery eyes glittered with raw exhilaration.

The element of primitive danger somehow gave the duel the element of seduction. Each time their blades rang together, Rhys felt a ringing peal in his soul. Each time Vivian retreated, he was driven to pursue her.

Desire throbbed in his veins like a beast at the verge of breaking the chains that restrained it. Vivian executed a movement that had their blades locked and her body inches from his. Her eyes locked on him and they both froze. Her breasts heaved beneath her woolen gown, seeming to beckon him. Her lips parted as she panted from the effort. For a moment, all Rhys could think about was a different sort of exertion.

Her pink tongue licked her lower lip as if in invitation, and Rhys smelled a hint of intoxicating feminine arousal. He bent and almost kissed her, then thankfully remembered what a disaster that would be. So instead of claiming those lush lips, Rhys twisted his blade free and stepped away, blocking her immediate responsive attack.

On and on they fought, while Rhys struggled between enjoyment at the duel and overwhelming lust.

His delight in the duel blinded his common sense. After what had to be an hour of sparring, he finally broke through his haze of rapture and realized that Vivian was reaching the point of exhaustion. Her legs wobbled slightly during her steps, and the tip of her blade quivered. Her hair was plastered to her forehead with a film of sweat and her breath heaved in long gasps.

Yet he still wanted to disarm her, carry her into the cave, and show her other ways in which they could be matched. From the whiff of desire he'd caught from her, Vivian likely shared the same inclination.

That would be folly. Folly that must be stopped for both of their sakes. The idea that had been whispering through the back of his mind now sang aloud in the forefront.

There was only one way to ensure that Vivian would fear him, and that the Lord Vampire of Blackpool would learn that he was dealing with someone on his level.

Every bone in his body ached with reluctance to cut Vivian's precious flesh, even a mere scratch, but he had to. Not only that, but he must end this dangerous desire sparking between them.

With his preternatural speed, Rhys brought his blade up and under Vivian's parrying arm, and nicked the side of her neck.

She dropped the blade and gasped as a thin, crimson stream trickled down her throat. Rhys stared at the ruby vintage and bared his fangs, now consumed by only one hunger.

As he stalked towards her, she held up a hand as if to ward him off. "What are you?"

He pulled her into his arms and let her have a good long look at his glowing eyes and sharp teeth. "I think you know."

Chapter Fifteen

Vivian froze like a frightened hare at the sight of Rhys's glowing eyes and sharp fangs. Yet she wasn't frightened, not really. Instead, a strange sort of elation filled her. At last was the explanation for all the odd things she'd noticed about him. How his gunshot wound had healed so fast, how he sometimes seemed to move quicker than what should be possible, his insistence on them all remaining inside the cave during the day.

Most of all, she finally had closure for the things she'd suspected about him. She hadn't been imagining things, not in the slightest. He was stronger than a man should be, and that first night, when she'd seen him leaning over Madame Renarde's bunk, blood trickling from his mouth had not been a dream. She wasn't cracked.

But when Rhys's mouth closed over her neck, she finally felt a trill of fear. His teeth stung as they sank into her flesh. Then, the pain vanished, replaced by a heavy, drugging pleasure that made her gasp and cling to him. She heard him swallow twice

155

and realized he was drinking her blood. She should struggle, but it felt so good.

Vivian heard Madame Renarde roar. Rhys released Vivian then, holding her shoulders for balance as her legs wobbled beneath her.

Sand flew through the air as Madame Renarde charged the vampire. With impressive speed, she picked up the sword that Vivian had dropped and thrust it at Rhys's heart.

His hand a blur, Rhys seized the blade. Blood dripped from his hand and he squeezed the sharp steel and Madame Renarde futilely tried to pull it back. "Let go of the sword, Madame, and we may speak civilly."

"How can I be civil when you've bitten my charge?" Madame Renarde snapped. "I told you that if you were to hurt her—"

"It didn't hurt," Vivian interrupted, not knowing what possessed her to defend the vampire. Especially with a sword prick and puncture wounds in her neck.

"I can heal her," Rhys said. Then that eerie amber glow returned to his eyes as he stared down Madame Renarde. "Release the blade and remain still."

The companion went stock still and the handle of the rapier slipped through her slack fingers. Rhys dropped his end and once more approached Vivian.

She braced herself to run, but then Madame Renarde cried out in panic, "I cannot move!"

"What did you do to her?" Vivian demanded, outraged at the thought of her dearest friend being trapped.

"I merely immobilized her. She'll be released in a moment." He gripped Vivian's upper arms with steely strength. "Now hold still."

He did not work his magic on her, though, since Vivian's knees quaked and her feet shuffled on the sand. For a moment she thought Rhys intended to bite her again, but instead he merely placed his bleeding palm on her wound.

After he stepped back, he turned his gaze on Madame Renarde. "You may move now."

The companion started to lunge at Rhys, then paused and instead rushed to Vivian. "Are you all right, Cherie?"

Vivian nodded. The sting in her neck was fading, replaced by a tingling sensation.

"*Mon Dieu!*" Madame Renarde gasped. "Your wound is healing."

Rhys grinned and held up his hand. The slash in his palm knitted back together before her eyes.

"Magic," Vivian whispered in awe.

"Yes," Rhys agreed in a self-congratulatory tone.

Madame Renarde regarded him with stormy fury. "You've doomed us! We are not supposed to know of your kind."

"And how do you know that?" Rhys asked with narrowed eyes.

"I used to be a spy," the companion explained. "I know many of the world's secrets."

The vampire seemed at a loss for words. He shifted back and forth on the sand for several moments before he cleared his throat. "We should probably head inside before one of you catches a chill."

Vivian bent and retrieved the sword Madame Renarde had dropped, though it likely wouldn't do any good. "And why should we spend another night under the roof of a monster that drinks blood to survive?"

To her shock, Rhys flinched. The word had hurt him. Then his jaw tightened as he favored her with a bitter smirk. "Aside from the obvious fact that you've been perfectly safe under my roof before learning what I am, I'll inform you that you were already biding under a vampire's care before I abducted you."

"Uncle is a vampire?" Even as her voice rang with disbelief, Rhys's words explained everything about her reclusive, nocturnal uncle.

"He'd be your great-great-great uncle at the least." Rhys gestured for them to follow him inside. "And he is not just any vampire, he is the Lord Vampire of Blackpool."

Vivian was tempted to refuse to return to the cave, but then she shivered as a chill wind picked up, piercing the sweat-soaked fabric of her dress to assault her skin. As if in agreement with the futility of the situation, Madame Renarde sneezed.

Reluctantly, she realized that Rhys had a point. Him being a vampire would hardly change the conditions of their captivity, aside from making the likelihood of escape much more dismal.

When they returned to the cave, Rhys added more wood to the fire and filled the tea kettle. The actions seemed so normal in the face of what she'd learned about him.

Vampire, her mind echoed. A vampire had abducted her. A vampire had talked and laughed with her. A vampire had taught her to curse. A vampire had dueled with her.

A vampire had kissed her.

A sudden thought jolted her. Had he used his mesmerizing powers to coerce her? Then she remembered the desire that flooded her when his lips had claimed hers that fateful night. Desire that returned when he'd held her in his arms earlier. No, she had kissed him willingly.

And that was a *much* more alarming thought.

So alarming that she'd temporarily lost the significance of the fact that her Uncle Aldric was also a vampire.

Now Rhys's words earlier this night: *"You had best pray to the heavens that you never learn what I know of Lord Thornton."*

Yet he'd now told them. And Madame Renarde had appeared to be more fearful of the knowledge of what Rhys was than of Rhys himself. Was there some sort of group of vampire authorities that killed humans for discovering their secrets? She thought there might be. And Uncle Aldric could be one of those authorities. Rhys said he was the Lord Vampire of all of

Blackpool. That must mean that he reigned over all the vampires who lived in that region.

What would Uncle do when he found out that Vivian and Madame Renarde knew what he was?

When Rhys handed her a cup of tea, she voiced her thoughts. "This is what you meant when you said that you and my uncle move in the same circles."

He nodded.

"And does my uncle know that Madame Renarde and I have been abducted by another vampire?" she prodded.

"No." Rhys said with a satisfied smirk. "And that is probably why he'd rather try to hunt me down than simply pay the ransom. He thinks he is dealing with a human, thus his pride prevents him from allowing me to win."

Madame Renarde coughed again. "Then this is your trump card. Letting Lord Thornton know that his foe is on equal footing. But if he has the same abilities as you do, why are you so confident that he won't find you?"

"That danger will increase once he is apprised of what I am," Rhys allowed, sipping his tea. "However, we are quite far from Blackpool, for one thing, and for another, Lord Vampires encounter difficulty travelling because they must secure permission as well as hunting rights from the Lord of each territory he passes through."

"What if he were to send one of his subordinates?" Madame Renarde asked, then blew her nose with her handkerchief.

Rhys shrugged. "He would still have to ask permission for their passage."

"And who was your Lord Vampire to grant you permission to travel to Lord Thornton's territory and abduct his kin?"

Rhys's eyes widened and Madame Renarde smirked. "Ah, you do not have a lord, do you? You're an outlaw even with your own kind."

Had Rhys's visitors the other night been outlaw vampires as well? While Vivian was certain that information would prove to be useful, another matter had her confused. "How is Uncle to learn that you're a vampire? Are you going to send him another letter?"

"Sending him a letter by post would have been ideal, though I would have to take care with the language in case it fell into the wrong hands." Rhys leaned back on his cot and rubbed the bridge of his nose. "*You* will write something, but I'm afraid the method of delivery will be different."

He was dallying, trying to draw out his words. Vivian's father did the same thing any time he had to deliver unpleasant news. "And what method will that be?"

The vampire heaved a sigh. "I am sending Madame Renarde back to Blackpool."

"What?" Madame Renarde's face went white as talcum powder as she set down her teacup. "You can't!"

"I have to," he said. "You're falling ill. I don't know if you feel it yet, but you have a fever. I can smell it. I will not be responsible for your death."

Madame Renarde did look feverish, Vivian realized. Her eyes were glazed, her cheeks ruddy, and beads of sweat gathered on her forehead.

Madame Renarde crossed her arms over her chest and shook her head. "I cannot leave Vivian alone with you! That would mean I failed in my duties."

"You'll fail if you die," Rhys replied bluntly. Apparently, he was done prevaricating. "If it will reassure you, Lord Thornton will be concerned about other matters than Miss Stratford's virtue when you tell him what I am."

Vivian remembered something else he'd said: *Just because I do not wish to sever your finger does not mean that I am incapable of doing other things that would horrify your uncle and that you would doubtless find unpleasant.* "Are you talking about draining my blood or turning me into a vampire?"

"The latter, of course," Rhys said. "It takes effort to drain a human, for one thing. For another, your uncle should rightly assume that I won't kill my hostage."

Before Vivian could recover from that gruesome information, Madame Renarde leapt back into her previous bone of contention. "And what if *I* am concerned with her virtue?"

Heat rose to Vivian's cheeks as she relived their almost-kiss before the duel, but Rhys seemed unaffected. "I'm a monster, but not one who ravishes maidens against their will. And now that Miss Stratford knows that I'm a monster, I don't think she will be in a hurry to welcome my touch."

Vivian nodded, more to reassure her companion than out of confidence in Rhys's words. Though she truly should be revolted at the thought of a vampire touching her. Any normal woman would be. Yet this was still Rhys. The man who'd captured her dreams with his kiss, the man who was trying to save his family's farm while doing as little harm as possible. The man who'd laughed with her, taught her foul language, and did everything he could to see to her comfort.

She couldn't help but notice that he emphasized two terms to place distance between them. He called himself a monster, and for once bowed to propriety in referring to her as Miss Stratford. Was he fighting the attraction as badly as she was?

Yes, she may be in danger to succumbing to his charms should he decide to work them on her. And the thought of being alone with him in this cave for lord knew how many nights did set her heart to pounding in a most improper manner. This was the first time she'd felt any stirrings with a male, the first time when a chaperone could be needed for her own good.

But Madame Renarde was ill. Damp climates never agreed with her, and Vivian had never heard such an ugly cough. There was no question, Madame Renarde must return to Thornton Manor, where her uncle could summon a doctor.

"No," Madame Renarde said, as if reading Vivian's thoughts. "I must stay."

Vivian realized there was another facet in her friend's stubborn refusal to leave. Madame Renarde did not allow doctors to examine her, lest her secret be discovered.

With that in mind, Vivian reached over and took her friend's hand, squeezing her palm in reassurance. "If you need treatment, my uncle will have to find a doctor who is discreet. After all, he has a bigger secret for you to hold over him."

Madame Renarde looked so hopeful that it was heartbreaking. "Do you truly think so?"

"I am," Vivian said with genuine confidence. "If he's survived so long as a vampire in the nobility without being found out, he must be well-versed in discretion."

Rhys nodded. "She's right," he said softly.

Hope gleamed in Madame Renarde's pale eyes, but her lips twisted in a frown. "What if he kills me or throws me out?"

Before Vivian could respond, Rhys spoke. "For the most part, it is illegal for a vampire to kill a human. Furthermore, although I will ensure that you do not know where this cave is, you have enough information for Blackpool—er—Lord Thornton for him to find it prudent to keep you healthy and safe."

Madame Renarde opened her mouth, whether to agree or to argue, they never found out, for she doubled over with another fit of coughing.

Rhys patted her back with a sympathetic frown and then took her teacup. "I'm going to give you some laudanum. It helps with coughing too." He fetched his brown bottle and poured a few drops into the tea. Then he went to the basket containing the fruit he'd stolen a few nights ago, took a lemon, then sliced it, adding a segment to the tea. After he added a large dollop of honey, he handed her the cup. "The lemon and honey will mask the laudanum and ease the pain in your throat. Now drink up, for you need to rest for our journey."

Vivian's heart clenched at Rhys's tender care for her friend. Her body warmed all over as she realized that he would treat her with the same gentle consideration, if she had fallen ill.

He may call himself a villain and a monster, but he acted like a hero. Vivian couldn't stop pondering the contradiction.

Once Madame Renarde finished her tea and was bundled up in her cot, Rhys built the fire to a cheery blaze that chased away the remaining chill of the cave.

"Thank you for caring for her," Vivian said softly as her companion's snores echoed off the stone walls.

Rhys gave her a slight bow. "It is nothing. Now I need you to compose the letter for your uncle." He rose and went to one of the shelves, fetching foolscap, quill, and ink.

When the writing implements were set before her, he dictated what he wanted her to write. Vivian fought to keep her hand from shaking as she penned the short missive, coded to inform Uncle Aldric that she knew what he was. Rhys didn't want

165

her to say any more than that, explaining that the consequences of Aldric not paying the ransom were implied. Vivian added her own coded plea for her uncle to be discreet and merciful with Madame Renarde.

Rhys read the letter and nodded with satisfaction. "This will do. Now I must go out and feed before the sun rises. If I come across some food or goods that you may enjoy, I will fetch them for you."

A laugh escaped Vivian's lips, though it held a hysterical edge.

The vampire cocked his head to the side. "What is so amusing?"

"You're going off to drink someone's blood and collect sweets or fripperies on the way." She shook her head. "I suppose it's not amusing, but you must admit it sounds odd."

"I suppose so." He chuckled and started toward the door.

"Rhys?"

He turned. "Yes?"

"Do you hurt them, when you….?" She trailed off with embarrassment, not quite ready to describe his fangs sinking into someone's neck. Her own flesh tingled at the memory of his bite.

His face contorted in what looked like pain, then he softened, regarding her with a long, almost tender stare. "No, I do not. Now you should sleep too. I extended our duel longer than I should have and you must be sore and exhausted."

She was, and she ached all over from her exertions. Never had she pushed herself so much. She remembered wondering why Rhys barely seemed winded. Now she had her answer. *Vampire*. The word whispered in her mind as she watched Rhys walk out of the cave to seek his next victim. Though if it was true that he didn't harm them, maybe victim wasn't the right word.

Donor, perhaps?

With a long shake of her head, Vivian pulled down the bamboo privacy screen, shrugged out of her gown and into the oversized night shirt that Madame Renarde had laid out for her before the duel. Then she lay down on her bunk and stared at the shadows and dancing firelight across the screen.

Madame Renarde snored on. The laudanum had put her out like a lamb. Too bad Rhys hadn't offered any to Vivian.

Sleep, Rhys had told her. *Ha!* How was she able to close her eyes after first learning that he was a vampire and her uncle was one as well? And then discovering that her best friend was ill? To top it all off, with Madame Renarde returning to Thornton Manor and informing Uncle Aldric that a rival of his kind held Vivian, and of all that had transpired, who knew how her uncle would react?

Which led to the most alarming realization that kept Vivian wide awake. After tomorrow night, she would be alone with Rhys, unchaperoned. Sleeping, bathing, eating, talking. All of those things would take on a different sort of intimacy, despite Rhys's assurances to Madame Renarde.

Alone with a vampire. Her heart thudded beneath the blankets.

Rhys's words earlier whispered in her mind: *"...now that Miss Stratford knows that I'm a monster, I don't think she will be in a hurry to welcome my touch."*

But was that true? Vivian recalled their kiss, then the times when he helped her mount the horse, the moment he pulled her against him to challenge her mocking his lack of villainy...and the closeness of their bodies as they'd dueled. Her belly fluttered as she relived each moment.

She wasn't so certain.

Chapter Sixteen

Sleep came hard for Rhys. Vivian's gaze had seared every inch of his body when he'd undressed to bathe. He hadn't realized that the tub was set back far enough that it wasn't hidden by the privacy screen. Had she seen... everything?

Lustful dreams plagued him whenever he managed to doze off. Even then, he was awakened constantly by Renarde's coughing. Dusk had him sitting up with a groan and rubbing his eyes.

He lit the lantern and saw that Renarde had already risen and dressed. Vivian remained asleep, her heart a steady beat, her breathing an even rhythm. Should he awaken her? He supposed he should, so she could say goodbye to her companion. But what if she told Renarde that she'd seen him undress? He could well imagine the companion's disapproval at that.

And then there was the constant reminder that when he returned from the journey, he and Vivian would be alone together.

Before he could speculate on the potential delights of that scenario, Rhys doused them with cold reality. He had to take Madame Renarde back to Thornton Manor tonight. Crossing territories was always dangerous, though as a rogue, he'd had many years of experience. But his progress would be slowed carrying a human.

And then there was the more alarming fact that Vivian would be completely alone. Fresh worries plagued him at that. What if another rogue vampire came by? Many would seek refuge with Rhys from time to time. Of course, if any had approached with Renarde watching over Vivian, it would have still been slim protection. He still worried that Andrew and Lucy, the fellow rogues who'd asked for refuge the other night, would gossip about Rhys's human guest to the wrong ears.

Madame Renarde broke through his fruitless musings. "Can you discern if she has caught my illness? You were able to smell mine."

Rhys nodded and carefully ducked beneath the bamboo curtain. The slumbering Vivian was a delightful sight, with the rise and fall of her breasts and her lush, parted lips. He bent down and the urge to kiss her ravaged him like a pack of lions. Restraining himself, he inhaled her scent. All he could detect was the sweat from last night's sword play, smoke from the fire, and her intoxicating womanly scent that was unique to her alone.

Before temptation overtook his senses, Rhys ducked back out. "She smells healthy."

"If that changes?" Renarde brought his attention back to more serious matters.

"I have ways of healing her," he said. "But I did not want to risk them on you. Your affliction is deep in your lungs, but you knew that, didn't you?"

Renarde nodded and muffled another ratcheting cough. "I've been stricken with pneumonia several times in my life. And I was a sickly child."

Rhys's heart constricted with sympathy. His mother had also suffered constant ailments of the lungs. "I hope you get well soon. I honestly mean that. Now bid your farewells to Miss Stratford."

He gave them a few minutes of privacy to spare himself from witnessing feminine displays of emotion, but unfortunately, when he returned to the cave to collect Madame Renarde, he discovered the two in a tearful embrace that tugged at his hardened heart. Poor Vivian was clearly desolate at the prospect of losing her closest friend, and Madame Renarde's brave front looked ready to crumble at any moment.

But Rhys would not have this unique woman's death on his conscience. Just because he was a rogue vampire didn't mean he lacked morals. "It is time," he said firmly.

Madame Renarde accompanied him outside with her satchel. "Are we taking the horses?"

Rhys shook his head. "It will be faster if I carry you. I will have to blindfold you."

Renarde nodded in comprehension. "So that I cannot lead Lord Thornton to your cave."

"Precisely." He tied a scarf around the companion's eyes.

When he lifted Renarde, he noticed with a pang of alarm that the stout lady's companion was quite a bit lighter than she'd been when he abducted her. He hoped he hadn't waited too long in deciding to send her back. As he ran with his preternatural speed, he also worried about the toll the chill wind took on her.

Halfway to Blackpool, he stopped near an inn and removed Renarde's blindfold. "We both need rest and sustenance."

The companion nodded, her ashen countenance alarmed him. At the inn, Rhys ordered a cup of hot tea, soup, and a tot of brandy to warm her. While she ate, he found an easy meal in a shadowy corner, where a drunk dozed in a chair.

Although Rhys knew they should resume their journey, he wanted to give Renarde more time to warm her chilled bones.

"When did you realize that you were meant to be a female?" he asked.

Renarde laughed. "Everyone who knows my secret asks me, and Vivian is one of the only people I've told. But very well, since I know your secrets, you may as well hear some of mine." She coughed and swallowed another spoonful of soup before she continued. "My father was a cruel, hard man. He wanted me to be the epitome of manhood, hard, unfeeling, and violent. Though I excelled in my fencing lessons, I failed in all other things. I loved poetry, music, and keeping the company of my mother, sisters, and female cousins. With them, I felt accepted for who I was."

"Your father sounds like he was an ass," Rhys said. He hadn't been particularly close with his own, either.

"He was. The first time my father caught me trying to learn embroidery from my sister, he thrashed me soundly and then forced me to wear a dress for the rest of the day." Madame Renarde smirked as if holding a secret triumph. "He thought I cried from the humiliation, but I cried because *Mama* was distraught over it. Dressing me as a girl became his preferred punishment for whenever I behaved in what he deemed a feminine manner. But something strange happened. I felt so much more comfortable in women's clothing than in shirtwaists and breeches."

Rhys suppressed a shudder at her father's cruel punishment. If his father had forced him to dress like a girl, he would have despised it. He was glad that the cruel action backfired in Renarde's case.

"During one such incident, my sister smuggled me out of my room while *Papa* went hunting for boar. She took me to her chamber and adorned my face most prettily with her paints, rogue, and kohl. Then she placed one of her powdered wigs on my head." Renarde beamed at the memory. "She thought it was quite the lark, but when I looked in her mirror, I saw the beautiful maiden reflected before me and thought, 'this is who I am supposed to be.'"

Rhys thought of how he'd felt when he first stood on the deck of a ship. Probably a poor comparison, but that was the closest he could come to relating.

Renarde continued her story. "We then went to call on one of her friends. My sister introduced me as her cousin, and we had a lovely time. Never had I felt so natural and free." Her smile dissolved into a frown. "But it wasn't until later when I was able to live my life as I wished. I was at a fencing club when I met *Le Chevalier D'Eon*. Her story was a revelation. We became constant sparring partners and close friends and she told me of how she'd first lived as a woman in the Russian court, acting as a spy. She then managed to secure me a position working for the King of France before she was exiled to England. I lived and worked as a woman, but my duties became too rigorous as I got older and the pneumonia afflicted me further. When the revolution began, I fled to England, but sadly, there was no royal pension for me as there was for *Le Chevalier*. So I hired myself out as a lady's companion and that is how I came to be with Miss Stratford."

Rhys couldn't help but note that Renarde never clarified what her royal duties had been. Likely a spy, as *D'Eon* had been. But he saw no need to pry. Just like his days as a royally-sanctioned pirate, Renarde's exploits were buried in the past.

He looked at the clock and realized with a jolt of alarm that they'd lingered too long. "I'm sorry, but we must go now."

Renarde lifted her chin bravely, but Rhys could hear the pounding of her heart. She was afraid of how Blackpool would treat her. Unfortunately, there was nothing to be done about it.

He carried Vivian's companion all the way to the edge of Blackpool's territory. When he set her down, guilt knotted his stomach as he told her she'd have to walk the rest of the way.

"Don't look so crestfallen," Renarde said with a smirk. "I may be ill, but I hardly think a mile's walk should do me in. When this debacle is all over, you truly should try to live a more respectable life. I'm afraid being a villain doesn't suit your constitution."

"You may be right about that." Once his family had their home restored, Rhys had originally intended to leave England and undertake the daunting quest to find a Lord Vampire willing to legitimize him. But he'd thrown away that hope when he'd told Vivian that her uncle was a vampire. For that crime, Blackpool would hunt him to the ends of the earth and execute him.

Renarde brought his attention back to the present. "Promise me you'll keep Vivian safe."

Rhys placed his hand over his heart and bowed. "I promise."

Yet as he returned to the cave, where he'd be spending Lord-knew-how-long in close quarters with a tempting, spirited beauty, Rhys wondered if he could keep her safe from himself.

***

An hour before dawn, Aldric was preparing to retire for the day when he heard footsteps pounding up the stairs. His heart quickened with hope. Had Vivian been found? Frantic knocking assaulted the door of his study.

"Enter," he called, wishing he could have run to the door and flung it open. But that was unseemly for a viscount.

"My lord!" Jeffries burst in, panting with exhaustion. "It's the companion!" He gasped and braced his hand on the doorframe.

Aldric's eyes widened with alarm at the gray pallor of the elderly footman's face. Tamping down the urge to demand the man keep talking, he gestured to the seat before his desk. "Sit down, Jeffries and catch your breath."

He poured his servant a glass of wine and wrestled with his impatience as Jeffries recovered from his dash up the stairs.

"What's this about the companion?" he asked when color returned to the footman's face. "Do you mean Madame Renarde has returned?"

"Yes, my lord!" Jeffries bobbed his head frantically. "I found her staggering down the drive. She's very ill, I'm afraid. Burning with fever and suffering the most terrible cough."

"And my niece?" Aldric demanded. It wasn't that he was unsympathetic to Renarde's plight, but his hope for Vivian's return could not be quenched.

Jeffries shook his head. "I did not see her."

Aldric rose from his seat. "Take me to Madame Renarde, and then organize the servants to search the grounds."

They went down to the kitchen and Aldric gasped at the sight of Vivian's companion. Renarde's face was gray and gaunt, her eyes glazed, and her frame trembled as if she'd been overtaken by palsy.

"Lord Thornton," Renarde said with a crooked smile. "I have been released due to my illness." Then she doubled over with a hoarse, racking cough.

"And Vivian?" he asked, though he suspected the answer.

Renarde shook her head sadly. "He will have his two hundred pounds, or die in the effort. But I assure you, Vivian is doing quite well under the circumstances." She swayed in her seat and grasped the table for balance. "There is one other thing that I must tell you in confidence."

Despite the feverish glaze, Aldric sensed an urgency that couldn't be denied. He dismissed the cook and the scullery maid.

Once they were alone, he leaned forward. "What is it you wish to tell me?" he asked, and that's when he smelled the answer. Beneath the stench of sweat and sickness, there was the unmistakable odor of something familiar. Something that chilled his blood.

Madame Renarde had been in close company with a vampire. A vampire who'd known precisely who he'd stolen from when he'd taken Vivian.

A low growl built in his throat. *That* was how Vivian's captor had carried off the abduction and managed to evade Aldric's hunt for so long.

But what Madame Renarde said next was not the information Aldric already gathered by scent, but something far worse. "I know what you are, Lord Thornton."

Aldric bared his fangs. "The bloody whoreson told you?"

The companion nodded, then exploded in another fit of coughing. Her pallid flesh whitened further aside from the crimson flags of fever on her cheeks. "Yes, and I will tell you all I know of him and where he keeps your niece if you will promise me one thing."

For a moment Aldric was tempted to tell the brazen companion that she was in no position to demand anything because he could simply drain the truth with her blood. However, he held back. In such a weakened state, to feed on her could kill her. Especially if the vampire that had held her and was still holding Vivian had already been feeding from Madame Renarde.

"And what promise would that be?" he asked, with a note of warning.

Despite Aldric's bared fangs and menacing tone, Madame Renarde reached forward and grasped his hand. Sweat beaded on her brow and she spoke in tremulous gasps. "That... the... doctor... you summon... will be... discreet with regards to... my secret."

The moment Madame Renarde finished her request, her eyes rolled back in her head and she toppled forward. Aldric caught her with a muffled curse and carried her out of the kitchen. "Jeffries!" he called.

The footman emerged from the parlor. "Yes, my lord?"

"Fetch Doctor Rosenfield at once," Aldric commanded. "And tell no one about this."

When Jeffries departed, Aldric carried Madame Renarde up to her room, silently praying that the companion's malady was not fatal. He needed the information she had about the vampire who held Vivian captive.

As he waited for the doctor, Aldric shuttered all the windows on the second floor and closed the curtains. Then he built a roaring fire in Madame Renarde's room and lit several lanterns. When Doctor Rosenfield arrived shortly after sunrise, he still complained about the lack of light.

"I am sorry, Doctor, the curtains must remain drawn." Aldric rubbed his temples. "The sun gives me a terrible headache. I can have more lanterns brought in."

"That is quite all right, my lord." Rosenfield shook his head and moved the lanterns closer. "I will examine the patient now."

"There is one more thing," Aldric said quietly. "There are certain attributes about this... woman... that require discretion should you encounter them. I do hope I can trust you in this matter."

Doctor Rosenfield stroked his chin and regarded him with a curious glance, but he nodded. "I am *always* discreet."

Aldric examined him for signs of a lie and found none, though his evaluations sometimes proved false. "Thank you, Doctor," he said and left the room.

Ten minutes later, the doctor met Aldric in the corridor. "Madame Renarde is suffering from pneumonia. If the fever breaks within the next day or two, ah, *she* should survive, but I recommend that... *she* ...remain in bed for at least a fortnight. I gave her laudanum for the cough and chest pain. Watered wine and broth should do for the next couple days, along with tea, honey, and soft foods." Doctor Rosenfield stepped closer and whispered, "She will also need a shave soon, if you wish to remain discreet about...her... ah... attributes."

"Of course." If Renarde was too weak to accomplish the task, Aldric would have to attend to it. "Is she conscious?"

Doctor Rosenfield shook his head. "She is delirious from fever. I was only able to rouse her long enough for her to tell me her name and where she felt pain before I gave her medicine. Then she fell unconscious again. That is a good thing, however. Sleep is the best of cures. Her heart sounds strong, and I have high hopes of a full recovery."

Aldric thanked the doctor and paid his fee as well as a little extra. He ground his teeth in irritation that his questioning would have to wait. As he retired to his chambers and undressed for the day sleep, the gravity of the situation weighed on his heart. Madame Renarde knew that Aldric was a vampire. Did that mean that Vivian had also discovered that fact?

The blasted cur who took them had broken one of the principle laws of their kind: *never* tell humans of the existence of vampires. If the Elders found out that Vivian and Madame

Renarde knew, they would order the women to be killed or Changed.

Aldric was most certainly unwilling to kill either one of them. But the alternative wasn't much more appealing. Renarde already felt trapped in the wrong body. Would it be fair to consign her to an eternity in that form?

And Vivian... Aldric's shoulders slumped in despair. His niece was supposed to have had her whole life ahead of her. A future full of sunlight, happiness, and hopefully children.

And now the whoreson who took her had cheated her of all that.

Chapter Seventeen

Vivian nearly went mad from worry as she waited for Rhys to return. A multitude of fearful scenarios flitted through her imagination. Madame Renarde had died on the journey and Rhys had to bury her. They'd both been caught by her uncle and Rhys was locked in a dungeon and being tortured. Or they'd been set upon by other rival vampires.

As the hours passed, Vivian's gaze constantly strayed to the clock at Rhys's bedside. How long was the journey supposed to be? She rubbed a crick in her neck from the constant turning, but couldn't seem to stop her pointless surveillance of the ticking minute hand. Dawn drew near, she could feel it. Because Rhys and her uncle remained indoors all day, she knew the myth that the sun was fatal to vampires had to be true.

Panic bloomed in her chest. If he didn't return soon, would that mean Rhys had perished? Or was he simply delayed, forced to take shelter in some crypt or cellar?

The click of the lock on the door made her jump. Then elation infused her being as Rhys strode into the cave, looking pale and exhausted.

She slipped off her cot and dashed across the cave to meet him, grasping his hands as if to verify that he was truly here.

"You've come back!" she exclaimed, and immediately felt insipid for stating the obvious. "I mean, how was the journey?"

Rhys's fingers, icy from the chill night air, brushed over her knuckles. "Long. We had to stop at an inn, so Madame Renarde could warm herself." Despite the coldness of his fingers, his touch seared her. "Your companion is a very formidable person."

That may be so, but worry churned her stomach as she recalled Madame Renarde's horrible, ratcheting cough and the clammy feel of her skin when she'd embraced Vivian and told her farewell. "Was she delivered back to Uncle safely?"

"I assume so." Rhys looked down at her with a deep frown. "I could not risk escorting her straight to the gate, but I brought her as close as I could."

His guilt-stricken face made her chest tighten. Vivian's grip tightened on his hands. "She was more ill than she let on, wasn't she?"

Rhys met her gaze directly. "Yes," he whispered. "Yet I made her walk to Thornton Manor all the same. I had no choice, if I were to return to you."

A bitter laugh escaped her. "Most men would have evaded the question and tried to reassure me with worthless platitudes to assuage my fears."

"You are not the sort of woman to be swayed by such men." He eyed her with what looked like respect. "And I am not the sort of man to have the patience to dither."

"Thank you for that," she said, holding his gaze. "All my life, people have danced around the truth instead of facing it with honesty. It is one of the things I detest about being a woman. People think I should be treated like a child, coddled and shielded from the harsh truths of the world." The impulsive outburst brought a flare of heat to her face. What was it about this man—vampire—that inspired her to blurt whatever thoughts crossed her mind? She brought the matter back to the present. "I ah, am pleased to see you returned safely as well."

His low laughter was like warm chocolate. "Are you saying that because you didn't want to be trapped in this cave, or because you had any concern for me?" He then pulled her into his arms, holding her so tight she could feel his heartbeat against her ear. "On second thought, do not answer. I wish to savor this warm welcome from a beautiful woman."

Shock reverberated through the core of Vivian's being. Not only at the sudden embrace, but at his question. It had not occurred to her that if Rhys hadn't returned, she would have been trapped in the cave. She'd been too consumed by worry for Madame Renarde and Rhys to have thought of herself.

Now, in the warmth of his embrace, with their hearts pounding together, Vivian's belly quivered with the same sense of excitement she'd experienced with his kiss. A chord of fear reverberated through her being. She'd read the old French fairytale of the beautiful woman who'd been held captive by a fearsome beast only to fall in love with him.

Was she falling in love this beast? A vampire who fed on the blood of innocents? Such would be folly. In the story, the beast held the beauty because love would break his curse. Rhys held her for money needed to save his family. And she doubted that love or anything else would break his curse and change him back to a human.

But oh, he felt so wonderful in her arms. So warm and safe. And the heavy thud of his heart made her suspect he felt the same.

A thought struck her. Weren't vampires supposed to be dead? She looked up at him. "You have a heartbeat."

"Yes." His lips curved in a mirthful smile. "Contrary to myth, we vampires are not reanimated corpses. Another sort of magic grants us our powers and eternal life."

"Magic?" She wanted to scoff at the word, yet she couldn't. Not with a creature from legend standing before her, holding her in his arms.

"I do not know what else to call it." He drew back slightly, though his grip remained on her arms. "There is something else, though."

"What?"

His lips curved in an impish smirk. "Your chaperone had only just departed and already we are in an improper embrace."

"Oh." She stepped back and regarded him with a frown. "But you initiated it."

"That I did." He walked further into the cave and gathered wood from the pile to build up the fire. "A mistake on my part. However, I'd expected you to be afraid of me after learning that I am a monster."

"I know I should be." Vivian suppressed her warring desolation at the breaking of their embrace and confusion at the emotions he'd wrought as she filled the tea kettle with water. "But you're simply not very monstrous."

He looked over at her and bared his fangs. His eyes glowed like banked coals. The effect was strangely beautiful. "I could be monstrous."

"But you're not." She ignored the tilt in her belly. "You cannot hurt me because you need that money for your family's farm. And speaking of, what monster cares enough for his loved ones to endanger himself to save them?"

Rhys took the kettle from her with a sigh and set it on the grate. "Very well, I admit to being soft when it comes to Emily and the children. But you are mistaken about yourself. While it's true that I will not kill or injure you, I have already hurt you."

"When you bit me?" She laughed even as a trill of pleasure flared through her lower body at the memory of his mouth on her neck. "Don't be silly."

Rhys shook his head and took two mugs from one of his myriad shelves. "No, my bite didn't harm you, but the knowledge that your uncle and I are vampires may destroy your future."

"What do you mean?" Vivian recalled Madame Renarde's words when Rhys had revealed his identity. *"You've doomed us all!"*

"It is forbidden for humans to know of the existence of vampires. We'd be hunted to extinction otherwise." Rhys prepared the tea, avoiding her gaze. "I do not know what your uncle shall do about it when you are returned to him."

Dread crawled up her spine. "What is he expected to do?"

"Typically, the human is to either be killed or Changed."

"Killed?" she echoed, rubbing her arms as a sudden chill swept through the cave. "You think my uncle might kill me?"

"No." Rhys shook his head quickly and handed her a steaming cup of tea. "I can tell that he cares for you too much to do such a thing. I assume that when you are returned to him that he will either arrange to have you Changed, or he will do like the primary Lord of London did when he married, and... bend the rules."

"What about Madame Renarde?" Vivian asked as a horrifying realization overtook her. "She's a servant, and an... unconventional person. Will Uncle kill her because you told us his secret?"

Rhys fell silent, hands cupped over his tea mug. "I have hopes that he will be able to vanquish her memory of what she's learned."

"That can be done?" While the core of her being revolted at the thought of someone manipulating her friend's mind, or her own for that matter, hope for Madame Renarde's life being spared was more important.

"Yes." Rhys continued to avoid her gaze and sipped his tea. "If the subject hasn't spent too long mired in our world, a vampire as old and powerful as the Lord of Blackpool should be able to make a person forget all about our kind. Few humans are immune to our influence."

"And if it's been too long?" Vivian set her tea aside and clenched her fists. Anger and fear suffused her soul. "Or if Madame Renarde is immune?"

Rhys sighed. "I do not know."

A red haze of fury fell like a curtain over her vision. Vivian launched across the few feet separating them and grasped the lapels of his coat. Hot tea sloshed all over their clothes, but she barely felt the scalding liquid.

"Damn you!" Her fists beat at his chest. "You put my only friend's life at risk on a pile of unknown assumptions? You *are* a monster. I thought you returned Madame Renarde to my uncle so that she wouldn't die from her illness, not so she could face a death sentence for something that is not her fault."

Rhys grasped her wrists as she struggled and cursed. "I apologize, but you must calm yourself." His grip was unyielding as iron manacles, but Vivian thrashed against him, blind with rage.

"Calm?" A hysterical laugh bubbled from her lips. "How can I be calm when you've told me that you may have sentenced my friend to death?"

She tried to kick him, but he was too quick. He pulled her closer to him and rolled so that he lay atop her, pinning her with his weight. "Be still!"

The shock of this new position knocked the breath from her body. She tried to buck beneath him, but only succeeded in becoming more aware of his solid frame.

"Why did you tell us what you are?" She fought for mental clarity under the dizzying sensation of his body pressed so intimately against hers. "You already held me as a hostage. Why risk our lives?"

Rhys closed his eyes in silent concentration before opening them to meet her gaze. "As I'd told you and Madame Renarde before, your uncle thought he was dealing with a mortal man. Now that he knows his opponent is another vampire, perhaps he'll take the threat of you being in my care more seriously, especially now that you lack a chaperone."

"You could have released her without divulging knowledge that endangered us!" Vivian shifted once more, trapped beneath his weight and iron grip on her shoulders. "What would be the difference between the threat of my being ravaged by a man or by vampire?"

She squirmed beneath him once more, then froze as she became aware of his hard length pressed between her thighs. Madame Renarde had told her that men's members grew large and firm when they were ready for the marital act.

Rhys seemed aware of it too, for he spoke through gritted teeth as if her movement had pained him. "Do not speak of my ravaging you. Not when you're... not now."

Was he not going to...? Some strange recklessness overtook her. "Answer my question," she demanded.

"The difference is that a vampire cannot marry you. Not unless he Changes you into a vampire as well." Rhys panted with ragged breaths as if he'd been the one struggling rather than her. "And either way, a vampire cannot give you children."

She frowned in confusion as his erection pulsed between them. "But you're not... ah... impotent."

He growled, and his eyes took on that eerie amber glow once more, yet Vivian wasn't afraid, even when he bared his fangs as he spoke. "Our bodies are capable, but our seed does not take root." He muttered what sounded like a curse in some foreign language. "You are making it very difficult for me to focus on the point." His lips brushed against hers so quickly she could have imagined it before he shifted off her and pulled them both back up to a sitting position. "If I release you, will you refrain from trying to pummel me?"

She nodded. Only when he set her beside him and moved his hands from her shoulders did she realize that the bodice of her dress was soaked with spilled tea. Rhys's shirt was also drenched. She could see the outline of his nipple through the damp fabric.

He turned slightly to conceal the bulge in his trousers and cleared his throat. "As I was saying, your uncle should be concerned that I may take it into my head to make you a vampire."

"Why, if he will have to turn me into one anyway?" The circular reasoning escaped her. The distraction of his presence had her mind at sixes and sevens. Her gaze narrowed on his face as she tried to avoid looking at his lap. Tried to avoid thinking of the effect their closeness had on him.

"He may be able to avoid turning you." Rhys handed her a handkerchief to blot at her damp bodice. "But if he did Change you, then you would be a legitimate vampire, under his authority and protection. Whereas, if I did so, you would be a rogue vampire."

His ominous tone made her shiver. "What is a rogue vampire?"

"Madame Renarde aptly read me," Rhys said, his face drawn as if confessing something heinous. "A rogue is an outcast among our kind. One who was banished by his lord for committing a crime not deemed severe enough for an immediate death sentence. But in a way, it is still a death sentence for many, because rogues are hunted and killed by most legitimate vampires. Sometimes, they are given a trial by a lord of a territory and even more rarely, granted legitimacy under the new lord. But those who were Changed by rogues do not have that good fortune. They are perceived as worse than bastards, for their Change was not sanctioned by a Lord Vampire."

Dizziness threatened to overtake her at this influx of information about this society of creatures she'd only just learned about. "What crime did you commit, to be banished by your lord?"

"I continued to disobey him and leave his territory without permission," Rhys said. "A vampire must always have a writ of passage from his lord before he travels out of a territory. But my former lord would not grant me leave to see my family. He firmly believed that vampires should abandon their mortal descendants. Emily and the children needed me. I had no choice but to go to their aid."

Vivian's heart constricted with sympathy. "Your lord exiled you for seeing your family? That is so cruel!"

"Many could see it that way." Rhys leaned forward, elbows on his knees, resting his chin on his hands. "However, it can also be regarded as pragmatic. Vampires are discouraged from maintaining connections to their human relations because the risk of our secrets being revealed is heightened and brings danger to both the vampire and their kin." His voice lowered. "Just as I've endangered you."

"And Madame Renarde," Vivian reminded him sharply. She was still furious and terrified to learn about the implications of that situation even though her companion could have died had she remained in the cave. Then something else niggled in her mind. "But my uncle is a Lord Vampire and he took me under his roof when I created a scandal during my London Season. A Season that he paid for when my last one failed to bring a match." In fact, she suspected that Uncle had paid for her previous failed Season as well. "Clearly, it is not an anomaly for vampires to care for their families."

Rhys shrugged. "Not an anomaly, but most certainly a privilege few can afford."

Undaunted by his cynicism, she pressed for solutions to his problem. "Are vampires permitted to move? To seek another lord?"

"In theory, yes." His mirthless laugh gave her chills. "But first one's lord must permit a vampire to seek a new territory. Then the vampire must apply to the lord of the place he wishes to move to and pray for acceptance. Do you think I would not have tried doing so before becoming an outlaw?"

Vivian flinched at his bitter tone. "Your lord refused to allow you to petition to move?"

"Oh, he allowed me to apply." Again, that bitter laugh erupted. "Yet he refused to provide me with a reference. The vampire who made me gave me one, but it wasn't good enough.

Blackpool and all neighboring Lord Vampires denied my applications with alacrity."

She sucked in a breath at his words. He'd tried to appeal to Uncle Aldric the honorable way first, but had been turned away. Much as she wished she could disapprove of him turning criminal, she could understand his motives. "References? You are like servants!"

"Serfs, more like." Rhys spat in the fire. "Servants have more rights."

His anger, justified as it was, alarmed her. Vivian tried to shift the topic. "Tell me about your family."

As she asked the question, she realized that she was honestly curious about these people who'd inspired such devotion from this vampire.

Rhys's furious countenance softened at the very mention of his family. "Emily is the strongest, most hard-working woman I know. Sadly, she is also the most soft-hearted, as well. She fell for a scheming ne'er do well who cleaned out her meager dowry and mortgaged her farm before having the good graces to get himself shot for cheating at cards. Yet while he did his utmost to neglect her and drain the farm dry, she has managed the farm on her own and kept up with the payments until a bad harvest set her back. All while raising her children to be honest, honorable, and as industrious as herself."

Vivian found it fascinating that he praised such qualities that he now lacked. Also, to her surprise, she experienced a pang of envy for his admiration of a widowed farm worker, someone of the lower classes that her father sometimes scorned. The memory of Father's disdain filled her with distaste. What had she or her father done to earn a living? They may have more wealth than the working class, but that had been inherited. They lacked any noble titles and were considered poor relations by most of Society, which was one of the reasons Vivian had trouble finding a husband.

Perhaps this was the source of ghastly green jealousy fermenting in her belly for this Emily. It couldn't be anything else. And yet... "How are you and Emily related?"

"She's the great-great granddaughter of my brother," Rhys said. "As I look too young to be an uncle, I merely introduced myself to her as my cousin when I attended her wedding. We've exchanged letters ever since."

Vivian's eyes widened at all the "greats" and she tried not to think about the fact that cousins often married, especially distant ones. "How old are you?"

"One hundred and twenty-six." Rhys regarded her with a challenging stare as if he expected her to be appalled.

She wasn't appalled, but she was astonished that he'd been on this earth for over a century. How many kings had he lived through? Three? Or was it four? "You must have seen much change in the world."

"I have. But now all I wish to see are the insides of my eyelids. It is past dawn and I wish to get out of these wet clothes."

He yawned and stretched, his fangs glistening deadly sharp in the firelight. She thought of all the times he'd covered his mouth before, when laughing or yawning.

Rhys rose from the cot and unbuttoned his shirt. Vivian remained frozen, rapt as his broad, muscular chest was bared to her. A chest that had been pressed against hers not too long ago. She swallowed as her mouth went dry and he turned and cocked his eyebrow. "You are not planning on sleeping in a gown soaked with tea, are you?"

"Of course not!" she left his cot and pulled down the privacy curtain in front of her bed. She pulled her rumpled night shirt out of the trunk where Madame Renarde kept their clothes and immediately encountered a problem. "Ah, Rhys?"

"Yes?"

Heat flooded her face. "I… cannot reach the buttons on this gown."

He cleared his throat. "Would you like for me to assist you?"

"Please." Aside from being damp, the garment was too tight in the shoulders and bodice and dreadfully uncomfortable.

He came behind the curtain and she turned her back, not only so he could reach the buttons, but so he wouldn't see her blush.

His breath was warm on the back of her neck as his fingers worked their way down the multitude of buttons. Though he unfastened the buttons briskly, making as little contact as possible, she shivered at every light touch of his fingers.

"That's the last one," he whispered, as he released a button at her lower back. "I'll leave you to it and build up the fire."

The moment he left, she felt the cold. Hurriedly, she struggled out of the gown and thanked the heavens that she didn't have to wrestle with stays. Then she shrugged out of her shift, donned the night shirt, and climbed into the cot.

Wrong as it was, Vivian peered around the curtain to see if Rhys had removed his trousers, and fought back disappointment to see his shadow through the barrier, climbing into his own bed.

As she lay in her cot, watching the light and shadows play across the bamboo curtain and cave walls, she worried about Madame Renarde. Had her uncle fetched a doctor for her, or had he killed her? No, he couldn't have. For one thing, Vivian refused to believe Uncle Aldric would be so cruel, vampire or no. For another, Madame Renarde was exceedingly clever. She would have withheld information to preserve her life, if needed.

Still, Vivian worried. She also felt her companion's absence in other ways. Without a chaperone, Rhys's nearness was a palpable thing. In fact, all propriety that had been observed with Madame Renarde's presence had been abandoned almost immediately. They'd embraced, then she'd tried to pummel him, gotten them both wet with tea, and then he'd been on top of her. He'd kissed her again too. She bit her lip as her lower body pulsed at the memory. And now he'd even helped her undress.

She was already beyond compromised. Yet she could not bring herself to regret it. In fact, she wanted more. Even his bite had been pleasurable.

Was he suffering from the same temptations as she was? Or was it only her blood he craved? Blood, she reminded herself. He was a vampire. He drank blood to survive. That prompted another thought.

"Rhys?"

"What?" he grumbled.

"Is it difficult for you, having me so close?"

She heard what sounded like his fist striking his pillow. "Difficult in what way?"

Her fingers tangled in the hem of her blanket. "Does it make you hungry?"

"Yes. In more ways than one. Now go to sleep, or I'll bite you." His bedcovers rustled as his shadow rolled over.

He would do no such thing. Vivian knew it. Unlike Lord Summerly and other so-called gentlemen that she'd known in her life, he would never hurt her, or try to ravage her against her will.

As her eyes closed, it occurred to her that it was a sad state of affairs when a vampire could be trusted more than most men to behave himself. And it was completely mad that she wasn't so certain that she even wanted him to behave.

Chapter Eighteen

The next night, Rhys returned from his hunt in a less than satisfied state. Vivian's words echoed in his mind as he slapped the newspaper against his hip.

"Is it difficult for you, having me so close? ...Does it make you hungry?"

His cock had hardened immediately when she'd asked those impudent questions and he'd licked his fangs in memory of the sweet taste of her blood. His thirst had been easy to tamp down, but his arousal had stubbornly remained throughout the morning, taunting him with memories of how her soft body had felt beneath his. The pounding of their hearts, the heat of her breath against his ear. The memories had turned to feverish imaginings of stripping off her gown, claiming her lush lips with his own, and their naked bodies entwined on his cot.

For all his admonishments for her to sleep, it had been an eternity before he'd been able to find his own slumber. Only to be tormented by erotic dreams.

By the time darkness had fallen, Rhys had to flee the cave lest he forget his vow to keep Vivian untouched. Slaking his bloodthirst on a tavern wench had only taken the edge off his feverish madness.

And now he had to return to the source of his hellish temptation. Some mad demon within looked forward to it. And to be truthful, Rhys had been lonely, such was the life of a rogue vampire. Having someone to converse with, to read with, and fence with had filled a void within him.

But it was all to end soon. If the Lord of Blackpool agreed to the terms of the ransom letter Rhys had sent with Madame Renarde, then Vivian would return home in four nights' time. An ache burrowed deep in Rhys's chest even as he cursed himself for the lowest of fools. He would miss her terribly.

When he returned to the cave, Vivian didn't rush to him and clasp his hands as she had last night. He tried to tamp down disappointment even as his gaze roved over her captivating smile and blushing cheeks. She was pleased to see him. Yet he should not care.

Still, he returned her grin and held up the newspaper. "Guess what I've brought?"

Her blue eyes widened, and she clasped her hands together with girlish glee. "More 'Two Hills?'"

He nodded and drew the paper back when she tried to snatch it from him. "I will only hand it over if you promise to read aloud while I prepare your breakfast. You are not the only one who wishes to know what happened to Constable Daleson."

"I promise." Vivian quivered with visible impatience. "Who do you suppose shot him? I think it was the Widow Josephine."

"Preposterous," Rhys snorted, though he always enjoyed her theories. Sometimes, she even guessed correctly. "She has no motive."

"I think that she thinks she does," Vivian argued. "But we shall see, won't we?"

Under the spell of her enthusiasm, he handed her the paper and removed a heavy pack from his shoulders containing more food, fresh water, and fuel for the lanterns. As Vivian read, he prepared a breakfast of ham, eggs, and porridge.

She handed him the paper when he offered her the plate and he picked up reading where she left off. To their disappointment, the mystery was not solved in this issue. Instead, they were left with more questions.

"Who was that large apparition who visited the constable?" Vivian asked when he set the paper aside. "Do you suppose he was a dream, or could he be one of the fairy folk?"

They speculated for at least a quarter hour, and then spent even longer trying to parse the riddles the apparition had told the constable.

Vivian sighed blissfully as Rhys cleaned the dishes and cookware. "Do you know what I love most about this story?"

He tried to tear his gaze away from her radiant face. "What?"

"That I have no idea how it will end. Most tales have a sense of where the characters will end up on their journey, but not this one." She reached for a basket next to her cot and pulled out one of his stockings, along with a needle and thread. "With all the strange events and blurred lines between fiction and reality, who knows what will become of these odd characters?"

"Yes!" Rhys exclaimed, delighted not only with her understanding of the appeal of such an eccentric story, but also with the sight of her mending his clothing. He tried to remind himself that the gesture meant nothing. Ladies sewed and embroidered to occupy their time. But the domestic picture she presented made his chest tight with yearning for the impossible.

Vivian stitched a hole in his stocking with deft practice and reached for another garment in the pile. "I'm reminded that our stories are similar in their unpredictability and ventures to the unknown. Only the good Lord knows how our journeys will end."

Her naïve optimism crushed his already flagging spirits. "No," he said coldly as he returned the clean pots and pans to their proper shelves. "I do know how they'll end. Even if I'm able to secure the money to save Emily's farm, your uncle will ensure that I am hunted down and executed. You'll be cheated out of a future with a husband and children, as your uncle will either

Change you into a vampire or set you up in a life of luxury to ensure your silence on his secrets."

Vivian flinched and stared at him with wounded eyes. Then her lips thinned, and she lifted her chin. "No. I refuse to accept that you'll die. I will talk to Uncle, do what I can to dissuade him from searching for you."

Rhys's lips curved in a grim smile. If only things were that easy. Sadly, no Lord Vampire would allow a rogue vampire to inflict such damage on his kin and be permitted to live. Not if he wanted to save face. "That is very kind of you, considering all I've put you through." Not wishing to spend what little time they had left arguing, he changed the subject. "You've been cooped up in this cave for too long. Why don't we fence for a while?"

Instead of an enthusiastic agreement, Vivian regarded him with a stormy glare. "Why should we bother? With your preternatural speed and abilities, you'll just win. I cannot believe you'd been toying with me this entire time, drawing out our duels when you could have defeated me in a trice."

Rhys chuckled at her blazing indignation. "*Why* should we bother? For one thing, swordplay is not about winning, Vivian. It is for the enjoyment of the dance. And I very much enjoy dancing with you. For another, just because you cannot move with a vampire's swiftness does not mean I cannot teach you new techniques."

Her lashes lowered and her cheeks pinkened at the mention of dancing. Then her anger melted like snow beneath a sunbeam. "You would teach me?"

"Yes." He unlocked his sword case and handed her a rapier. "And you may have some tricks I have not learned."

They sparred for two glorious hours. Rhys remained in awe of Vivian's already formidable skill coupled with her quick grasp on the new moves he taught her. She even contributed a few new steps and attacks to his repertoire. Only when she was panting from exertion did he declare a stop.

Invigorated from the lessons, he escorted her back to the cave. "You did very well."

"If I were a vampire, I may be able to defeat you," she teased with a cheeky grin. "Perhaps if I become one, I'll track you down for another match."

Rhys's blood went cold at her cavalier manner. "Do not jest about becoming what I am. Pray your uncle will have another solution to the problem I caused."

Vivian paused, startled as she placed her rapier back in its case. "Is it truly so terrible, to be a vampire?"

At her wounded eyes, Rhys immediately regretted his harsh tone. "It does have its benefits, but I've lost so many things that I took for granted in my mortal days."

"How *did* you become a vampire?" she asked as she rummaged through the cupboard where he stored the food.

Should he tell her? Rhys hadn't spoken of that fateful time of his life since he'd lived under the rule of the Lord of Manchester and had friends with whom to share stories of their Changes.

He'd already broken several vampire laws where Vivian was concerned. What was one more? "I'll tell you under one condition."

Her eyes narrowed with suspicion. "And what would that be?"

"You tell me anything I ask about yourself." He knew it was not only callous, but also fruitless to learn more about her, but the mysteries she withheld continued to tantalize him.

Vivian's expression remained shuttered as she buttered a scone. After a long silence, she nodded. "Very well. I suppose if I can pry, so can you."

"Let's not think of it as prying on either side." Rhys filled the kettle with fresh water and put it on the grate. "We're only trading tales to pass the time, not so much different as reading Two Hills."

She chuckled and took a bite of her scone. "That's nothing like it and you know it. Two Hills is fiction. We're discussing our lives."

Rhys shrugged and took a piece of wood he was carving out from under his cot. "Very well, have it your way. In 1726, I was a privateer for the Royal Navy. However, we were indeed more like pirates, raiding any Dutch and Austrian merchant for their goods, using the Spanish War of Succession as justification. I loved the sea. The smell of the salt air, the excitement of keeping afloat during a storm, the rainbow of the sun across the endless blue water." He smiled at the memory as he withdrew his carving knife. "I loved it so much that my wife left me."

She sucked in a breath. "You had a wife?"

He shrugged. "In a manner of speaking. I was honor bound to wed her after I sheltered her from a storm when her carriage was overturned. We rarely saw each other, as I was away at sea almost all the time. I was also unfaithful to her, for there were tempting beauties at every port, and I was young and feckless, so I could hardly fault her for finding happiness elsewhere. I granted her an annulment and returned to my first love, the sea. Sadly, that love was taken from me soon after."

"Why?" she asked somewhat sharply, doubtless disapproving of his infidelity.

Rhys grinned, happy to confess one of his more honorable moments. "I relieved my captain of some of his cargo."

Her eyes narrowed. "You stole from your own captain?"

He shook his head. "I do not see it that way. You see, he was attempting to add slave trading to our illicit side ventures. While I did not object to pillaging vessels from enemy nations, this was too immoral and far out of the bounds of our royal duties. So, I released the slaves when we made port in Plymouth." His chest tightened as he recalled the pitiful conditions of the captives and the wretched smell of their tight quarters. "I was sacked immediately. However, I also reported the captain's unlawful activities to the Crown and he was arrested for piracy and unchartered trading."

"And the slaves you released?" Vivian's disapproving countenance had softened, replaced with an aching sympathy.

"I only encountered two afterwards. One set up a thriving business as a costume maker for the theater. The other joined the Royal Army. I know that others only wanted to return home, and I pray they found their way safely." Rhys still wondered about their fates from time to time. His own was more dismal after his deed. "As for me, no captains would take me on after what I'd done, so I was forced to return home to Blackpool. Unfortunately, my father was outraged at both my annulment and my loss of my position. We'd never got on well in the first place, so it was easy for him to order me to leave the farm and never return. My brother inherited the farm after that. We exchanged letters after I settled in Manchester and labored on a small farm. I'm afraid I became a bit of a wastrel at the time, drinking my wages." He favored her with a self-deprecating smirk. "One good thing came from it, I suppose. I made a friend. I cannot tell you his name, for his secrets are not mine to reveal. He was an odd fellow, nursed the same pint for hours at a time, but we conversed about topics of every nature. He was also one of the only people who saw honor in freeing the slaves and turning my captain over to the crown." Haunting sadness crept into Rhys's memories at the mention of this friend.

"We met at the same pub for years. Then one night, I'd won a large purse on a hand of cards and was knifed in the back by a thief. Just when I thought I'd bleed to death in the alley behind the pub, my friend bit his wrist and healed my wound with his blood. That is how I discovered that he was a vampire. He then took me before the Lord of Manchester and I was given a choice for having my life saved. Either die, or become a vampire." Rhys frowned, now knowing he was denied the third option. "I only learned later that my friend should have been able to erase my memory instead. I never got up the nerve to ask him if I was one of the rare mortals who are immune to mesmerism, or if he simply wanted me to join him so badly that he misled me."

"What happened to him?" Vivian leaned forward, rapt with fascination.

"He was the one who told the Lord of Manchester that I was leaving the territory without permission." The betrayal still stung. "He was the one who recommended that I be exiled."

"But he was your friend!" Outrage rang in her voice.

Rhys nodded. "Yes, and he was a great mentor as well. However, he seemed to feel that since he Changed me, that meant that he had the right to control every aspect of my life. At first, I did not notice how controlling he was, because I was so grateful to him for not only teaching me everything about my powers and how to live as a vampire, but also for granting me a life of more wealth, comfort, and education than I ever would have been able to achieve without him. He even took me to see the world, once we had leave from our lord. But as the decades passed, living with him became more constricting."

"Did he have an… ah…" Her cheeks flushed crimson. "…an interest in you that was more than mere friendship?"

Rhys's jaw dropped in astonishment that she knew of such things. Madame Renarde must have told her. He coughed. "I'd sometimes wondered, but he never gave any indication that he thought of me in *that* manner, and as far as I was aware, he took female lovers." Rhys hadn't thought of John in years, of how their friendship had bloomed, then soured. "He lost interest in me after the first century, and began his quest to find a new companion more to his liking. Or maybe only more malleable. Yet he must have kept some attention on me, as my visits to my family were carried out with the utmost discretion. But one night, six years ago, I was arrested by the Lord of Manchester's second and third in command, and forced to confess everything with my former friend standing by and supplying any information I left out. At his recommendation, I was exiled. I've been robbing carriages to help Emily regain the farm ever since." Rhys set down his tea cup. "And that's my tale as of now. Rather dull, I imagine."

"Not at all," Vivian said fervently. "To have lived such a long life, to have adapted to a new society and different challenges of survival is very fascinating. You must have seen and experienced so many things. Did you ever fall in love?"

"I thought I had, a time or two." Rhys tried to ignore the twinge of heat at her saying that word. "But with mortals, you quickly realize that not only can you live without a person, you must. With other vampires..." He shrugged. "Most are already attached, and those who are not are generally disinclined towards devoting themselves to one being. Not when they've tasted freedom that mortal women cannot fathom."

"Freedom." She breathed the word like a prayer. "I would very much like to know how that feels."

"From me?" That should he his first assumption, but something in her tone made him think she was talking about so much more. He remembered the conversation he'd overheard between Vivian and Madame Renarde. "Or from your marriage prospects?"

Although her reluctance to talk about her fears of marriage had nothing to do with their situation and were likely rendered invalid for her future, Rhys remained perversely curious about her unconventional views on the matter. Especially when she hadn't so much as blinked when he'd told her that he'd likely cheated her out of having a husband. Emily's distaste for the prospect of remarrying, he could understand, given how her first husband had destroyed her life. But Vivian had no such compass to steer her in the direction of spinsterhood.

When she avoided his gaze, he grasped her chin and tilted her face towards his. "You promised you would answer any question I am inclined to ask."

For a moment, she looked as if she'd protest, then she sighed with resignation and drew back from him. "Very well. You'll think me silly and spoilt, I warn you."

"I've learned long ago not to discount a person's feelings as silly, I assure you."

She regarded him with a cautious smile as she refilled her tea cup. "I'm my father's only daughter, and by the time I was born, my brother was already nearly full grown, so we never had a chance to become close. Mother died when I was only four, and I was given over to the care of my nanny and tutors."

"That sounds rather lonely," Rhys said. At least when he was younger, his father had been attentive. His mother had doted on him and his older brother had been his favorite playmate.

"It was." The statement was matter-of-fact as she sipped her tea. "I hardly ever encountered other children, so I imagined playmates from the stories I read. That is likely why I was always so fanciful. Father took little interest in me until my seventeenth birthday. At first, I was overjoyed that he at last took notice of me and turned myself inside out to please him. But when he made it clear that his wish was for me to find a husband, I realized he only sought to rid himself of me." The hurt in her eyes made Rhys long to take her in his arms. "Aside from Madame Renarde becoming my companion, three years ago, my introduction to Society was a resounding disappointment. With my plain looks and meager dowry, I was passed over in the Marriage Mart, year after year."

"You are *not* plain!" Rhys interjected, outraged at the thought of this beauty speaking so dismally about herself.

Vivian laughed drily. "That is kind of you to say, but my father mourned the fact all my life. His worries proved correct as I languished as a wallflower. The man who wished for me to be his mistress flat out told me."

"Well that proves the lie," Rhys said, arching his brow in challenge. "Why would he want a plain mistress?"

Her hand froze with her teacup halfway to her mouth and she gave him a stunned look as if the thought had not occurred to her. "Perhaps it was my dowry that was plain."

"Tell me more of this cad and his insulting proposal." Rhys would love to wring his neck. "Was he the source of the scandal you and Madame Renarde alluded to?"

"Yes. Lord Summerly cornered me in the conservatory and attempted to…" Her features contorted in a grimace of disgust. "His hands were everywhere. Then Lord Falton and his wife opened the door and I was so humiliated and angry that I challenged Lord Summerly to a duel." Her lips quirked up. A smile at last, but it vanished quickly. "Everyone was outraged at my challenge, while Summerly's behavior was ignored. My father sent me off to Blackpool to stay with my uncle until the talk died down. Unfortunately, Uncle Aldric seemed to be just as eager to have me married off to be rid of me."

"Likely to ensure you did not remain long enough to learn his secret." Rhys could not believe that he was defending the vampire who was his enemy. The cold-hearted villain who would see Emily and the children forced from their home. Yet he had to admit that the Lord of Blackpool's reasons for wanting to see Vivian wed was for the sake of her safety and his, rather than any dislike of his niece.

Furthermore, he could not stop himself from offering comfort. "I am certain Blackpool—er—Lord Thornton, is fond of you and cares for you very much."

It was a discomfiting realization, that Rhys and the Lord of Blackpool had that in common, caring for mortal kin. The knowledge made it difficult to hate the man.

"If he cared so much, why hasn't he paid the ransom?" Vivian asked with an accusing glare.

"The point of a ransom is that the hostage is not harmed, so he knew you were safe. Now that the stakes have changed, I am certain he will be in a hurry to deliver the money." Rhys changed the subject, not wanting to dwell on what life would be like with her gone. "You still have not told me why you were so afraid of marriage."

She attempted to hide an exasperated frown with her cup. "All my life, I've been told what I should want, but I've never felt that I do want those things. I know that I am expected to run my husband's household, serve as a hostess for his parties, and bear his children. Yet little is said about sharing interests, a meeting of minds, or even fondness. And there seems to be no expectation about what a husband is supposed to do for me."

"A lifetime of thing-hood," he said, repeating the words he'd heard her say.

"Yes." She nodded. "I do not wish for my husband to be like my father. Treating me like an inconvenient and uninteresting pet."

"I am certain there are countless men who wouldn't treat you in such a way." Namely him.

"I do believe that. However, I spent so much time alone that I find it difficult to go about discerning which men would be inclined to enjoy my company." Vivian set her cup aside and hugged her knees. "And it isn't only about the men. I do not even know what I want, or what makes me happy. I know I enjoy reading, and Madame Renarde gifted me with a love of fencing, but other than that?" Her shoulders hunched. "How am I supposed to find a man who suits me when I don't even know who I am?"

Rhys placed his hand atop hers. "I know who you are. You are a strong, courageous woman with an insatiable curiosity, quick mind, and a passion for living. You're also a great beauty. All you require is confidence and a freedom to explore various interests to learn what incites your passion. I've seen how decisive you can be."

"Do you truly believe so?" The hope in her voice tugged his heartstrings. He couldn't bear to tell her that he'd likely ruined her marriage prospects.

"I do." He squeezed her hand. "And if I didn't need the money for my family, I would have instead demanded your hand in marriage as my ransom." The admission slipped out before he thought.

Silence fell between them as she stared at him in shock.

He cursed under his breath. "Forget I said that."

"Rhys?" Vivian's imploring eyes were large enough to drown in. "Could you show me what marital affection is like?"

Rhys froze. She couldn't mean what he thought she meant... *could she*?

Chapter Nineteen

Vivian watched Rhys freeze like a startled hare in the woods. She didn't know what reaction she'd expected to her brazen request, but it hadn't been this look of fear. Not after he'd blithely admitted that he would wed her under other circumstances.

Rhys cleared his throat. "Ah, what exactly do you mean?"

"What I mean is that despite your kind words about finding a husband who I will get on well with, I do not think that can happen anymore." She held up a hand before he could spout off another round of heartfelt apologies. "Between holding me alone with you in this cave and revealing the secrets of the existence of vampires, I know I must be compromised beyond all hope."

His features contorted with guilt. "I am—"

"Don't you dare apologize." Vivian cut him off. "I am grateful to you for sparing me from the parson's mousetrap. Especially after tasting freedom from societal mores and expectations. Whether I become a vampire, or am permitted to

216

live out my days as a spinster, either is preferable to marriage. Aside from one thing."

He steepled his fingers below his chin. "And that is?"

"If I may be candid, I must say that I very much enjoyed your kiss, as well as the feel of your embrace." Her cheeks heated as she uttered the confession. "I want more. I want you to show me all the pleasures a man and woman can share together."

Rhys's eyes glowed molten copper, his desire blatant and palpable as he licked his lips. "I do not think that is wise," he said raggedly.

"Why not?" She moved toward him, placing her hands on his shoulders. "I am already compromised, staying with you unchaperoned. Why not enjoy the very things that will be assumed anyway?"

"Your uncle—"

"If he did not want this to happen, then he should have paid the ransom immediately." Another spear of hurt pierced her heart that Uncle Aldric had indeed placed his pride above her safety, but she forced it down. "He deserves to be taught a lesson."

Rhys shook his head. "That is not a reason for us to…"

"Of course not," she said with an agreeable smile. "I only mention that because it remains a fact. Besides, you threatened to cut off my finger. I'd much prefer to lose my maidenhead than a digit."

His frown deepened. "I wasn't serious about your finger."

"I know you weren't." She shook her head dismissively, wanting to get back to important matters. Matters between him and her. "Never mind about uncle. I know you desire me, and I feel the same. Just because I wish to live as a spinster does not mean I wish to remain a virgin."

"You cannot know whether you'll be permitted to live as a spinster." Rhys's hands slid to her waist, but then he snatched them back as if he'd been burned. "You do not know what your fate will be."

"I know that no one has ever given me a choice with regards to my fate." The old anger coiled in her gut and she spoke more sharply than she intended. "For once I want to make a choice. And I want that choice to be which man I lie with. My choice is you."

Boldly, Vivian leaned forward and pressed her lips against his. For a moment, he remained stiff and unyielding, aside from a nearly imperceptible quiver in his muscles. Then, his arms locked around her body and he pulled her roughly against him. His mouth moved with hers hungrily, a low growl reverberating in his throat. Vivian slid her hands down his back, reveling in the feel of his firm muscles. Electric shivers rippled through her body as his tongue slid across the seam on her lips and she opened her mouth to yield to his exploration.

Time seemed to vanish as they kissed and stroked each other, hands and bodies surging to become closer. Desire flared from her belly down, converging between her thighs in a fiery pulse. Rhys pulled her into his lap, and she gasped at the feel of his hardness pressing against her throbbing core.

His lips trailed down her jaw and across her neck. Frissons of pleasure resonated from her flesh. The sensations he wrought were most divine.

No wonder ladies were supposed to remain chaperoned whenever they were alone with a man, Vivian thought dizzily as her fingers plunged into Rhys's silken hair. She'd been told that men possessed an animalistic nature and could not be trusted not to act upon their base instincts if granted the opportunity, but she'd never imagined that women also succumbed to the same primal needs.

If she didn't feel Rhys's bare skin against hers soon, she felt she'd go mad.

Suddenly, he drew back with a ragged gasp. His fangs glistened in the firelight. "It's been too long since I've last fed. I'm afraid that if we continue, I may not be able to refrain from…"

"It's all right." She recalled the tantalizing pleasure of his bite. "I want you to drink from me tonight. You've provided me nourishment these past several nights. Why not let me do the same?"

That hungry growl rumbled in his throat once more and he licked his fangs. "Why must you tempt me so?"

She threaded her arms around his waist and pulled him close. "Because I wish to please you, as you've pleased me."

His fangs grazed her throat, making her shiver. "Not yet. Not until I've pleased you. This is your first time, and I want to make it... beautiful for you. Then..." He sucked in a shuddering breath. "Then I will taste you."

Vivian's heart pounded beneath her ribs. He was going to do it after all. He was going to make love to her. Sudden nervousness imbued her. Not about the act and the potential pain she'd heard about, but that she would be disappointing to him.

Her face heated again. "Do you wish me to disrobe?"

Rhys laughed, a low and sensuous sound. "I would very much appreciate the pleasure of undressing you. But all in good time." He grasped her hands and rose to his feet, pulling her with him. "Come here."

He led her towards his cot and paused to place another log on the fire. Once she was seated, he knelt on the floor and slid his hands up her skirts, caressing her calves and shins. Vivian gasped at the new sensation, never guessing that her legs, even through the thin fabric of stockings, would be so sensitive.

Rhys favored her with a wicked grin as he shifted her skirts up higher. "Would you like me to continue?"

"Please." The word came out in a gasp.

That sinful smile broadened as his fingers danced above the tops of her stockings, stroking her thighs in whispering touches that made her tremble. As his fingertips neared the juncture between her thighs, her center began to tingle with anticipation. Yet he did not touch her there, and Vivian had to bite her lip to hold back a whimper of disappointment when he instead ceased his teasing caresses and sank back on his heels.

"Christ, you have the finest pair of legs I've ever touched," Rhys said.

Vivian warred between triumph that for once she'd been declared the best, and envy at the other women who'd been in his bed. All her thoughts swept away like the tide when he sat next to her on the cot and pulled her into his arms once more.

"I want to hold you again," he whispered against her ear and sank them down on the thin pallet together.

The bed was narrow, so they had to stay pressed close together. Vivian did not mind. It seemed she could not get enough of this achingly close contact with him. His hands moved up from her back to her hair, and he began to loosen her braid. Her scalp tingled with pleasure that she'd never felt when her companion had performed this simple task.

"I want to see your magnificent hair spread across my pillow," Rhys whispered.

Joyous disbelief filled her at his words. All the times her father and other men had praised the appeal of blondes had always stung. But Rhys called her brown hair magnificent. Yet another reason why she wanted him to be the one to take her maidenhood.

Though as she studied the sculpted planes of his cheekbones, his rakish long hair, copper eyes, and sensuous lips, Vivian couldn't deny that the fact that he was devastatingly handsome also played a factor in her decision. Recalling her stolen glimpses of his bare chest, Vivian longed to feel his solid flesh beneath her fingers. She reached for the buttons of his shirt and unfastened the top one. When he did not object, she moved to the next.

When she'd undone all the buttons, Rhys shifted and shrugged out of his shirt, at last treating her with the view she anticipated.

"May I touch you?" she asked softly.

His knuckles brushed her cheek. "Only if I may return the favor."

"Oh, yes," she breathed, then splayed her hands against his bare chest, noticing how his nipples hardened immediately. When her thumb brushed across the dark nub, he sucked in a breath. "Does that feel agreeable?"

He nodded, and she continued exploring his sculpted form, feeling his heart pounding beneath her palm. Just like hers was beating fast. She delved down to his flat stomach, enjoying the feel of his heated flesh. But when she moved lower, to the fastenings on his trousers, he stopped her.

"Not yet." He moved her hand aside. "Now I think it is time to help you out of your gown."

This dress, one of the garments Rhys had stolen, opened in the front. Something she'd been grateful for this afternoon when she'd been able to put it on herself without asking for help. Now, as his fingers worked each button free, revealing her bodice inch by inch, Vivian trembled with anticipation.

Rhys paused and regarded her with a concerned look. "Do you want me to stop?"

She shook her head. "Please continue."

He unfastened the remaining buttons and worked the dress over her head, and tossed it across the cave onto her cot. She lay beside him in only her chemise and stockings, yet he did not give her time to dwell on her diminished garb.

Rhys cupped her heavy breasts through the fabric of her chemise and she gasped at the heat of his palms. His thumbs grazed her nipples, turning them into swollen, sensitive peaks.

He slid the top of her chemise down, baring her to his hungry gaze.

She'd thought that breasts only served to fill out a gown and feed infants, but she'd been wrong. Oh, so wrong.

"So beautiful," he whispered, then lowered his head and covered her mounded flesh with kisses. His fingers continued to stroke the sides of her breasts as his tongue circled her areola before flicking over her nipples, sending jolts of electric pleasure coursing through her entire body.

His mouth and fingers worked their way lower as he tugged her chemise down her waist and down her hips. For a moment, everything she was taught cried out that she should be ashamed to be unclothed before a man, but then, as she looked up at Rhys's adoring gaze and felt his gentle touch, she realized that nothing was more natural than this.

"Perfection," he muttered, and lay down beside her, pulling her into his arms. For a long while, he just held her. The feel of his arms around her and the warmth of his bare flesh against hers filled a void within her, an ache she'd endured since time immemorable.

Vivian trailed her fingers along his back, reveling in the texture of his masculine flesh. She tilted her chin up and he answered the unspoken plea by claiming her lips with his. They kissed for a blissful eternity, tasting and exploring each other.

Rhys's hands caressed her hips and teased her thighs above the tops of her stockings. She shivered at the sensations he wrought and shifted her hips closer. When her center grazed his hardness, a pulse of heat flared through her core. Rhys groaned at the contact.

"Did that hurt?" She didn't want to cause him any discomfort.

"No," Rhys hissed through his teeth, yet his expression did indeed look pained. "Let me show you what it felt like."

His fingers shifted up from the top of her stocking and delved between her thighs. Vivian gasped at the contact. She'd never imagined that men would touch women *there* with their hands. She thought they only wanted to touch them with their parts. It was as if he'd lit a sort of fire there, making a strange ache coalesce in her most secret place. She'd pleasured herself this way before, but him doing so felt completely different. The pad of his thumb circled the nub at the top and she cried out.

He gave her words back to her. "Did *that* hurt?"

She shook her head. "I don't know how to describe it." She reached up and stroked his cheek. "I only know that I do not want you to stop."

Rhys's smile was sin incarnate. "Then I will continue until you ask me to."

His fingers wrought magic, pulses of ecstasy that intensified with every stroke. Vivian pulled him to her, kissing him to silence her cries. The sensations built and spiraled through her being and then shot through her like bolts of lightning.

Rhys pulled her tighter against him with his free arm and continued his ministrations until she gripped his shoulder, shuddering from the magnitude of his touch. "No more."

Immediately, he withdrew his hand and licked his fingers. The sight of the carnal gesture made her blush.

"I would like to taste you there," he said. "To bring you to climax with my mouth."

She quivered in his arms, imagining the feel of his tongue on her sensitive flesh. "I do not think I could bear that."

"Perhaps tomorrow." He grinned wickedly. "Right now, I would very much like to make love to you."

Her eyes widened, remembering the purpose of what they were doing. He would be inside her. Would it give her the same pleasure?

Rhys loosened his grip on her shoulders. "If you do not wish me to, I will not."

"I do," she said, pulling him closer. "I am only a little frightened. I am told that there is pain the first time."

He closed his eyes, silent for a moment before meeting her gaze. "Yes. I would do everything possible to lessen it. But we don't have to—"

"Yes," Vivian said. She reached down and cupped the hard ridge in his bulging trousers. "I want more of you. I want all of you."

Rhys's eyes glowed copper fire as he unlaced the fastenings and slid his trousers down his hips, releasing his swollen length. Vivian sucked in a breath at the sight, so different than what was depicted in paintings. Long and thick, with a drop of moisture beaded on its ruddy tip, she could only stare at it in awe.

Then he covered her body with his, infusing her with the heat she'd already begun to crave on her skin. She felt the tip of him press against her tender core. He withdrew, then slowly pressed into her further. So far, it did not hurt. In fact, she rather enjoyed the sensation of him sliding across her wet flesh.

When he came to a point where there was resistance and a slight bit of discomfort, paused. "Do you still wish for me to drink from you?"

She blinked at his whispered question, then understood, remembering the pleasure of his bite. He wanted to distract her from her pain. "Yes."

His fangs pierced her neck at the same time he thrust inside her. Vivian still felt a second of pain, but it was drowned with the hypnotic bliss of his bite. The pleasure throbbed as he drank, pleasure that didn't last long enough. After a few swallows, he lifted his head from her neck and licked the blood from his lips. The sight should have been horrifying, yet instead, she felt a deep satisfaction that she was able to provide something he craved.

He remained still within her, his heart pounding so hard she could feel it.

"Is this all it is?" Vivian asked, somewhat disappointed. All those poems and bawdy songs were about a few moments?

Rhys chuckled, though it sounded strange. "No. I only wish for you to become accustomed to me, so I do not hurt you further."

"Oh." The sensation of having him inside her was indeed overwhelming. Yet beneath the slight ache, there was something else. Instinctively, she shifted her hips and gasped at the twinge of pleasure.

Vivian moved again, and this time Rhys moved with her until their hips rocked together in a hypnotic rhythm. She clung to him, reveling in the heat and strength of his embrace. The arcs of pleasure strengthened and reverberated like a melody.

Rhys kissed her neck and whispered, "You feel like heaven."

She trembled in his arms, awash with the sense of poignant closeness. As her pleasure built, she arched her hips as the pleasure built higher and higher, cascading into a crescendo of earth-shattering sensations. Her lips formed his name as she shuddered beneath him.

Rhys held her tighter, stroking her hair as he kissed her and murmured endearments. Then he let out a primal growl of satisfaction before his mouth locked over her neck. The rhythmic pulses of his drinking echoed the tempo of her climax. She cried out, not sure she could bear any more of this exquisite ecstasy.

He drank a little more than he had during his first bite, and when he withdrew his fangs, she had to refrain from trying to pull his head back to her neck. The realization of the danger of such a desire sobered her. She didn't want him to take all her blood.

"Are you all right?" he asked. Blood trickled from his lower lip, but it wasn't hers. She saw a gash.

"Yes. Are you?" she reached up and cupped his chin. "You bit your lip."

"That was intentional. I used my blood to heal your puncture wounds." Slowly, he slipped out of her body and rolled on his side, pulling her with him. "Are you certain I didn't hurt you?"

"I'm certain." She nuzzled her cheek against his chest and stroked his back. "You were so gentle, and the experience was so…" she trailed off with a sigh. "Now I understand the meaning behind some of my favorite poems and songs."

Rhys arched a brow. "What sorts of songs has a gently-born maiden such as yourself heard about lovemaking?"

Vivian sang in French. *"When moonlight comes, my lover arrives. Our bodies become one as we engage in the oldest dance.*

In his embrace, I become incandescent. My petals open to receive his honey. Without his love I shall wilt."

He chuckled. "Madame Renarde taught you that song, I presume?"

"Not exactly." She regarded him with a coy smile. "I overheard her singing it when she worked on her embroidery or strolled through the garden. I didn't understand the words until after two years of her French lessons." She swallowed and added softly, "And it wasn't until tonight before I truly comprehended their meaning."

A look of mingled melancholy and longing suffused his handsome face. "Did I truly make you feel that way? Incandescent?"

Heat flooded her face. "I know, I sound like an utter greenhead. You must have done this with many women, and I'm sure everyone feels that way after…"

"No." Rhys kissed her firmly as if to emphasize the word. "Such passion is a rare gift." Another kiss, sweet and lingering. "And I've never experienced passion like I have with you this night."

Vivian's heart clenched at his haunting tone and soulful eyes. Could he possibly mean that? She'd been warned that most men, especially worldly rakes would say anything to convince a woman to yield her body, and there could be no one more worldly than a vampire who'd lived for well over a century.

Yet she'd been the one doing the persuading, and he hadn't spoken of passion until after he'd already had what he wanted. Her breath tightened. Did he feel the same way she did about him? But what did she feel for him?

Love. The word struck her like a blow to the ribs. She'd fallen in love with him.

That was the real reason she'd given herself to him.

"Are you all right?" Rhys broke through her thunderous realization.

"I'm wonderful." She smiled and boldly kissed him. There was no way she dared confess the depths to which he'd stolen into her heart. "I ah, need to use the chamber pot." The words had been intended as a reason to extricate herself from the warmth of his embrace before she blathered like an infatuated twit.

"Oh." He pulled them both into a sitting position and she put a hand over her eyes as a wave of dizziness engulfed her head. Rhys frowned. "Dear God, I took too much from you. I am so sorry."

"No, I am all right." To prove the point, she swung her legs over the bunk and got to her feet, swaying for a moment on weakened legs.

Rhys grasped her shoulders to steady her and did not release her until he walked her to the chamber pot. "I'll fetch water for your bath and you must eat and drink something to combat the blood loss." His tone brooked no argument. With a kiss on the forehead, he released her. "I will return soon."

Vivian attended to her business as soon as he left. The place between her thighs was sore, but at least there was no blood as she'd been warned was a possibility. She must have broken her maidenhead one of the times she'd had a rough ride on horseback. Madame Renarde told her that often happened and advised her to prick her finger on her wedding night and let the blood drip on the sheets instead.

Well, there would be no wedding night for her.

Yet she didn't regret it in the slightest.

The chilly air of the cave made her remember that she was clad in nothing but her stockings and garters. There were no more clean night shirts left, so Vivian brazenly helped herself to one of Rhys's shirts. The garment hung down past her knees. She wished she had a pair of slippers as walked on the cold stone floor to the little larder. Filling a mug with cold water from the jug, she moaned in pleasure as the cool liquid slid down her parched throat.

Rhys returned, hefting the massive cauldron of water as she was wiping the crumbs from her lips. His eyes raked down her form, clad in his shirt.

"You look quite fetching in that. Enough to stir my hunger anew," he said as he set the cauldron on the grate above the fire and added more wood. "I've brought you fresh water from the river this time. I didn't want the saltwater to sting."

As the water heated, Vivian ate. Despite having a scone earlier, she found that she was ravenous and quickly devoured a crust of bread, a chunk of cheese and some salt beef. By the time Rhys filled the tub, her dizziness had abated.

"Would you prefer that I leave you in privacy to bathe?"

She shook her head. "You've seen all of me." That, and she took primal pleasure in the way his eyes followed her as she undressed.

He tried to busy himself with other things while she bathed, but he kept stealing heated glances. His attention brought a sense of power.

Just after she washed and rinsed her hair, he cursed suddenly. "I am the greatest of fools."

"What?" she spluttered as her heart froze in her chest. Did he suddenly regret what they'd done?

But then he laughed and grabbed her cot, sliding it from its place at the wall and moved it against his. "We could have been much more comfortable earlier, had I a single thought in my head."

"Oh." Relief curled her lips upward. "Perhaps next time."

"Vivian?" His face suddenly went somber. "Would you sleep with me? Dawn approaches and I would like to hold you longer."

The thought filled her with a joy she could never imagine. "Yes."

Quickly, she dried off as best as she could and donned Rhys's shirt once more. He removed his own, along with his boots and trousers, clad only in his smalls. As she slipped beneath

232

the blankets, she wondered if he wished to take her again. Part of her wanted to allow him while the ache between her thighs protested.

But Rhys only pulled her against his chest and rested his chin on top of her head. "Heaven," he murmured.

As her body relaxed against his warmth, she could only agree. If only it could last forever.

Chapter Twenty

Aldric stood over Madame Renarde's bedside and frowned as the companion thrashed and moaned in the throes of her fever. She had not awakened since their talk in the kitchen last night.

He thought of the kidnapper's last ransom letter. The one containing the lock of Vivian's hair. *"Next time, it will be her finger,"* it had read.

Instead, the man had sent back Vivian's companion. Had it been only because Renarde was ill? A servant wasn't valuable in a ransom situation, aside from the purpose the villain had outlined in his first missive. To vouch for Vivian's virtue.

That made Aldric wonder if Renarde had been released as a message that the kidnapper intended on compromising Vivian, along with the other message he did indeed deliver.

"I know what you are," Renarde had told Aldric before she collapsed.

The man who held Vivian hostage didn't only want Aldric to know that Vivian was now alone, unchaperoned with a man. He also wanted Aldric to know that she was alone with a vampire.

Aldric's fists clenched at his sides as the possibilities of what the vampire could do to his niece flitted through his mind. The vampire likely already had fed from her. An action that filled Aldric with distaste, though he could accept that because she at least wouldn't endure lasting harm for it.

But a vampire could also mesmerize Vivian with his mind and make her do… whatever he wanted. And leave her with no memory of bending to his will, if he was merciful.

Impotent rage curdled in his gut as he imagined his dear niece being at the mercy of such a dangerous creature. True, most of their kind were imbued with laws and morals. However, whatever vampire that had taken Vivian had already flouted the law when he'd abducted two humans and revealed his nature to them. What care would such a creature have for lesser laws, like the prohibition of rape?

The urge to call his people and spread out to all neighboring territories and demand that all Lord Vampires account for their subjects roared forth once more. Yet Aldric had to refrain from such a foolhardy move. No one could know that he harbored a human who knew of their kind. And most of all, no one could learn that his niece knew.

Aldric would have to learn the identity of the culprit on his own. An easier feat when Madame Renarde was awake and able to tell him all she knew, but there were things he could deduce on his own.

His first thought was that a rival lord had taken Vivian, but Aldric immediately dismissed the notion. He hadn't made any direct enemies of any lords, though he supposed the Lord of Grimsby and the Lord of Liverpool may bear him ill will for fighting against them during London's little civil war when another vampire tried to overthrow the interim Lord of London. A Lord Vampire would demand more than two hundred pounds. Most Lords wanted more land to rule over, not money.

A common vampire was more likely, but Aldric had determined from the last Gathering that none of his own were guilty. They had all been at the Gathering the night Vivian and Madame Renarde were taken, for one thing. Furthermore, he was generous in his loans, so if any of his people needed money, he knew they would not hesitate to ask.

Would a vampire of one of the neighboring territories dare risk his own lord's wrath by committing a grave crime against another lord? Aldric doubted that very much.

All those facts led to the conclusion of what sort of vampire Aldric was dealing with.

A rogue vampire.

He shuddered at the thought. Unfortunately, logic dictated that this was most likely the case. Rogues could not stay in the same place for long, lest they risk being hunted down, so they were always in need of money. Two hundred pounds would be a king's ransom for that sort.

And since rogues were already exiled for breaking the law, they had no reason to live by the rules. Aldric loathed the system. It only bred more crime, in his opinion. So very few could be reformed, so it was best to kill them if they were caught on his land. He'd only made citizens of a handful during his two-hundred-year reign over Blackpool. One an alleged thief, who Aldric believed innocent, another who'd had an affair with his lord's mistress, and the last, a vampire whose only crime was to have been Changed by another rogue.

Aldric stiffened as the memory brought him back to the present. What if that was this rogue's threat? What if the rogue intended to Change Vivian if he did not pay the ransom? That would be far worse than if he defiled her. Naturally, Aldric would legitimize her, but he wouldn't be able to do so without notifying the Elders.

Then the Elders would naturally inquire as to how it had come about that his niece had been Changed by a rogue. That would be a blow on their regard to his leadership. A blow he could not afford. Not with older, more powerful vampires arriving from the Continent and eyeing new lands.

He had to awaken Madame Renarde. He needed every bit of information the companion had to locate the rogue and save his niece from the vampire's clutches before the unthinkable happened.

Yet when he looked at Renarde, his stomach sank in dread at the sight of her ashen pallor and fever-reddened cheeks. Although she was a large woman, she'd clearly lost weight. Her rattled breathing and intermittent coughing battered his ears. Vampire blood could heal, but for a lung ailment as severe as Renarde's, it would take time to cure her without Changing her, something he still hoped to avoid. A vampire could only Change one human every hundred years. Aldric wished to conserve his power so that he would be able to Change Vivian if he had to.

But perhaps a few drops now would be enough to rouse Madame Renarde.

Aldric pierced his finger with one of his sharp fangs and placed the digit between Renarde's lips. For a moment, she didn't respond, and his heart quickened with fear. Then her mouth tightened around his finger and she suckled the blood from his wound.

Her lashes fluttered and at last her eyes opened, still glazed with fever.

"Thirsty," she croaked.

Aldric grasped the glass of water from the bedside table and held it to her lips. She managed two greedy gulps before her head fell back on the pillows.

Her eyelids began to close and Aldric seized her shoulders. "Madam! The man who took you and Vivian. Tell me his name."

She groaned and sweat beaded on her forehead. Her pupils contracted and dilated as she struggled to focus on him. Her lips trembled with effort to form a word. "R-Rhys," she gasped at last.

"Rhys what?" A full name would help immensely.

A brittle sound that may have been a laugh clacked in her throat. "*Je... ne... pas.*" She'd reverted back to French, but Aldric was thankfully fluent. *I don't know.* She licked her lips. "He... was careful not to... give his surname."

Another of those racking coughs exploded from her lungs, deep enough to make the bed shudder. Aldric wiped the phlegm from her mouth and thanked the heavens that there was no blood in her spittle. That gave him hope that she'd recover. Also, the sweat soaking her garments gave sign that her fever was breaking at last.

He frowned suddenly. She was still garbed in the clothes she'd been wearing when he found her last night. That could not be comfortable

"Madame Renarde," he said, gently as possible, "I'm afraid if we're to keep your secret, I will have to undress you. You'll be more comfortable in a bedgown."

For a while, Renarde lay so still that he thought she hadn't heard him. Then she nodded, and her hand flapped on the counterpane as if to say, *Get on with it.*

Physically male she may be, the task still felt like undressing a helpless female. Aldric kept his eyes averted as much as possible, rolling her and lifting her as necessary to unfasten and take off her gown. He cringed at the sight of the corset, binding her stomach and chest. Little wonder she had difficulty breathing.

After no small amount of struggling with the laces, he removed the offending garment. The chemise and stocking came off easier, and he managed to avoid glimpsing anything private, unless one counted her chest, which was hairless and had enough paunch that it was no wonder they passed for breasts.

At last, he pulled a soft linen bedgown over her head and helped her get her arms through the sleeves before tucking her back under the counterpane.

"Much… better," she panted. "Thank you."

Her eyes closed once more and Aldric debated whether or not he should attempt to question her. It would be cruel in her weakened state, and possibly misleading, as she was almost certainly delirious.

Suddenly, she seized his hand and jerked her head toward the pile of her discarded clothing. "*Le…*" She coughed and took a breath. "*Le…*" Her face reddened and contorted in effort to speak. "*Lettre*," she gasped, and then collapsed on the pillow.

"There's a letter?" he asked, but Renarde was already snoring, exhausted from her feeble efforts.

Aldric snatched Madame Renarde's dress from the floor and ran his hands all over the wool until he felt the crackle of paper. He withdrew the missive from a cunning pocket in the skirts and returned to the chair beside the bed to read it.

Instead of the kidnapper's handwriting, he recognized that this missive was penned by Vivian.

Dearest Uncle,

I hope you are well and not too worried about me. My host has provided the utmost hospitality, but due to my stay being extended, he found it necessary to tell me some things of a rather personal nature.

Uncle, I know your secret. The man who I am with is like you. My host had intended to send a letter to you informing you of that fact, but since Madame Renarde has fallen ill, he was gracious and compassionate enough to instead send my dearest friend and companion home with this letter so that you may send for a doctor.

Please take care of Madame Renarde and treat her gently. She is very dear to me and more discreet than you know. Go to Bamber Bridge on Sunday and bury the money beside the gravestone of Anne Blackburn and I will be returned to you the following Tuesday.

With love,
Vivian Stratford

The two-night delay between the payment and Vivian's return did not surprise Aldric in the least. The rogue vampire was clever enough to know that Aldric could have his people surround the graveyard and seize Rhys the moment he arrived. Likely the rogue would employ a mortal, or Vivian herself to collect the money during the day. Then he would take Vivian to another location, leave her there, and send a note to Aldric telling him where he could collect her. If Rhys had not been working against him, Aldric could almost admire his wit. Every communication had come from a different source, and he'd given different locations for Aldric to deliver the ransom each time, so that there would be little hope of tracking down his location.

Rhys also acknowledged Aldric's own intelligence. That was clear in the note he'd doubtless dictated to Vivian, for this time, there was no threat if Aldric did not comply with the rogue's demands. After all, it wasn't needed, given that Vivian now knew that Aldric was a vampire. Some of the words did seem to be Vivian's own, however.

He glanced over at his resting patient. The request to treat Madame Renarde gently stung in a way. Did she believe that he would kill the companion, either for what she knew, or simply for her failure to protect his niece? And what did Vivian mean,

242

that Renarde was more discreet than he knew? Was it a promise that she would not reveal his secret, or a subtle request to not Change her into a vampire? Or was there some other coded meaning?

Perhaps he would learn from Renarde herself. He would give her more blood tomorrow and pray that she would be recovered enough to speak with him.

Chapter Twenty-one

Rhys awoke with hunger raging through him like wildfire. The scent of blood, so near, so sweet and tempting, made his upper lip curl, baring his fangs. As he moved forward to strike, a thought struck him. Since when had he awakened with a meal so close? His eyes snapped open and the sight of Vivian curled up beside him stole his breath.

The previous night and morning roared through his mind in a torrent of images and remembered sensations. He'd lain with her, taken her virginity, something he'd never intended on doing, yet something he'd been too weak to resist.

He'd fed from her as well, drank enough of her sweetness to make her dizzy. And yet his bloodthirst tore through his body with a fierceness he hadn't experienced since he was a young vampire.

Rhys drew away from her and slowly made his way off the two cots he'd placed together so that he could hold her.

As his bare feet touched the cold stone of the cave's floor, he realized that he was still naked. His gaze strayed to Vivian's bare shoulder and the memories of her smooth warm skin and her lush body entwined with his brought forth a different sort of hunger. God, he'd never made love to a woman the way he had with her. The experience transcended the carnal. It was nearly spiritual.

"Rhys?" Vivian murmured sleepily and leaned up on the bed. The blanket slipped down, baring her round, creamy breast.

The sight stirred his cock. Rhys forced himself to look away before he fell upon her in a frenzy of mad lust. He walked to the shelves where he kept his clothing and grabbed his trousers, tugging them on and tucking away his erection. "I must go out and hunt."

"But you can—"

"No!" He tamped down the temptation at what she'd been about to offer. "You'd be weakened if I drink from you twice in a row."

She flinched at his harsh tone and pulled the blanket over her breasts. "Oh. When will you return?"

"In an hour or two." Rhys turned away and donned a shirt, pausing a moment when he noticed the fine stitching where Vivian had mended a tear in the sleeve. "I wish to bring you a hot meal."

Her tone brightened. "That would be heavenly."

The gratitude in her voice made a shroud of guilt press upon him with a leaden weight. He'd imprisoned her, subjected her to living conditions well below what she'd doubtless been accustomed to, destroyed her future, and taken her virtue. Vivian may have offered herself to him, but he was supposed to have been the older, wiser party, who was well aware of the consequences.

"Rhys?" She said as he pulled on his boots. "Do you regret what happened last night... or rather, this morning?"

His chest tightened like it was clamped in a vice. "That's a rather complex question, I'm afraid."

Her indrawn breath tugged at his soul as she looked up at him with wounded eyes. "D-did I displease you? I know I'm inexperienced... and—"

"No! You pleased me more than any woman has before." Despite his better wisdom, Rhys crossed the cave and grasped her shoulders, bending down so they were face to face. "I do not regret making love with you. What I regret is the fact that I had no right to do so. I was supposed to leave you untouched."

Vivian's lips, swollen from his kisses, drew downward in a pout. "You speak as if I had no say in the matter. I *asked* you to touch me. It's what *I* wanted, and I have no regrets." She gripped his forearms and fixed him with a pleading gaze. "Please do not wallow in undeserved remorse because you think you've ruined me in some way. As I said before, I was already compromised, and I was already intending to remain unwed. Rather than taking from me, you've given me a gift. Moments of pleasure I could not have fathomed. I will cherish the memory forever, and welcome new ones this night if you are inclined to indulge me."

Rhys's resolve crumbled under her impassioned words. He claimed her lips with a kiss that transfused all his longing and despair. The sound of her heartbeat beckoned him like a forbidden melody. Before he gave into the siren's song of her embrace, he released her. "I *have* to go now."

Before she could protest, he grabbed his coat and fled the cave.

The cold, salty air did little to cool the heat in his blood. What he'd shared with Vivian had been more than mere coupling. When he'd joined his body with hers, he'd felt as if they'd become one. Magic had been wrought between them. Somehow, either inside her slick heat, the melding of their lips, or the hot rush of her blood on his tongue, Vivian had bound him to her with invisible threads that pulled taut with every step he took away from her.

Eager to return to her as soon as possible, Rhys ran in a blur, cresting hills and dodging trees, until he reached Southport. Normally, he avoided areas so close to his cave so that the vampires of villages near the no-man's land did not take notice of him, but he needed to feed and wanted to find a hot meal for Vivian. He came to a hotel and made his way to the restaurant, full of humans dining on their own suppers, but thankfully no other vampires.

Instead of finding a patron to slake his thirst, Rhys stole into the kitchen, mesmerizing the first servant to see him before the lad could cry out.

When he'd drunk his fill from the kitchen boy, he turned his attention to Vivian's meal, gathering fruit, cheese, and a hot roll. These he stuffed into his pockets before he encountered the cook. He froze the man with his gaze and stole a capon and wrapped the roasted bird in a handkerchief before tucking it under his arm to keep it warm. As he dashed out of the kitchen, some of the hot juices soaked through into his sleeve.

He'd made a spectacle of himself, but hopefully not a significant one. Mortals had a way of dismissing things that were out of the ordinary.

When he returned to the cave, he realized that for the first time, he'd left the door unlocked. Vivian could have escaped, yet here she remained. The welcoming light in her eyes when he entered the cave pierced his soul. No longer naked, she was dressed in a plain gray gown from the trunk of clothing he'd stolen. Yet she remained just as desirable as when she'd been bare before him.

"What is that delicious smell?" she asked.

He presented her with the capon. "I've also brought you an orange, some cheese, and a roll."

She tore into the capon with her white, even teeth, occasionally pausing to lick her fingers, making soft, blissful noised that forced him to smile at her delight. When the bird was reduced to bones, she devoured the bread and then made short work of the orange. The cheese she set aside in the small larder he'd accumulated for her before she washed her hands in a barrel of salt water.

While watching Vivian enjoy the sort of meal that she'd long been denied, Rhys once more warred between guilt at what he'd taken away from her and elation at what he'd been able to give her. When she returned to her cot, still joined with his, he studied her with a mixture of awe and confusion.

He may have abducted her, but she'd stolen his heart. Why had she given herself to him? Was it simply a matter of convenience and proximity since she didn't believe she'd have an opportunity to be with another man? Was it some sort of subversive reaction to her captivity? An attempt to gain some control over the situation? Or could she possibly feel the same way he did about her?

The last thought made his heart swell with mingled hope and despair. It was best that he never learn about her true feelings, because a future for them was impossible. However, Rhys had to know, for some self-punishing reason.

"I left the door unlocked. You could have run away," Rhys said. "Why didn't you?"

"Because I support your cause to save your family." Vivian said, eyeing him as if he'd lost his senses. "And I *want* to stay with you."

Rhys shook his head with disbelief. Had captivity driven her mad, or had last night borne the same effect on her? "I cannot comprehend why you would wish to do so."

She reached for his hand and threaded her fingers through his. "My time with you has been a revelation of excitement and freedom."

"Freedom?" he echoed with a disbelieving frown. "I've kept you a prisoner for nearly a fortnight."

"Look at my hands." Vivian pulled their intertwined hands towards him. "I haven't had to wear gloves. You cannot fathom how liberating that has been." Her lips curved in a coy smile and she peered at him beneath her long lashes. "I'm also not wearing stays."

Rhys's gaze raked across her body and his mouth went dry. "You are driving me mad with such talk." He looked away from her tempting figure and pulled his hands away. There was only one way to know what was in her heart. And only one way to appease his conscience. "I should release you. My honor demands it. I broke the agreement with your uncle when I took you."

He rose from their makeshift bed where they'd slept in each other's arms and tried to ignore the stabbing pain in his heart. He opened the cave door. If she left, he'd lose the ransom money and have nothing but a broken heart. But at least he'd have done something honorable. He couldn't hold the woman he loved against her will, no matter the cost.

He spoke through the lump in his throat. "You are free to go."

Vivian blinked at him. "I told you, I wish to stay with you. And to hell with my uncle. He made no agreement. He made that clear when he refused to pay the ransom in the first place."

"But—" He broke off his feeble protest as the selfish imp within danced with triumph. She wished to remain with him, of her own free will.

She rose and strode from the bed to the door and slammed it shut before he could react. "You need that money, Rhys. And I need a few more memories to cherish before we are parted." She took a deep, shuddering breath, and a sudden vulnerability flooded her eyes. "Unless, you don't want me anymore?"

Her words crumbled the walls around his heart. He pulled her into his arms and buried his face in her silken hair. "I want you more than I've wanted anything in my long life." He trembled in her embrace as the confession held locked in his heart tumbled from his lips. "I love you."

"I love you too," Vivian whispered, stroking his back. "I wish—"

He silenced her with a kiss, unable to venture down the road to tragedy. "Wishes are never granted. We only have now."

Her arms tightened around him as she rose up on her toes to silently beg for another kiss. Rhys indulged her, feeding at her mouth, reveling at her taste of fruit and honey. Even through the fabric separating their flesh, the feel of her breasts pressed to his chest gave him a thrill of delight.

Vivian broke the kiss only to brush her lips across his neck. "I am so glad you don't wear a cravat." The breath of her whisper made his flesh tingle. "Could we... go to the bed?"

His cock stiffened further. If he hadn't deflowered her only last night, he would have hiked up her skirts and taken her against the wall. However, she was probably still sore and required gentler treatment.

In answer to her request, Rhys lifted her and carried her to the joined bunks. As they kissed and caressed, slowly their clothing was cast away until Vivian's body glistened naked in the firelight.

Just like the first time, the sight of her beauty stole his breath. Rhys took his time licking and nibbling every inch of her, from her delicate neck to her lush breasts, across her belly, and at last to the place he so desperately wanted to taste.

"May I kiss you there?" he asked.

She bit her lip and nodded, her cheeks rosy with delightful blushes. Rhys lowered his head and inhaled the tantalizing fragrance of her arousal. When his mouth closed over her mound, her hips arched up and she gasped. He slipped his tongue between her nether lips and reveled in her feminine cry of delight.

Rhys circled her swollen bud, holding her thighs down as she bucked and wiggled, not so much to restrain her, but so he didn't risk grazing her with his fangs. Vivian moaned with every movement of his tongue. With his lips and fingers, he played her like a fine musical instrument, bringing her cries and shudders like an ethereal symphony. The sweet taste of her nectar filled his mouth like a forbidden elixir, nearly as addicting as her blood.

Vivian screamed his name as she climaxed. The sound was music to his ears. Rhys tightened his grip on her hips as she thrashed beneath him, relentless as he continued his ministrations.

When she fell back against the pillows, limp and trembling, Rhys released her. He moved up on the bunk and pulled her against his chest.

"My goodness," she gasped. "I had no idea that it could be so…" A light laugh escaped her. "I don't have the words."

"You're stoking my pride so much that I may burst with it." Rhys glanced down ruefully. "Of course, that wasn't the only thing in danger of bursting."

Vivian caught his quick look and frowned. "But what about your satisfaction? Do you want to take me again?"

"Very much, but you are still sore from the previous night, so I think it best for me to refrain." Especially with the state he was in. Rhys very much feared that he'd lose control and take her too roughly.

Her fingers wrapped around his shaft, making him suck in a breath. "Then perhaps I should pleasure you as you have with me."

"You would truly wish to do that?" Rhys stared at her in astonishment. He never imagined a well-born lady would willingly touch a man's anatomy in such a way. Hell, his wife had only been a fisherman's daughter and she'd told him that if he wanted his knob polished, he could go find a whore at the docks.

Vivian squeezed him, eliciting another gasp from him and peered up at him with a blush. "You did the same for me."

She moved down, placing feathery kisses along his chest and stomach before leaning over his throbbing erection. Her warm breath over his swollen head brought goosebumps all over his body. The unabashed fascination in her eyes as she regarded his hard cock filled him with primal satisfaction.

All thoughts fled when her lips closed over his tip. Rhys groaned with pure bliss as her tongue swirled around the sensitive flesh. She explored him with her mouth and fingers, tentatively at first, then with increasing confidence at his pleasured noises and muttered words of encouragement. He tangled his fingers in her hair and guided her lightly, but not forcefully.

His pleasure at her ministrations built until he thought he'd go mad from it. "Vivian," he growled through gritted teeth. "For God's sake, please stop, or I'll spend."

She lifted her head and regarded him with a sinful smile. Her grey eyes were dilated with lust. She tossed his words back at him. "I want to taste you."

Then her mouth locked over him and she took him deeper, sucking his length with erotic pressure. Rhys exploded, his fist bunching in her hair, his hips bucking beneath her. Vivian drank down every drop, sending pulses of pure ecstasy through his body. At last, she withdrew and licked her lips.

"It was salty," she said and moved back up on the cot to nuzzle against his chest. "But not at all unpleasant. Why didn't you want me to finish?"

"Many women find it disgusting," he replied, stroking her back.

She frowned and shook her head. "Many women are fools then."

A combination of wonder and melancholy swirled through Rhys's heart. How could he have found such a perfect woman only to be destined to lose her?

Chapter Twenty-two

The next evening, Aldric found himself engaged in a task that he'd never imagined doing: shaving Vivian's lady's companion. It was quite a different experience than shaving his own face, and he had to pause and draw the blade away every time it seemed Madame Renarde was about to cough.

Just as he was scraping the stubble from her neck, Renarde opened her eyes. "Thank you," she whispered through cracked lips. For once, her eyes looked clear and shone with recognition.

"It is nothing," he said, and rinsed the shaving razor in a bowl of warm water. "I would have done it sooner, but you were thrashing from your fever and I did not wish to cut you."

"Afraid it would make you hungry?" Renarde's chuckle dissolved into a bout of coughing.

Aldric shook his head. "My control is far better than that. Besides, we prefer to feed on the strong, not the sickly. Speaking of, how are you feeling?"

"Much better." Renarde struggled to sit up and Aldric shifted her pillows behind her back. "The past few days and nights were a bit of a blur to me." She looked down and touched the sleeves of her bed gown. "I vaguely remember you undressing me. I hope the sight did not injure your sensibilities."

"My sensibilities are rather sturdy, I should think." Aldric chuckled at the memory of the awkward process. "Though I must say that the corset was quite a trial. It was no wonder you had trouble breathing."

Renarde studied him as if searching for a hint of censure or disgust. "While I am grateful for your tender care, I cannot help but wonder if it will last, once you've gotten what you want from me."

Aldric brought the blade to her other cheek and carefully resumed shaving Madame Renarde. "I will have every bit of information you can give me regarding Vivian's captor. But if you are concerned that I will do away with you after you've told me all you know, you can dismiss that worry. There are ways around our laws, and I am not in the business of killing those who help me or my loved ones."

"But… I failed to protect your niece." Pain and remorse radiated from her eyes.

Aldric snorted in dismissal. "You came up against a cunning rogue vampire with powers far superior to your own. There was nothing you could do. Cast away such foolish self-recrimination. It will not help in seeing Vivian returned to us." He reached for the snifter of brandy he'd had Jeffries bring in earlier. "Would you care for a glass?"

Renarde's taut features relaxed as she nodded. "I cannot tell you where he is holding her. I was unconscious when he took us there, and blindfolded when he returned me. All I know is that he has a well-furnished cave by the sea."

"And this country is an island. There are countless caves along the coasts. I doubt he is as far as Cornwall or Kent, but a vampire can range far and fast," Aldric said bitterly as he poured their glasses. "Still, I suppose I can learn which areas are no-man's-lands and track him from there."

Madame Renarde shook her head and accepted her glass. "I know it is not my place, being a servant, but I would advise you to pay the ransom so that Vivian may be returned as soon as possible."

Her grave tone gave him pause. "Do you think she's truly in danger?

Renarde nodded. "I do, but not in the way you think."

Aldric suddenly suspected he'd missed an impending threat. "What do you mean?"

"My profession depends on the ability to closely observe things, such as the way two people interact with each other."

Renarde's intense eyes implored him to listen. "I've seen the way Rhys looks at Vivian, but that was of little concern as I also observed his efforts at restraint."

"Well I most certainly see it as a concern!" Aldric tossed back a hearty swallow of brandy, even knowing it would give him a devil of a bellyache later. "Especially now that he has been alone with my niece for the past two nights and days. You yourself said she is in danger."

"Yes, but from her own heart and desires." Madame Renarde sipped her brandy with more delicacy than he had. "I also observed the way she looks at him. How she smiled when they conversed and the sparks between them when they practiced fencing."

Aldric blinked in disbelief. "He is fencing with her?"

"Yes. He sparred with me as well. Something to bide the time, I suppose. However, with them, it was like a dance. Both share a deep passion for swordplay." Madame Renarde sighed and took another drink. "They also read together. They're utterly captivated with a serial story in the papers and discuss it as if they are trying to decipher the chapter of Revelations." Renarde sighed and took a deeper drink. "The point I am trying to make is that Rhys did not act the villain with us. He has been very kind. Furthermore, while I was treated as an honored guest, he treated Vivian as if they were the best of friends, something she's never experienced from a man in her entire life. And from what I've learned about her life before I came along, she'd been very lonely

259

and never had a friend until I came into her father's employment."

Horror twisted Aldric's gut as he grasped her meaning. "You think she is falling in love with him?"

"I do," Renarde said levelly. "There is a tangible spark between them. There is something else you must know. Rhys was the highwayman who robbed us on our way to your estate. The reason he did not steal her necklace was because he stole a kiss instead. She's fancied him since that night, but now that they've had time to become acquainted, I'm afraid her fancy has developed to something more than girlish infatuation."

"Good God!" Aldric nearly choked on his brandy. Renarde's tale was worsening every moment. "*He* was the highwayman?"

When Vivian had told him about their carriage being robbed that first night, he'd reported the theft to the constable, who had told him that there'd been other robberies, but assured him that his officers were closing in on the thief. Aldric hadn't thought much of Vivian's robbery since very little had been stolen and Vivian herself hadn't been particularly alarmed.

Because the whoreson wooed her with a kiss, he raged inwardly.

The incident had been forgotten in the wake of her being abducted and Aldric had been an utter fool not to make the connection. And Vivian had been infatuated with the thief. Madame Renarde was right. His niece was in far worse danger than he'd previously contemplated. If Vivian fell in love with a rogue vampire, she would be tempted to allow him to Change her. "You do not believe he will Change her into a vampire?" he asked.

Renarde shook her head emphatically and sneezed. "From the way he described his life as a rogue vampire, I would say no. He cares for her too much to subject her to a possible death sentence."

"That is a measure of relief at least." But what if Vivian convinced him to go through with it? During the short time she'd spent under his roof, Aldric had discovered that she could be very charming. Which of course, led him to another concern, one that he'd already had before he'd learned of Vivian's feeling towards her captor. He struggled for a delicate way of phrasing his worry. "You think they will act upon their mutual attraction, don't you?"

"If they haven't already." Madame Renarde's lips thinned into a grim line. "Which is why you should abandon your pride and pay the ransom. Many women form deep emotional attachments to men after they've been intimate. The longer you delay, the more attached Vivian will become. Rhys as well. A most untenable situation for the both of them."

"You sound as if you're sympathetic to Rhys as well," Aldric noted with disapproval.

Madame Renarde shrugged. "I am a human with a human's sense of compassion and empathy. I have not had the benefit of centuries of feeding on the blood of innocents to harden my heart."

"I do not believe I deserve such talk. After all, my heart is why you remain alive." Aldric softened his tone even as he writhed with frustration. "But I do not wish to quarrel. Removing my niece from this rogue vampire's clutches is my utmost concern." His hands tightened on his empty glass until it cracked. "Why does Rhys want money from me anyway? If he was already making a career as a highwayman, why make the fatal mistake of abducting a Lord Vampire's niece for a pithy two hundred pounds?"

"Such a sum may be pithy to you, but not to others. That is ten times my yearly allowance." Madame Renarde eyed him with scorn of the likes Aldric had never been subjected to. "But it can be salvation for others. My understanding is that Rhys wishes to give the money to his mortal relations so that they may pay off a mortgage. Much like Robin Hood."

"Blast it, no wonder Vivian has romanticized him," Aldric growled.

Then the companion's words sank in. Aldric held a few mortgages in Blackpool, but only one that was going to be foreclosed in a week. He had been on the right path to begin with. If he'd only probed further…

His lips curved in a bitter smirk as the final piece of the puzzle clicked into place. "Very well, Madame. I will heed your advice and pay off the scoundrel."

"Thank God," Renarde murmured, and quaffed the last of her drink. "I pray that Vivian is safely returned and undamaged from this ordeal. Will you Change her into a vampire when we have her back?"

Aldric's triumph at coming to a decision deflated as the other dilemma was once more thrust upon him. "I will deal with that matter when she is back under my care. As for you…" He gathered his powers and fixed her with his gaze. "You will forget that the highwayman is a vampire. You will forget that I am a vampire."

At first, Renarde frowned at him in puzzlement, but then her eyes glazed just like those of the mortals he fed upon. "Forget…" she echoed.

"Yes." Aldric focused his will on her mind. "Only remember that you and Vivian were taken by a highwayman. Remember that you are concerned that Vivian is infatuated with him. When she returns, your duty will be to convince her to put that cad out of her mind."

"Yes," Madame Renarde's eyelids drooped. "The cad."

Aldric released his hold on her mind and tried to fight back worry. The longer a human spent in a vampire's company, and the more they knew of the secrets of his kind, the more difficult it was to banish their memories.

Renarde blinked and rubbed her head. "I apologize. I must have dozed off. What were we speaking about?"

Aldric's shoulders relaxed slightly. So far, this was the usual reaction. "I've agreed to pay the ransom as you've advised."

"Splendid." Madame Renarde yawned. "I cannot wait until my dear Vivian is home. Poor, sweet girl. I vow to do everything I can to help her forget about the highwayman who abducted her. Such a dreadful affair."

"Indeed." Aldric bit back a satisfied smile at her lack of mention of vampires. One problem appeared to be solved. "Now you should take your tonic and rest so that you may be of help to Vivian when I bring her home."

"*Oui*. I am terribly exhausted." When Aldric took the bottle of tonic from the bedside table, she favored him with a weak smile. "I am sorry to have been so much trouble to you. Doubtless you've never had to play nursemaid in your life."

"You are correct in that assumption." Aldric grinned as he held the medicine spoon to her lips. "But I regard it as a new experience. Something an old curmudgeon like me could benefit from time to time."

Renarde chuckled as she fell back against the pillows. "Pish-tosh. You are still a young man. Perhaps instead of finding a husband for Vivian, we should seek a match for you."

"I am a confirmed bachelor, I'm afraid." Some Lord Vampires took female vampires as wives, either out of love, or simply an arrangement to keep Society from pestering them. Aldric preferred to avoid that sort of complication. "Now get some rest and I shall look in on you tomorrow evening."

"Promise me you will not treat Vivian too harshly if she has been seduced by Rhys," Madame Renarde said sleepily.

"I promise." Aldric extinguished the lamps and left the room.

His mental exertions on banishing Renarde's memories had drained him. He needed to feed again. After ordering his valet to fetch his coat, Aldric went out to the seedier part of the village.

A woman's scream boiled his already heated blood and he bolted down the alley to find a man with a barmaid pinned against the wall, a bucket of slops overturned on the cracked stone cobbles. For a moment, he envisioned the besieged maid to be Vivian, and a red haze of rage distorted his vision.

With a roar, he seized the assailant by the scruff of the neck and yanked him off the barmaid. The woman squeaked in terror at Aldric's blazing eyes and fled back to the safety of the tavern.

Aldric slammed the man against the grimy brick wall and tore into his throat in a fury. Hot blood gushed in Aldric's mouth and he drank deeper than he had in decades, glutting himself on the last dregs of a wastrel's life.

When the body went limp in his grip, Aldric hefted the corpse over his shoulder and wove through the alleys until he reached the wharfs. Technically, it was illegal to kill a human, except in cases of self-preservation, but if a killing was not discovered or proven, the Elders tended to look away.

Still, shame flooded Aldric. While he felt no remorse for killing a man who would force himself on a woman, his loss of control revolted him to the core.

The idea of Vivian being deflowered by a rogue vampire infuriated him more than he'd thought. But Madame Renarde's words about Vivian falling in love with one alarmed him even more. The companion had urged him to hurry before it was too late, but there were two more nights before the ransom was due. If the situation was as ominous as Renarde perceived before she left Rhys's lair, surely things had escalated further now that Vivian no longer had a chaperone. In fact, Aldric had the sinking feeling that the die had been cast.

Many centuries ago, in the glow of his mortal youth, Aldric had fallen under the potent, cruel spell of love. It was not a malady easy to recover from.

Chapter Twenty-three

Vivian and Rhys spent the day in each other's arms, kissing and touching and laughing together, treasuring each bittersweet moment. At dusk, he took her with him when he went out to hunt, showing her that a vampire's bite did not harm a person. That relieved Vivian more than any verbal assurances he'd given her. If she were to become a vampire, she never wanted to hurt anyone.

Rhys also took her to a restaurant, where she dined on roast beef and buttered potatoes. She felt a slight twinge of guilt when he used his preternatural powers to convince the proprietor that they'd paid. Did all vampires do this, or was it only rogues who were forced to steal?

When they returned to the cave, she asked him.

"Legitimate vampires are usually set up for some manner of employment by their Lord. I imagine the less wealthy ones don't hesitate to filch money and things from time to time, but that is generally frowned upon." Rhys built up the fire and then came to sit beside her. "Are you afraid of what life will be like if your uncle Changes you into a vampire?"

"Yes." Vivian had to pry the word out. She'd tried to conceal her trepidation at the prospect of becoming a blood-drinking immortal, but the realization that she and Rhys would soon be parted compelled her to confess. "Could you tell me how the process works? I mean, will it hurt?"

"Some," he admitted. The sympathy in his eyes made her wish she could take back the question. She did not want him to pity her. "When your fangs grow and the magic spreads through your body, it hurts a great deal. The first hunger for blood is painful as well, but not as bad as the teeth growing. That was the worst, from what I remember. Thankfully, it doesn't last long, and your uncle will have a fresh source of blood on hand for your first feeding." He grasped her hand and squeezed it. "I wish I could be there for you during the transformation. Teach you to wield your powers, the joy of the hunt, and show you the beauty of the night."

"I wish you could be with me as well." Vivian threaded her fingers through his. "But you still have not fully answered my question. How is the magic done?"

"Your uncle will drink as much of your blood as he can, then he will cut his wrist and feed it back to you," Rhys looked down at his boots, as if avoiding her censure.

Vivian cringed at such a macabre process. However, at least it was straightforward, and did not sound like a long, ceremonial affair. "If it is so simple, why isn't the world full of vampires?"

"Because it takes a century or thereabouts for a vampire to build the power to make another. And they can only make one at a time, for the most part. Although I did hear of an ancient vampire Changing mortal twin boys on the same night, hundreds of years ago." Rhys filled the kettle for tea. "Also, one must petition their Lord Vampire before they are permitted to Change a mortal."

Vivian blinked. If her uncle was already a Lord Vampire, then... "Who is my uncle's lord?"

Something flickered in Rhys's eyes that looked like fear. "I'll let your uncle tell you."

"Why?" Curiosity bubbled within her at his sudden reluctance to divulge information.

"Because there are some aspects of our world that even I won't risk discussing. Certain parties whose attention I do not wish to attract." His voice quaked with definite terror.

Vivian dropped the subject with Rhys, but she would most definitely discuss it with her uncle. Vampires must have a higher authority than lords. A king, perhaps? Or maybe some sort of parliament? Whoever they were, they frightened Rhys like a boggart from children's tales. "You said that the first craving for blood is painful. Does it always hurt?"

Rhys shook his head. "It is only painful for the first few weeks, as you learn to control it. Because of that, a new vampire must always be accompanied by an older mentor, to ensure that they do not accidentally harm a mortal during feeding. Since you are such a quick learner, you should master the hunt in no time."

"Your confidence in me is reassuring." She poured the tea when the kettle whistled. "I pray it is not misplaced. What can kill a vampire?"

Again, his expression shuttered. "You've already observed that the sun is one method, but I will leave the rest to your uncle to explain."

"You're not giving me much reason to be optimistic." She frowned into her teacup. "Can you share any positive aspects of your existence?"

"Oh yes." Rhys favored her with his first genuine smile of the night. "You will be able to move faster than the blink of an eye. You'll never sicken or grow old. If you are wounded, you will heal rapidly. You'll be able to see and hear things that humans cannot perceive. And you will have the strength of ten men. Some vampires can read people's thoughts. Others can make objects move with their minds. A few can even fly."

"Fly?" she echoed in awe. "Can you?"

He shook his head. "Thus far, I am not so blessed. Some say it is an ability gained with age, others say it depends on the bloodline of who Changed you."

For the rest of the night, he regaled her with tales of him reveling in his powers, the knowledge he'd gained, and the benefit of having time at one's disposal. Vivian could tell that he was skirting around the less pleasant facts about being a vampire, and only doing his best to reassure her.

However, she was grateful for everything he could tell her. She drank an entire pot of tea as she listened to him. They then went out to the beach to fence for their last time before dawn. After Rhys shut them inside for the day, he made love to her with such fervent devotion that tears sprung to her eyes.

She tried to stay awake as she held him, savoring her last minutes in his arms. Tonight, Rhys would visit the human he'd instructed to collect the ransom. If the money was there, that meant that Rhys would take her to an inn tonight and her uncle would collect her tomorrow.

But sleep was relentless and sucked her down into a world of fractured dreams and incessant fears.

When Rhys kissed her awake, she clung to him, not wanting to let him go. "What if my uncle has laid a trap?"

"Then it will be him who returns here instead of me." Despite his attempt at dismissing her worry, she detected a note of trepidation in his tone.

"Take me with you to meet with your contact then." If Uncle Aldric tried to capture Rhys, maybe Vivian could persuade him to see reason.

"No. It is far too dangerous. If any vampires see a rogue in company with a mortal woman, it won't take long to reach the ears of your uncle. I'm fortunate that the rogues who tried to take shelter with me haven't spread the gossip." He kissed her somewhat roughly before leaving the bed to dress. "With luck, I'll be back shortly."

After he departed, Vivian paced the cave, wringing her hands with worry that Rhys would be caught. Between praying that he would receive the ransom money and return safely, a selfish part of her hoped that her uncle would again refuse to pay. If that proved to be the case, then perhaps she could convince Rhys to let her stay with him. Maybe they could both go to the Americas and build a life together and Rhys would be safe.

What about Madame Renarde? Vivian's conscience prodded her. Guilt knotted her belly. She'd hardly spared a thought for her dearest friend in the past few nights. Was her uncle taking care of her and had he sent for a doctor? Was he treating her with kindness or cruelty?

Vivian slumped back on the cot and sighed. She couldn't abandon her best friend. But she didn't want to be parted from Rhys either.

Why did this situation have to be so hopeless?

A key rattled in the lock of the cave door. Vivian's heart leapt in her throat. Rhys had made it back safely. She ran to his side the moment he entered the cave.

"He paid the ransom," Rhys said hollowly, withdrawing a sack of jingling coins from his pocket. He took out a few pounds and put the sack in a hidden compartment behind his bunk.

For a few moments, Vivian's heart refused to beat. It lay frozen and aching in her breast. Her time with Rhys was over. In mere hours, she'd never see him again.

She struggled to form a smile. "Your family is saved at last."

"Yes." He did not sound as pleased as she'd expected. "Soon I will have accomplished all I set out to achieve. Emily can pay off the mortgage, and the farm will be restored to my family at last."

"Where will you go after you've given the money to Emily?" Impossible as it was, she hoped there was some slim chance that she'd see him again.

"I will have to leave the country. It is no longer safe for me to remain here after what I've done." Something in his tone conveyed less optimism than his words. "I'm going to try to find passage for the Americas. I'm told that rogues can find a fresh start there."

"I hope you make it there safely and no longer have to run." Still, a sudden anger filled her. It shouldn't be that way in the first place. "It's not fair. My uncle will be getting back the money he paid, and you will have to flee anyway. I wish there was some way that—"

"There is no way." Rhys paced in front of the cave door, his head down so his hair concealed his expression. "What I've done is unforgivable in vampire society. There is no Lord Vampire who would shelter me. Even most rogues would slay me if they knew of my deeds."

When he looked up, Vivian saw the hopelessness in his eyes. She remembered that he'd been resolved to die the last time they'd spoken of his fate after the ransom was paid. Only now he tried to reassure her, but she knew the truth. He didn't expect to make it out of the country. He expected to be caught and killed. If his family didn't need the money, she would have begged him to take her with him. Perhaps together, they could be safe and happy.

With utmost reluctance, she abandoned that dream. Besides, she couldn't leave Madame Renarde anymore than Rhys could allow his family to lose their home. "When are you returning me to my uncle?"

"Tonight." Rhys's voice sounded hoarse. "I will take you to an inn in Lytham, where you may send a note to him tomorrow morning."

She gasped in shock. "So soon? But I thought we'd have a little more time together."

Rhys shook his head, his features contorted with pain. "I'm sorry. The journey is long, and I must be able to return to the cave before sunrise." He took a shuddering breath. "Let's pack your things."

Vivian opened her mouth to refuse, but the bleak reality froze the words in her throat, reducing them to a heavy lump.

Together, they filled a valise he'd previously stolen with a nightgown, the dress she'd worn the night he abducted her, and the carved animals she and Madame Renarde had chosen.

"I also want you to take my sword," Rhys said. "Not only in case anyone tries to accost you during the day while you wait for your uncle, but also because you're the only one I know who will appreciate it."

He unlocked his sword case and withdrew the blade from an intricate tooled leather scabbard. The rapier's hilt had an elaborately crafted silver hand guard that she'd admired when they'd dueled. The pommel was carved in the shape of a queen chess piece, something she hadn't notice before.

She spoke through the heavy lump in her throat. "It's beautiful."

"I took it from the captain of a Spanish galleon in the late seventeenth century." Sadness infused Rhys's smile. "It's the only thing I have left from my mortal life."

"I will treasure it always," she said as he handed her the blade and scabbard. Not even the sword that Uncle had given her was so fine and well-balanced as this one.

"You should give the other to Madame Renarde."

"No!" Vivian said quickly. "Not that she wouldn't appreciate another sword for her meager collection. But you must have something to defend yourself with."

He sighed. "You have a point, though I fear it will do me little good if Lord Thornton catches me. I will not harm your kin."

"He can heal quick as you," she said, unable to hide her bitterness. "I'm afraid I cannot feel charitable towards him if he seeks to kill the man I love."

Rhys uttered a humorless laugh. "The man you love is a criminal whom your uncle is fully justified to execute." He tilted her chin up to meet his gaze. "But I don't want to spend our last moments quibbling."

"I don't either." Vivian wrapped her arms around his waist. "Make love to me one last time?"

He undressed and had her clothing off so quickly it was like magic. Kissing her hungrily, he lifted her against the wall of the cave and thrust inside her so hard she gasped. Vivian clung to his shoulders and gave herself over to the new sensations.

From this angle, her pleasure was threefold. She felt him reach a place deep inside her that sang with every thrust, even as the walls of her sheathe clenched his hardness. But the best part was that the base of his shaft ground against her swollen bud, which sang with the sweet friction of his movements.

The climax swept over her in a sudden storm, making her scream his name as lightning seemed to flicker through her clitoris while a heavier explosion erupted deeper within.

"I love you," Rhys groaned and shuddered inside her, his thrusts rocking her into another cascade of bliss.

Too soon, it was over, and he set her down. Vivian placed her hand on the wall to steady herself as she caught her breath and willed her knees to stop quaking.

Adoration shone in his eyes as he smiled. "I wish there was time for another round, but we must go now."

After they dressed, Rhys shoved her valise in his pack, along with the sword. "I'm sorry, but I'll have to blindfold you again."

Vivian's heart sank as her last hope of somehow finding him again was crushed. "Why?"

"It is very likely that Lord Thornton will drink your blood to see your memories. I'd rather them not lead him back here." Rhys pulled a scarf from his pack and tied it behind her head.

He lifted her in his arms and she jolted as he took off running. She couldn't feel his footsteps, only a rapid jouncing and a strong wind against her face and body. How fast was he going? After what seemed like an hour, he set her down, panting with exertion. If not for his firm grip on her shoulders, she would have toppled from dizziness.

When he removed the blindfold, Vivian saw a sign with a carved owl swinging in the wind. The Owl Inn, it read. Rhys pressed a few coins into her palm. "This is where I must leave you, so the innkeeper doesn't see me."

Her chest ached with the sense of impending loss as she threw herself into his arms. "Oh, Rhys, I can't bear it!"

"You'll have to." He kissed her long and deep, and Vivian sought to memorize the taste of his mouth and the softness of his lips.

Tears ran down her cheeks as he released her. "Forever," she whispered, her soul contorting with grief. "My love will be forever."

"Goodbye, Vivian," he said. "I'll love you always."

And then he was gone.

Numb with agony, Vivian shouldered the heavy valise and trudged into the inn. The innkeeper regarded her with a querulous glare at her late arrival, but changed his tune when he saw her coin.

After a servant led her up to her room, Vivian collapsed on the bed unable to hold in her sobs. Only minutes after being parted from Rhys and she already missed him like a severed limb.

A creaking sound made her lift her head. The window had blown open. She began to rise from the bed to close it when strong arms enfolded her.

"Not just yet," Rhys whispered, pulling her into his lap. "It will be the death of me, but I'll stay until dawn."

Vivian couldn't summon the words to voice her joy. Instead, she covered his face with kisses and plunged her hands in his long, silken hair. He removed her dress and worshipped every inch of her with his hands and mouth. She tore at his shirt, impatient to have him bared before her one last time.

As he thrust inside her, he looked down at her and smiled. "It feels so good to have you in a real bed."

And have her he did, long and well. He had her a second time, and a third, giving Vivian more memories to cherish.

"I love you," he whispered again and again as he held her in his arms.

She fell asleep listening to the beating of his heart.

But when she awoke in the morning, a ray of white light streamed through the window across place where Rhys had been only hours ago.

Vivian had never hated the sight of the sun as much as she did that moment.

Chapter Twenty-four

When Aldric rose for the night, Fitz, the butler, greeted him in the parlor. "My lord, this note arrived for you this afternoon."

"Thank you, Fitz." Aldric took the note and tried to maintain composure as he opened the envelope and withdrew the sheet of foolscap.

The sight of Vivian's handwriting made his hands tremble with anticipation. The words were short, but sweet.

Dearest Uncle,

I am staying at the Owl Inn in Lytham. I am faring quite well, but I would be most obliged if you would fetch me home.

Sincerely,

Vivian Stratford

Aldric heaved a sigh of utmost relief. The promise had been fulfilled. At last, Vivian would return to the safety of his home. And then he would be able to deal with the rogue vampire without risk of her being harmed.

"Fitz, tell Jeffries to ready the carriage," Aldric told the waiting butler. "Then tell Madame Renarde that Miss Stratford will be arriving shortly."

"Very good, my lord." Fitz bowed and strode off to complete his duties.

Aldric gnashed his teeth with impatience as he waited for the carriage. While it was practical for a vampire to have elderly servants, it was not efficient.

At last, Jeffries came through the front door. "The carriage is ready, my lord."

Although Aldric wanted to go straight to Lytham, precautions must be made. "Take me to the Gordon's Pub," he directed once he was seated in the conveyance.

Once they arrived at the tavern that his second in command owned, Aldric found Bonnie in her usual corner.

"My niece has been released and is staying at an inn in Lytham," he told her. "Will you come with me to collect her?"

"Of course, my lord." Bonnie set her book aside and rose from her overstuffed chair. She regarded him with an arched brow. "You paid the villain off?"

Aldric nodded. "Yes. But if I have my way, he will not keep his ill-gotten gains and all his efforts will be for naught."

When they went out to the carriage, Bonnie commanded Jeffries to sleep and took up the reins. The eight-mile drive seemed to last an eternity. If it weren't for nosy neighbors and his servants, Aldric would have ran to Lytham himself and carried Vivian home.

At least Bonnie was as efficient a driver as Jeffries and they arrived at the inn at a quarter to seven.

"Would you like me to accompany you?" Bonnie asked. "Another woman's presence can be reassuring."

Aldric shook his head. "Stay with Jeffries."

The last thing he needed was one of his people to witness an emotional outburst if Vivian was indeed traumatized by the events of her abduction. Or worse, fear or revulsion at knowing what he was.

Aldric froze in the doorway of the Owl Inn. Just as promised, Vivian sat at the polished wooden bar, nursing a cup of ale, and reading a newspaper. His heart and lungs suddenly felt like they were clamped in a vice. Until this moment, he'd never realized how much he cared for her, how much he'd worried for her safety.

From her straight spine and relaxed shoulders, she appeared unharmed, though the downward turn of her lips and the crease between her brows radiated melancholy.

"Vivian?" he said softly.

She turned and Aldric braced himself for a look of fear, accusation, or both.

Then, to his disbelief, she rose from her seat and ran into his arms. "Uncle, I am glad you came."

He marveled at her lack of fear of what he was. Not caring that they were in a public place, he kissed the top of her head. "I am sorry I did not pay the ransom sooner," he whispered. "I was—"

"Rhys explained your reasonings," she said with an offhand wave.

"Oh?" His eyebrow lifted. This rogue presumed to know his mind? "Let us depart and you can tell me what he said about my reasoning at home." He set a guinea on the bar, took her elbow, and led her outside.

Vivian squinted curiously at Bonnie and the sleeping Jeffries, but before she could question that, Aldric handed her up into the carriage. Now that they'd left the inn, with its miasma of food and beer and humans, the other vampire's scent radiated from Vivian. Aldric suppressed a growl. His primitive instincts to find the interloper and drive a sword through his heart clanged through his head like the peals of a bell.

His niece seemed to sense his ire, but held her tongue through the rest of the ride. Aldric was thankful for that, since he did not wish for Bonnie to be privy to just how sticky this situation had become.

And Bonnie was indeed squirming with curiosity. Aldric gave her a warning glare as Jeffries was awakened near Gordon's Tavern. She departed with a bow that was more cheeky than meek.

"Who was that woman driving the carriage?" Vivian asked.

"It's not important right now." Aldric leaned forward and spoke to Jeffries. "Please take us back to Thornton Manor."

"Very good, my lord. And may I say that it is a delight to see Miss Stratford again?"

"Thank you, Jeffries," Vivian called up from her seat. "I'm pleased to see you as well."

The remainder of the ride home passed in silence, but once they arrived at Thornton Manor, Vivian asked to see Madame Renarde.

Aldric shook his head. "She is recovering from her illness and still resting, and we must talk."

Once they were seated in his study, Aldric poured them each a glass of wine. As she sipped her wine, he studied her, frowning at her shabby attire, ungloved hands, and wistful eyes. The reek of the other vampire continued to taunt him. The cad hadn't Marked her, but he may as well have. "Now what exactly did this rogue tell you about my end of our dealings?"

Vivian spoke in a soothing tone, as if to placate Aldric. "Rhys said that you originally believed him to be a human, and so it would be damaging to your reputation as a Lord Vampire to allow a mortal to best you."

That was true, yet Aldric stewed with vexation that a strange vampire had been able to assess him with such accuracy. "Why did he even bother trying to explain my original refusal to pay?"

"Because at first I was hurt and thought you did not care about me." Vivian regarded him with a sad smile. "He wished to assure me that you did."

Aldric closed his eyes and rubbed the bridge of his nose. Ever since he'd found Vivian to be missing, and received the first ransom letter, nothing had gone as he'd expected. This rogue, Rhys, had been concerned about his captive's feelings. Yet another indication that Rhys was too soft to be in the business of kidnapping. Sadly for him, that horse had already left the barn.

Soft as he may be, the rogue had still abducted the blood kin of a Lord Vampire and extorted money. And from what Madame Renarde had said, Rhys had likely done more than that.

"Did he feed on you?" Aldric demanded, eager to gather up sins to lay at the rogue's feet.

"Twice." Vivian lifted her chin as if proud of the fact. "Once when he showed me what he was. The second time was because I asked him to so that he did not have to risk going out."

"How do you know it was only twice?" Aldric pressed, even though part of him knew it was cruel. "A vampire usually banishes his victim's memory after he feeds."

"I was *not* his victim." Red flags of anger streamed across her cheeks.

"You were, though." Aldric couldn't stop prodding her apparent wound. Her look of besotted heartbreak filled him with righteous indignation. "He took you from the carriage and held you against your will to extort money out of me."

"He did it to save his family!" Vivian retorted. "And I know he didn't feed from me without my knowledge because Rhys had honor, even if he is a rogue, as you call him." Her eyes narrowed and she her lip curled in a grimace. "Did *you* ever feed from me?"

"Certainly not." Aldric held up his hands, aghast at the notion. "You are my kin and were under my care."

"I was under Rhys's care as well. One does not wish to harm a hostage." Her tone was victorious as she pressed her argument. "He went out for his meals, same as you. And I do not see why it matters. As you can see, I am unharmed from the ordeal."

"*Unharmed*?" Aldric echoed, stunned at her lack of comprehension as to the gravity of the situation. "The whoreson has ruined your life and placed you in grave danger! He compromised you the moment he abducted you. I may have been able to salvage the situation and keep that sordid fact secret had he not shown you his fangs. In doing so, he's ruined any hope of you finding a husband and living a normal life. And if I did not care for you as much as he'd wagered, he very well could have signed your death warrant. Humans cannot know of our kind and be permitted to live."

Vivian's rebellious countenance softened. "Are you going to Change me into a vampire then?"

He sighed and buried his face in his hands. Mentoring a youngling was among the last things he wanted to do for the next few decades. "I do not yet know what I am going to do. Blast it! What am I going to tell your father? You were supposed to return to London in the Spring, but now, you cannot."

"Father never cared for me much." Although her tone was sublime indifference, there was a flash of old hurt in her eyes. "Before I'd learned that you were in a rush to marry me off, I'd planned to ask you if I could remain with you at Thornton Manor and care for you in your dotage."

"My dotage?" He snorted. "I may be there already." The remainder of his words registered. "You didn't wish to wed?"

"I did not." Vivian crossed her arms over her chest and stared daggers of accusation in his direction. "Something easy to discover had anyone bothered asking me what I wished."

A twinge of remorse pricked him, but Aldric shrugged it off. "Well, now you are spared the parson's mousetrap," he said with a sigh. At least the settlement he'd prepared for Vivian's dowry also included a trust with a provision for it to belong to her, in case she remained a spinster. A settlement that would bring justice to her, though she wouldn't know it. "And I suppose you may write to your father and express your wishes to remain in Blackpool. If he refuses, I'll convince him to change his mind."

Vivian's mutinous countenance softened. "Do not look so dismal, Uncle. I am sure we will get on well enough."

"You're the one who looks dismal," Aldric fired back. Madame Renarde's concerns rang in his mind. "The rogue didn't bed you, did he?"

"What would it matter if he had?" The crimson flood in her cheeks proclaimed the truth. "I was already compromised. You said so yourself."

Aldric's fists clenched at his sides as he rose from his desk and paced the study. "It matters because you're a highborn lady and your virtue should be reserved for the bonds of matrimony. It matters because you're my niece and I care very much if some blackguard takes advantage of you."

"He did *not* take advantage," Vivian said through gritted teeth. "I was willing. But I find this conversation to be unseemly and do not wish to speak of something so personal."

"It's not the conversation that is unseemly. It is this whole sordid affair." Still, Aldric didn't truly wish to know the intimate details. He had his answer. Vivian had indeed fallen for the rogue vampire, the rogue had reciprocated her feelings and as Madame Renarde had predicted, the two had succumbed to temptation. The only positive aspect of this disaster was that at least vampires were sterile, so Aldric did not have to worry about her carrying a bastard. "You are right. We will not discuss this further. The sooner you can forget about that blasted rogue vampire, the better."

And Aldric would do his best to ensure that she did indeed forget. He gathered his power, fixed Vivian with his gaze, and commanded her to forget all about vampires. "Forget that you loved your captor. He was nothing but a lowly thief and now that you are home, you only wish you get on with living a normal life."

Vivian blinked and rubbed her temples. Aldric held his breath and silently prayed that his mesmerism has worked just as effectively as it had with Madame Renarde.

"How dare you!" she hissed. "How dare you try to make me forget the only love I'll ever know?"

"For your own safety." Aldric returned to his desk and slumped in his chair, defeated. His last hope of eliminating Vivian's involvement in his world had drifted away like gossamer in the wind. She'd spent too much time with the rogue vampire, had learned too many secrets, and had been intimate with him. Just as Aldric had feared, the memories were permanently etched in her mind and heart. "Didn't your 'love' tell you that a human who learns about vampires must be killed or Changed?"

Vivian crossed her arms over her chest. "Yes," she said quietly. "He even told me you'd try to make me forget. But I can't forget. Not after all I've been through and what I've shared with him." Tears pooled in the corners of her eyes. "Did you banish Madame Renarde's memories?"

"Yes." Aldric shifted in his seat, uncomfortable with Vivian's display of emotion for a vampire who'd ruined her life. "She only remembers that you were abducted by a highwayman and that I paid the ransom and that we must be discreet lest another scandal breaks out. *Please* do not say anything to her that could make her remember any other details. Her life depends on it. A vampire can only Change one human every hundred years."

"I won't breathe a word," Vivian promised. "May I go see her now?"

Aldric nodded. "She is in her room. I will have the servants draw you a bath while you visit with your companion." Now that Aldric had the rogue's scent, he wanted it washed away from his niece as soon as possible.

Vivian darted from the study, in a rush to see her friend. Aldric shook his head. Only a fortnight away, and she'd already forgotten how to speak and walk like a lady. He took a deep drink of wine before ringing for the housekeeper.

His previously peaceful life had been upended beyond comprehension. His niece had fallen in love with a rogue vampire who'd abducted her for ransom to prevent Aldric from evicting a widow who couldn't manage the land she lived on. Aldric had spent the past several nights nursing a woman who'd been born a man. And now that he'd finally gotten Vivian back, his niece had been flat out hostile towards him.

What would he do with her? When he'd taken his niece under his wing, it was supposed to have been a brief idyllic reconnection with family and a satisfactory endeavor of finding her a prosperous match and ensuring his family line could continue.

Now he couldn't return Vivian to her father, he certainly couldn't marry her off to a mortal, he couldn't even give her the land he'd settled on her, for as long as she knew his secrets, it was too dangerous for her to leave his home. He would most certainly have to Change her, and spend the next few years teaching her and helping her adjust to life as a vampire.

But to Change her, he'd have to petition the Elders. That was the law for all Lord Vampires. Aldric shuddered with dread at the prospect of corresponding with the oldest and most powerful vampires in the world who oversaw the laws of their kind. Although it was unlikely that whatever lie he fabricated for his reasons to bring his niece into the fold would be detected, there was always the slim chance that the Elders would send a representative to hear the case in person.

After he ordered Vivian's bath to be drawn, Aldric left his office and looked in on Vivian's reunion with Madame Renarde. He prayed Vivian was holding to her vow to keep her silence about all things pertaining to vampires.

He paused in Madame Renarde's doorway and watched the two exchanging an affectionate embrace. Madame Renarde's palpable joy and relief to see Vivian brought an unexpected lump to Aldric's throat. How long had it been since he'd felt such a closeness for someone? At least two hundred years. Vivian had burrowed her way into his heart and Renarde had gained his respect and admiration in ways Aldric had not anticipated. As he observed Vivian's protective concern over her companion's illness and listened to her questions about how she was treated, he felt a pang of melancholy.

That was yet another tangle in this disastrous affair. Vivian's foray into the vampire world would cleave their friendship like a stone slowly cut by rushing water in a river. No longer could she talk with her companion about everything in her life. Only Aldric would be safe to talk to and since he'd separated Vivian from her lover, he didn't anticipate her confiding with him.

Especially when he was finished dealing with said lover. Damn that rogue to hell.

Vivian rose from Madame Renarde's sickbed and levelled Aldric with an accusing glare as she strode to the door. "You cannot grant me a moment's privacy with my companion?"

Aldric ignored the sting he felt at her angry tone. "Actually, I only came by to let you know that I must go out tonight and ask you to remain here with Madame Renarde."

Her stormy countenance softened slightly. "Oh. Well, have a satisfactory hunt, then."

"Lower your voice," he admonished with a whisper. "And you are not to leave the house until I've decided what to do with you."

Vivian visibly bristled once more. "I recant my words regarding our prospects of getting on well together." Before she could utter another biting set-down, the housekeeper appeared in the corridor to announce that her bath had been prepared. Vivian gave him one last furious glare and flounced to her chambers.

Aldric's shoulders slumped with despair. He had to find a way to repair their relationship before he Changed her. Alas, there was little chance of that, for if Vivian discovered his next course of action, she would hate him for all eternity.

Chapter Twenty-five

Rhys hugged his arms as he trudged through the mud to the Berwyn Farm. He could have used his preternatural speed to cover the miles from his cave to Emily's house, but he simply did not have the spirit to run. He knew he should feel happy and victorious that he'd managed to secure the money to save his family farm as well as cause havoc with the Lord of Blackpool for his cruelty in trying to force Emily and her children from their home.

Yet after spending time with Vivian, reading, talking, and laughing with her, kissing her, making love to her, and ultimately falling hopelessly in love with her, the victory felt hollow.

A cold, ragged hole resided where his heart used to be. If not for his duty to protect his kin, Rhys would have been tempted to take Vivian and flee England. Leaving her at that inn had been the hardest thing he'd ever done in his life.

Almost as difficult as lying to her had been. Rhys knew that Vivian's uncle would never forget the insult borne against him. The Lord of Blackpool would ensure that Rhys would be hunted by every vampire Blackpool could employ. If Rhys didn't leave the country before dawn, his life was likely forfeit.

Remembering that fact, he willed his feet to carry him faster, running in a blur until he entered Blackpool's territory. For a moment, the temptation to turn towards Thornton Manor to see Vivian and make sure she was safe reverberated in his bones. But he knew that was folly. Blackpool would most certainly have his vampires guarding the perimeter. Still, his constant worries refused to abate. Had Vivian been Changed? If so, how was she coping with the situation? Would her uncle be a compassionate mentor?

Or if Lord Thornton had decided against Changing Vivian, what did that mean for her future? Would Vivian be kept a virtual prisoner, isolated from the world so that she couldn't tell anyone of the existence of vampires?

What about Madame Renarde? While Rhys knew that Aldric wouldn't kill his own niece, he wasn't so certain that Vivian's companion would be spared.

God, he'd been such a fool. Although revealing himself and Lord Thornton as vampires had certainly resulted in Aldric capitulating to the ransom, Rhys should never have endangered Vivian's and Madame Renarde's lives with such a dangerous action.

But there was nothing he could do about it. The only thing he could do was fulfill his original mission and take care of his own family.

He paused at the edge of the Berwyn Farm and scented the air. A shuddering sigh of relief escaped him when he didn't smell any other vampires. He'd knock on Emily's door, give her the money, and have her awaken the children so he could tell them all goodbye.

His chest tightened as the fact sank in that not only would he never see Emily, Jacob, and Alice again, he'd also never set eyes on any of his mortal descendants again. Not so long as the Lord of Blackpool lived.

At least the farm remained in the Berwyn family. Rhys had made certain of that. He reached in his pocket and felt the reassuring weight of the hundred and ninety-eight pounds in coins. Two pounds had gone to Vivian's room and meals at the Owl Inn and Rhys would give all but five pounds to Emily, so that not only could she pay off the mortgage, she'd also be able to purchase food and perhaps seed or livestock to begin the arduous process of making the land profitable as it once was.

That would be the only comfort Rhys would have as he lived the rest of his doubtlessly short life running from the Lord of Blackpool and his allies. With a heavy sigh, Rhys started forward to deliver salvation and bid his farewells.

Suddenly, he was seized from behind. Firm hands gripped his upper arms like iron manacles.

"You didn't think you'd be able to win this game, did you?" a cold voice hissed in his ear.

Rhys's stomach sank with dread. "Blackpool."

"The very same, but you will address me as Lord Thornton." The other vampire jerked his arms further back, and then real manacles were clamped over Rhys's wrists. "And you are Rhys Berwyn, a rogue vampire. You are under arrest for kidnapping, extortion, and the cardinal crime of revealing our existence to not one, but two mortals. You also compromised my niece. Although that is not technically a crime, I will see that you pay dearly for it. To start, I am foreclosing on that farm tomorrow."

As Rhys was dragged away, his soul contorted in agony. After all his efforts, sacrificing what little honor he'd had left, and sacrificing the love of his life, he'd failed.

Berwyn Farm was lost to his family, Emily and her children would be tossed out into the cold, and Rhys would die in vain.

"I did it for love," Rhys muttered. "Every bit of it."

"Save your prattle for when I question you," Aldric growled before he shoved Rhys into the luggage boot of his carriage.

Rhys closed his eyes and sighed with yearning as he detected a hint of Vivian's scent. At least she'd been brought home safe. Had her uncle Changed her yet? Rhys doubted it, for there wouldn't have been much time between the transformation and the first feeding before Aldric had tracked Rhys down and arrested him. Not to mention that Lord Thornton would have been weakened by the process. From how easily the vampire had restrained Rhys, he must have conserved his strength thus far.

When the carriage halted, Rhys was hauled outside. For the first time in his life, the sight of Thornton Manor did not inspire a sense of hatred. Instead, abject longing emanated from his heart like a beacon before a storm-swept ship. Rhys lifted his head and smelled the air, desperate to take in his last scent of Vivian. She was *here*, his senses screamed, and every cell of his being surged to break free and go to her. He caught Madame Renarde's scent as well, faint, and not as sickly as before. Thank God Aldric hadn't killed her. Vivian's love would have twisted to loathing if he'd been responsible for the demise of her dearest friend. He looked up at the windows, wishing more than anything for one last glimpse of Vivian.

Aldric's fingers clamped down on the back of his neck, breaking off Rhys's search. "If you make a sound, I will forego your trial and put a bullet in your brain."

A trial? A jagged laugh caught in Rhys's throat. What was the point? He was guilty as sin. The Lord of Blackpool must be a stuffed shirt indeed to bother with such an empty formality. Unless, Rhys thought with dawning horror, Blackpool's idea of a trial involved torture.

Yet still, Rhys did not struggle, for in case Vivian was peering through the window, he didn't want her to see him killed right then and there.

Lord Thornton led him to a stone staircase at the rear of the house and hefted Rhys over his shoulder so suddenly, it knocked the wind out of Rhys's lungs.

He carried Rhys down the steps with one arm as if he weighed no more than thistledown. Rhys probably could have struggled free, but the smell of a gun—no doubt holstered near Thornton's free hand—told him what would happen if he tried.

Instead, Rhys remained still as Aldric unlocked an iron door and carried him into a pitch-black cellar. Even with preternatural sight, it was hard for Rhys to make out the details of his surroundings, though the creak of metal hinges was familiar enough.

Without warning, Aldric tossed Rhys across the room. Rhys's back slammed against a solid wall and he grunted, the wind knocked out of him.

Stars danced before his eyes as he heard the strike of a match. Lord Thornton's unforgiving features were illuminated as he lit a lantern outside the bars of the cell he'd tossed Rhys into. Rhys glanced around at the sturdy, stone walls and blinked in surprise at the sight of a pallet on the floor and the clean floor. Blackpool's dungeon was far more comfortable than Manchester's.

Still, Rhys noted the thick iron rings bolted into the ceiling, made for suspending a captive in the air. Comfort did not promise mercy.

Aldric reinforced the notion when he strode across the dungeon and opened a cabinet, pulling out a massive gun meant to shoot elephants on safari. He entered Rhys's cell and aimed the gun at his chest. "Why were you exiled by your original lord?"

The question threw Rhys off guard. "I beg your pardon?"

"I am asking how you came to be a rogue," Blackpool snapped from behind the enormous gun barrel.

Rhys leaned against the wall, unable to see why it mattered. "Because I continued to leave my lord's territory without a writ of passage."

Lord Thornton raised one eyebrow. "Why?"

"My great-grand niece needed me." Rhys glared at the other vampire. "Her wastrel husband had mortgaged the family farm before cocking up his toes. I was giving her money so that she could stave off eviction. I thought you already knew this, being that you hold the mortgage and denied my application to move to Blackpool so that I could help her."

"I've received dozens of applications over the last decade." Aldric's frown deepened. "I can only accept so many, since my territory can only safely sustain a limited number of vampires. If your disobedience was mentioned, or if you had no references to recommend you, I would have issued my standard rejection."

Rhys's former best friend, John, was supposed to have written a commending reference. Now Rhys realized that John had betrayed him. There could be no other explanation, as Rhys had obeyed his lord until his application to Blackpool had been denied. And now, Aldric's indifferent tone rubbed further salt in the old wound. Rhys's future and the fate of his family had been nothing but a jot of discarded paper to him.

"Who was your former lord anyway?" Thornton asked, oblivious to Rhys's pain.

"Manchester," Rhys spat the name. "Are you going to turn me over to him?" If so, then at least perhaps he could curse John to the lowest circle of hell before he was executed.

"And deprive myself of making you answer for your crimes against me?" Aldric snorted. "I think not." He stalked around Rhys like an angry lion, keeping the elephant gun trained on him the entire time. "It is unfortunate that you chose robbery and extortion as your effort to help your family. Although I frown on disobedience, I would have been willing to listen to an appeal, and at the very least, granted your niece an extra year to catch up on her payments. I am not an unreasonable man."

"How was I supposed to know that? You rejected my petition when I thought you knew that I had mortal kin in your territory who needed my help." Rhys pulled at his chains. "You care for your family, why don't you understand that I care for mine?"

Lord Thornton regarded him with an imperious glare. "If you truly cared for them, you would have done something other than extort the money needed from the very Lord Vampire who held the mortgage. A Lord Vampire who was bound to catch you in the end. Your spite won over your reason." He pointed the gun like a wagging finger of condemnation. "Did you target me because you thought it clever to bilk me out of the money for a mortgage that I held, or was it out of anger that I denied your petition for citizenship?"

"Both." The admission tore from his lips.

Crippling humiliation forced Rhys to his knees. Lord Thornton was right. Rhys's pride and anger had made the choice to target the Lord Vampire of Blackpool for ransom money. If he'd set aside his anger for one moment, he would have chosen a safer course of action. Robbed a mortal nobleman, perhaps. Hell, he could have sneaked into one of London's hallowed clubs and cheated a thick-pocketed earl in a game of cards.

But Lord Thornton wasn't finished with his castigations. "And on top of all that, you forced my niece into our world, thus destroying any hope of a normal future for her. You defiled her body and broke her heart."

"I did not rape her!" Rhys would not allow that untruthful abomination to be laid at his feet. "She gave herself to me willingly. If I could have wed her first, I would have gladly. I *love* her!"

Lord Thornton bared his fangs and growled. "The thought of a union between my precious Vivian and a low-born, thieving scoundrel like you makes me ill!" He strode toward Rhys, eyes glowing red with unholy wrath. "Bloody hell, I can still smell her on you." The vampire closed his eyes and took a few deep breaths, visibly struggling to collect himself. "I think I've questioned you enough. "I, Aldric Cadell, the Lord Vampire of Blackpool charge you, Rhys Berwyn, of kidnapping, extortion, theft, trespassing, and revealing the secrets of our kind." Thornton pressed the gun barrel to Rhys's heart. "How do you plead?"

"Guilty," Rhys stated flatly. "To all charges."

He closed his eyes, awaiting death. "Goodbye Vivian," he whispered.

Chapter Twenty-six

Three days later

Vivian wiggled her hairpin in the lock and cursed as it once more skittered uselessly in the keyhole. Her fingers ached like the devil, but she refused to give up.

A cough sounded behind her. "What are you doing?" Madame Renarde asked in a chiding tone.

"I'm trying to get inside Uncle's study," she answered through gritted teeth. "As soon as I can pick this bloody lock. And you should be resting. The doctor only permitted you to be out of bed yesterday."

Although Vivian was pleased to be reunited with her best friend, and relieved that Uncle hadn't killed her, she still felt a sense of loss. Because Uncle had banished Madame Renarde's memories of everything pertaining to vampires, Vivian not only couldn't tell her closest friend about the true depths of her heartache, and uncertain future, she also had to endure Madame Renarde rubbing further salt in the wound by admonishing her to forget about the wicked thief who'd seduced her.

And oh, how Vivian missed that wicked thief. Rhys haunted her dreams and every waking thought. She would give anything for one last glimpse of him, her very soul for one more moment in his arms. Had he gotten away safely? Was he thinking of her? Did love always hurt so much?

Madame Renarde interrupted Vivian's inner mourning. "Why are you trying to break into Lord Thornton's study?"

"Because I need to look at his ledgers and deeds. I need to know if Rhys's niece received the money and had her farm restored to her." As the nights passed with no visitors from solicitors and no word from her uncle about the farm, Vivian's worry grew. She had to know if Rhys's family had been saved. That at least the consequences of her abduction had been worth it. It was the only closure Vivian could hope to receive.

Besides, Rhys would want her to make sure that Emily and the children were all right. Since he had to flee England, he had no way of knowing.

Madame Renarde made a tsk of disapproval. "You have that pin bent all wrong. Give me another one and let me try."

Vivian blinked in surprise. Was her companion an ally after all? From the way Madame Renarde spoke during suppers with Uncle Aldric, Vivian thought that her companion hated Rhys for what he'd done.

Only seconds after Vivian handed Madame Renarde a new hairpin, her companion bent the slim piece of metal, inserted the pin, and with a twist, the lock clicked free.

"I've picked dozens of locks of this style," Madame Renarde said with a smirk.

Vivian smiled for the first time since Rhys left her at the inn. Sometimes, it was useful to have a companion who'd once been a spy.

Together, they entered Lord Thornton's office. Vivian lit the lantern on the desk and Madame Renarde closed the door behind them and locked it in case a servant overheard them. Vivian made her way to Uncle's large mahogany desk, but her companion stopped her with a hand on her shoulder.

"He will likely keep property deeds in a locked box." Madame Renarde scanned the room. "Probably in that cabinet."

Vivian found four locked boxes in the cabinet. Madame Renarde had a bit more difficulty unlocking them, but she managed to spring the first one, which contained a fortune in bank drafts. The deeds were in the second box. Vivian's eyes widened at the formidable stack as she carried them to the desk to read. Her uncle owned farms and estates not only all over Blackpool, but also in London, Scotland, and even property in Italy and France.

Madame Renarde rifled through the papers with a frown. "The majority are deeds he owns outright." She came to a smaller stack with different seals and signatures. "Ah. Here are the mortgages. But how are you to know which one belongs to Rhys's family when we don't know his surname?"

"His niece's name is Emily." Vivian's heart sank. "But it would have been her husband who mortgaged the place. Rhys only referred to him as a wastrel. Which he most certainly was, to sell off his wife's land like that."

Madame Renarde continued to scan the documents. "Lord Thornton may have had her sign it if he was allowing her to make payments before. Ah!" She held up a paper. "Berwyn Farm, first signed by a William Horne, then later by Emily Berwyn Horne."

"Rhys Berwyn." At last, Vivian knew her love's full name. "He was Welsh."

Her companion arched her brow. "Do not tell me that you broke into Lord Thornton's study simply to discern that thief's surname."

Vivian suppressed her wistful smile and shook her head. "No. I want to know if Emily had the farm restored."

"Since the deed is still here, signed over to Lord Thornton, I'd say not." Madame Renarde shrugged. "However, there is no telling if or when Rhys was able to deliver the money. Furthermore, I imagine it would be difficult for a widow with two small children to have the time and ability to make her way here to deliver the payment. She may be waiting for your uncle to come to her."

"Then there is only one way to find out." Vivian took one of her uncle's quills and a sheet of parchment from his desk drawer and wrote down the address of the farm from the deed. "I shall have to pay her a visit."

Madame Renarde fixed her with a stern frown. "Your uncle said you were not to leave the house."

For a moment Vivian almost slipped and said that her uncle wouldn't be able to stop her, since vampires could not go out in the day. "If he rises before I return, you will know nothing about my leaving or anything disturbed in his study. You're supposed to be resting. I will take Jeffries with me." She stormed down the stairs before Madame Renarde could protest.

The footman, unfortunately, was also privy to her uncle's orders and tried to refuse. It was only when Vivian threatened to saddle her own horse and go alone that he complied. "His Lordship will hear of this, Miss," he admonished.

"I expect he will," Vivian replied and dug her heels in the horse's flanks.

The afternoon sun was painfully bright after weeks of only being out at night. Still, the day was beautiful and green, the sky blue as cornflowers and the November sun surprisingly warm on her back. Vivian shivered as she realized that soon she would never be able to experience the daylight again.

That was, if Uncle would indeed Change her. He'd avoided the subject for the past several nights, instead trying to charm her into their previous congenial interactions as if her time with Rhys had never occurred. Vivian couldn't be swayed by the act. Not only because she was still angry at him for his callous dismissal of her feelings, but also because it was impossible to observe frivolous niceties when her future was in purgatory.

Berwyn Farm lay only four miles from her uncle's estate. As she and Madame Renarde rode up the rutted drive, Vivian's first sight of the farm made her stomach sink. The cottages meant for the field hands had tumbled down, their timbers rotted away. The gray wood of the barn was swollen and warped, its roof had a gaping hole where the beams had collapsed.

Yet Vivian remembered the fondness that had radiated from Rhys's features when he'd spoken of the place. *"The property is forty-three acres. I spent half my childhood working them, and the other half climbing trees in the orchard, swimming in the pond, and fishing in the brook."*

After uttering a silent prayer, Vivian dismounted and bade Jeffries to remain at the end of the drive with the horses and approached the farmhouse. Despite its peeling grey paint and missing roof shingles, she could see the cozy charm of the home.

When she knocked on the door, Vivian drew in a breath, wondering what Rhys's niece would make of her. *Cousin*, she corrected herself. Rhys told her they were cousins.

The door opened to reveal a tall auburn-haired woman. Even her shabby, tattered dress and the lines of exhaustion around her eyes and mouth couldn't obscure her breathtaking beauty. Copper eyes, the same color as Rhys's, narrowed on Vivian and her companion with suspicion. "Who are you?"

"I am Miss Vivian Stratford." Vivian curtsied.

Emily's suspicion warped to outright malice. "Come to admire your dowry already? Lord Thornton may have foreclosed on me day before yesterday, but he gave me another fortnight to make arrangements for myself and the children."

Foreclosed? Vivian's heart clenched as her worst fear was confirmed. "Rhys didn't bring you the money?"

Emily's eyes widened, as her mask of bitterness melted into panic. "You *know* Rhys? Have you seen him? He was supposed to come by three nights ago."

Vivian didn't know what she could say to reassure the woman, but she had to say something. Furthermore, she also wanted to know why Emily assumed this farm was her dowry. Marriage was out of the question for her. "Ah, may I come in?"

"Please do." Emily's face was white as linen.

Once they were seated at the scarred maple dining room table, Emily poured two cups of cider with shaky hands. "Tell me how you know my cousin."

Vivian hesitated. "Where are your children? This is a subject too delicate for their ears."

"They're in the barn, playing with the kittens." She peered out the window just in case and lowered her voice. "You know what means he used to support me, don't you? Was he arrested by a constable?"

Vivian shook her head. "Not to my knowledge." Though she feared that if her uncle or another Lord Vampire had caught Rhys, an arrest by human authorities could be the only explanation offered to this poor woman. "As to how I know him, he abducted me for ransom."

Emily gasped. "He thought to bilk Lord Thornton out of the funds needed for the mortgage that he himself held?

"Yes." Vivian tasted her cider. It was delightfully sweet for such a bitter conversation. "And he succeeded, to my knowledge. My uncle paid Rhys, and he returned me the following evening. He was supposed to come straight to you to deliver the money."

"And he never arrived." Emily fell into a pensive silence and sipped her cider. "But why have you come if you thought I'd paid off the mortgage?"

"Because Rhys said he'd have to leave the country after what he's done, so I thought he would want someone to make sure that his family was safe." Vivian's throat tightened as she stared into the woman's copper eyes, remembering how he'd looked at her the same way when they'd discussed the mysteries in the "Two Hills" stories. "We fell in love, you see... and—"

"Oh my!" Emily exclaimed, hand over her throat. "My cousin is a good-hearted man, despite his thieving ways, and quite charming, so I can see why a maid would lose her heart to him... but the circumstances are tragic. I imagine His Lordship was furious."

"Absolutely livid." Vivian agreed with a bitter smile.

"And yet you care enough to come here to see if I had received the money," Emily said softly. "Even though if that were the case, this land would not be yours."

"I'm not certain it *is* mine," Vivian said. "Uncle never said anything to me about it and as I told you, I am quite compromised. What makes you think the farm is my dowry?"

"Because he told me he intended to give it to you when he came to tell me that I had to pay by months' end." Emily frowned over the rim of her cup. "He said that he would ask that your husband would allow me to stay and work for you as a housekeeper."

"Housekeeper?" Vivian echoed in outrage. "When you're the mistress of this land? I hope you threw that insulting offer back in his face!"

Emily chuckled. "Rhys said the same before he announced that he had a plan. I never imagined that it involved kidnapping Lord Thornton's niece." She shook her head, a mirthful smile just like Rhys's curving her lips. "I do not think you are supposed to be on my side."

"Well I am," Vivian declared. "I will speak to my uncle tonight and try to convince him to return the deed to your land, or at the very least, grant you more time. Perhaps Rhys is merely delayed."

"Or perhaps your uncle had him arrested." Emily's face was etched with worry.

"I will find out," Vivian promised. "No matter what, I promise that I will do everything in my power to ensure that you do not lose your home."

Emily sighed and shook her head. "Women have no power in this world."

"Then we should all do our utmost to change that." Vivian rose from the table. The sun hung low in the sky and would set in less than two hours. "I will return when I have news." She held out her hand and was gratified when Emily shook it. "It was an honor to meet you. Rhys has told me so much about you."

Emily managed a watery smile. "You will have to tell me more about yourself and the tale of how you came to love him."

"I would like that." Vivian curtsied one last time before departing. On her way back to the horses, she silently vowed to continue Rhys's mission to protect his family, no matter the consequences.

Jeffries protested as Vivian raced her horse back to Thornton Manor, but she refused to slow and left the footman in the dust. What had happened to Rhys? And if Uncle Aldric intended on giving her Berwyn Farm for a dowry, what did he intend to do with it now that Vivian could no longer wed?

If she'd only known about the dowry, she would have eloped with Rhys. Then he could have given the deed to the farm back to Emily. Uncle would have still been angry, but at least it would have been legal.

Or at least, it would be if Rhys hadn't been a vampire.

Madame Renarde waited in the parlor, wringing her hands, an embroidery hoop in her lap. "Did you meet Mrs. Horne?"

"I did." Vivian reached into the sewing basket for something to do while she waited for her uncle to rise for the night. "Rhys didn't deliver the money on time and Uncle Aldric foreclosed on the farm."

"Oh, that is unfortunate." Madame Renarde said with genuine sympathy. "That means he risked his life for nothing."

"Uncle Aldric intended on giving me the land for my dowry." Vivian threaded a needle and blinked back tears at the memory of mending Rhys's clothes. "I am going to see if I can find a way to restore the land to Emily."

"You would truly take up that man's quest?" Madame Renarde gaped at her in surprise.

"My conscience depends on it." Vivian stabbed the needle through the hoop. "And since we cannot be together, this is the only way I can display my love for him."

Before Madame Renarde could respond, Aldric entered the parlor.

Vivian tossed her embroidery aside and stood. "Uncle, may we speak in private?"

The wary look in his eyes indicated that he heard the cold anger in her voice. "Very well. Let us head up to my study."

The moment they were alone, Vivian slapped her palms down on Aldric's massive desk. "Why didn't you tell me that you intended to give me Berwyn Farm for my dowry?"

He rubbed the bridge of his nose and fetched two brandy snifters. "Forgive me, but there was so much else going on that such a trifle matter didn't cross my mind." He poured an inch of amber liquid in each glass and slid one across the desk to her. "How did you learn about it?"

"Emily Horne told me when I went there to see her." Vivian crossed her arms over her chest, despising him for his obvious lie. He had to have thought of the farm as he'd recently taken possession of it. "And I hardly think that forcing a woman and her children out of their home is a trifle matter."

"Damn it!" Aldric tossed back his drink. "I told you that you were not to leave the house without me."

Vivian ignored the outburst. "How is the place to become my dowry when Mrs. Horne was supposed to be able to pay the mortgage with the ransom money?"

"She wasn't able to pay." Aldric said through clenched teeth. His fangs glistened in the light of the lantern. "I caught the rogue on his way to the farm and arrested him three nights ago."

Her heart thudded with dread. "Where is he?"

Aldric's voice was cold as a winter grave. "Did Rhys not tell you the fate of rogues when they are captured?"

Vivian gripped the edges of the desk as white spots danced in her vision. Rhys was dead. Her uncle had killed him. Memories of his smile, his embrace, the tender way he'd said, *"I love you,"* flooded her mind. And now he was gone? Her knees threatened to buckle, but she willed herself to remain standing.

"How could you?" she whispered through numb lips.

"I'm sorry, but the law is clear." Aldric reached for her hand and frowned as Vivian pulled away. "I cannot allow a rogue to go unpunished and expect to retain loyalty from my people."

"But did you have to kill him?" she pleaded, as if he could magically take it back. "He was only trying to care for his family as you are caring for me."

For a moment, something in Aldric's eyes flickered, as if there had been another option, one he didn't wish to explore. Then his expression shuttered. "Something that set me and him at cross purposes. And continuing to care for you is all I can do." He moved as if to try to reach for her again, then his shoulders slumped, and he pushed her untouched brandy glass towards her. "I know that losing a love is an excruciatingly painful event. I know that you probably despise me right now. But we must get on with our lives, and if there is anything I can do…"

"There is nothing you can do to atone for what you've done to me." Vivian took the glass and quaffed the brandy, coughing as the fiery liquid slid down her throat. Then she remembered her purpose for talking to him before he'd shattered her world. "Although one thing might help.   Give me the deed to the Berwyn Farm."

"Why do you want the land?" Aldric cocked his head to the side. "You cannot marry anymore, not after becoming involved with our kind."

"So I can return it to Emily, of course." Vivian fumed. How could he be so obtuse? "That way, Rhys's death won't be in vain."

"You speak of him as if he was a hero, rather than a criminal who sought to steal my money and cheat me out of land that was by rights to go to me." Aldric leaned back in his chair and closed his eyes. "And what do you suppose this poor widow will be able to do once her land is restored? You saw the farm. The land has gone fallow for lack of a plow, and the buildings are falling down over her ears. She has no hope of restoring the place. You think I am the villain for taking it from her, but I am not. I would rather see someone bring the farm back to its former prosperity, and allow her to remain with gainful employment so she may feed and shelter her children."

He had a point, Vivian admitted ruefully. Still, it didn't mean the situation was right. "Then let me be the one to restore the place. I will need somewhere else to live anyway."

Aldric opened his eyes and stared at her. "And why is that?"

"Because I hate you for what you've done." Vivian spoke slowly, imbuing each word with palpable animosity. "And I cannot abide one more night under your roof."

Aldric flinched, but then his eyes went cold. "I'm afraid you have no choice in the matter. For one thing, you are privy to our secrets and thus must remain with me. For another, a new vampire has extreme difficulty controlling their hunger. Do you wish to risk accidentally killing Mrs. Horne or one of the children?"

"No." Vivian shook her head with dawning horror. She wanted to save Rhys's family, not hurt them.

"I thought not." Aldric rose from his desk and approached the cabinet containing the locked boxes that Vivian and Madame Renarde had broken into earlier in the day. "I am afraid you will have to endure being under my roof for a while longer. As for the Berwyn Farm, there is something I can and have already done."

He unlocked one of the boxes and withdrew a sheet from a stack of documents that Vivian and Madame Renarde had not examined. "This was not only a dowry, but also a trust. If you do not marry before the age of twenty-five, the farm will be yours rather than passed to your husband. Since you no longer can marry, you may take over the farm in two years. By then you will have learned to control your hunger and will no longer require my constant supervision." He handed her the document. "After that, you can do as you please with the place, even sign it back to the Mrs. Horne."

"And what is Emily to do until then?" Vivian asked.

Aldric shrugged. "With her being foreclosed, she no longer owes mortgage payments, so what little income she has from the farm can be used to feed her children. And if you wish to use your pin money to aid her cause, I cannot stop you."

Relief that she would be able to fulfill her vow and care for Rhys's family melted the edges of Vivian's animosity. But she could not forgive her uncle for killing Rhys. "Thank you for displaying at least a scrap of humanity."

"I'll accept that grudging praise." Aldric sighed. "We will inform Mrs. Horne of her new circumstances tomorrow night. And I will write a petition to the Elders to Change you."

Vivian was tempted to ask about these Elders that Rhys had been so reluctant to talk about, but her grief and anger choked off the inquiry. She couldn't bear to be in the same room with the man who'd murdered her love. At least she'd ensured the safety of Rhys's family.

With a curt nod, she left the study and fled to her room. Tears flowed unchecked down her cheeks. She couldn't believe that Rhys was dead. Even though he'd had to leave her, she'd clung to the small comfort that he was out there somehow, thinking of her. Now even that had been ripped away.

Vivian pressed her fist to her mouth to muffle her strangled sobs. Strange, she'd never been one to give into tears before, but now that her heart had been reduced to a ragged hole, she could do little else.

Her door opened, and Vivian lifted her head to curse her uncle, but relaxed as she saw Madame Renarde.

"He isn't dead," her companion whispered.

Vivian's breath froze in her lungs. "What?"

"Lord Thornton has Rhys imprisoned in the cellar behind the house." Madame Renarde crossed the room and sat on Vivian's bed. "From what I've observed, he's still alive. He even fed him night before last."

Vivian leapt from her bed. "Then we must free him at once!"

Madame Renarde nodded. "Yes, and quickly, while your uncle is out hunting for his meal."

"Wait." Vivian froze with her hand on the door handle. "I thought Uncle erased your memory."

"He tried, and for my own self-preservation, I allowed him to believe his magic worked." Madame Renarde said with a smirk. "While I do not think he has the stomach to do away with me, it is best to err on the side of caution."

Even though Vivian quivered with the need to go to Rhys, she held back. "But if Uncle Aldric finds out that you helped me free Rhys, he'll know of your ruse, and you'll be at risk."

"I cannot sit idle and watch you drown in heartache. I'd at first believed that you merely suffered from a childish infatuation with Rhys, and I was gravely wrong." Madame Renarde took her hands. "Especially since it was my fault that Rhys was captured in the first place. My fever and the laudanum I was given for my cough loosened my tongue and I told Lord Thornton why Rhys wanted the ransom money. I won't have his death on my hands, if I can help it."

Vivian threw her arms around her friend. "I love you, Jeanette! No one has ever been blessed with such a good friend as you."

As they rushed down the stairs together, Vivian's heart bloomed with hope as she clutched her dowry settlement. She would see her love in moments, save his life, and god willing, they could be together at last.

Chapter Twenty-seven

Rhys recoiled in dread at the sound of the cellar being unlocked. But when the door opened, a most welcome scent filled the dungeon.

"Vivian?" His voice cracked with hope.

"Rhys!" She ran down the stairs and thrust her arms through the bars. Tears glistened in her grey eyes. "I thought Uncle Aldric had killed you."

He took her hands and placed kisses all over her wrists and palms. Honestly, he did not know why Aldric hadn't killed him yet. After Rhys had admitted guilt to all the crimes the Lord Vampire charged him with, Lord Thornton had struck him with the butt of the gun and walked out of the dungeon. The next night, Thornton had unlocked his manacles, released a live pig in the cell, and walked back out without a word.

Last night, Lord Thornton had removed the pig's carcass and brandished Rhys's application for citizenship, questioning him about the character flaws and disobedience outlined in the letter that John had included. A letter that was supposed to have been a recommendation rather than condemnation.

Rhys had explained his relationship with the vampire who'd made him, utterly perplexed as to why Aldric cared. But the moment Rhys asked about Vivian, Lord Thornton struck him with a backhanded slap and stormed out of his cell. There was no pig that night. Rhys had to make do with a rat that came into his cell.

Aldric had to be torturing him. That was the only explanation. To be so close to Vivian, yet never able to see or touch her again had tormented him to near madness.

Now, Vivian stood before him, and despite his ravening hunger, the temptation to kiss her was much stronger than that to bite her.

Madame Renarde tapped Vivian's shoulder. "Move aside so I can deal with this lock."

"I visited Emily," Vivian said as her companion set to work.

Rhys's chest tightened at the mention of his niece. "How is she?"

"Worried sick about you, just as I was. Uncle foreclosed on her last week." Before Rhys could react to that dismal news, Vivian withdrew a sheet of parchment from the pocket of her cloak. "I also discovered that he'd given me the farm as my dowry, but placed in a trust so that if I do not marry, the land will become mine on my twenty-fifth birthday."

His jaw dropped. "You own the land?"

Vivian nodded. "And then you will own it after we're married."

"Married?" A parade of fanciful visions of waking up beside her every evening, sharing a house, and making love to her every day marched through his mind. He couldn't stop a smile from forming. "Are you asking for my hand?"

Vivian shook her head and returned his grin. "I am demanding it."

The lock clicked and Madame Renarde swung the cell door open. "You'll have to elope to Gretna Green," the companion said. "I do not think you can acquire a special license."

Rhys caught Vivian as she threw herself into his arms. The bloodthirst reared up, but he suppressed it with the sheer joy in holding her. When his lips touched hers, his dreary cell faded away and he was transported to heaven. Vivian returned his kiss with unchecked hunger. Her low moan was a joyous serenade. Only when he was in danger of becoming aroused in front of Madame Renarde did Rhys regain his senses. With agonizing reluctance, he broke the kiss.

"A journey to Scotland will be dangerous," he said, trying to maintain practicality in the face of being offered his most fervent desire. "And I cannot Change you unless we find a Lord

Vampire willing to legitimize me. I refuse to sentence you to life as a rogue."

"But you *must* marry me!" Vivian's pleading voice tugged at his soul. "I love you, and cannot bear living without you."

"I love you too." Rhys buried his face in her hair. "Which is why I cannot risk your death."

Madame Renarde cleared her throat. "I have an idea."

Rhys and Vivian turned to face the companion. Rhys had assumed that Lord Thornton had been able to banish Renarde's memories. Apparently, he'd failed, but did Thornton know it hadn't worked? If so, what were his plans for her?

"Rhys should leave for Gretna Green immediately." Madame Renarde brought his attention back to the present. "And Vivian and I will leave separately and meet you there. You can then wed, and Vivian can return here to help your niece manage the land in your name. If her uncle still Changes her like he plans, you can write to her when you find a lord vampire to legitimize you and you can reunite then."

Vivian nodded eagerly. "That could work."

Rhys frowned. "But what if Thornton refuses to Change her after helping me escape?"

"Perhaps your new lord will allow you to Change her when you're legitimized," Madame Renarde said. "After all, she'll be your wife."

"What if Lord Thornton catches you and Vivian on your way to Scotland?" As tantalizing as Renarde's plan sounded, Rhys couldn't stop weighing the risks. "What if he kills one or both of you? It's simply too dangerous."

A dreaded voice sounded behind them, crushing Rhys's spirit. "Do you truly believe that I would harm my own blood?" Aldric strode down the stairs. A longsword hung from his hip. "Though I do agree that running off to Scotland is indeed too dangerous. I won't allow it."

"Uncle!" Vivian leapt in front of Rhys, trying to shield him with her body, even as he moved to protect her. "Please, don't hurt him!"

Madame Renarde moved to Rhys's side as well. The foolhardy gesture humbled him.

Rhys pulled both women against him and faced Lord Thornton over Vivian's shoulder. "I am not naïve enough to plead for my life, but I will plead for Vivian, and Madame Renarde, and for Emily. Please, my lord, don't punish them for my attempted escape."

"He didn't try to escape!" Vivian told her uncle. "I tried to free him."

"And I am the one who told her that Rhys was here." Madame Renarde lifted her chin in defiance, but Rhys felt the light tremble of her shoulders. "I picked the locks, and as you overheard, he has refused to go."

Her courage filled Rhys with wonder, but he wouldn't allow Vivian's loyal companion to sacrifice herself. "My lord—"

Aldric held up a hand. "God blast it all, you win!"

Rhys sucked in a breath. "I do?"

"Not you, you bloody knave. Her." Lord Thornton pointed at Vivian and spoke to her. "If I kill this sod, you'll hate me for eternity, as you did when you thought I'd already done the deed. I can't leave him locked in my dungeon either. Which gives me no choice but to legitimize him, loath as I am to do."

Was he dreaming, or was this some sort of cruel jest? Rhys knew he was gaping like a village idiot, but could not close his mouth.

Vivian wrapped her arms around Rhys's waist as if she feared he would be torn away from her side. "Oh, Uncle Aldric, thank you!"

The Lord Vampire of Blackpool heaved a long-suffering sigh. "Even this elopement idea will work in our favor. Your father will want nothing to do with you afterward, and we won't have to worry about London Society or my neighbors here in Blackpool any longer because they will shun you for such a scandalous thing. However, we don't need to bother with a trip to Scotland. I will secure a special license after I legitimize your rogue."

Rhys sank to his knees. "Thank you, my lord."

"I don't want your thanks," Blackpool snarled. "I want to mitigate the damage you've done, and for you to stop causing me trouble."

"You will have my utmost obedience." For the safety of his family, marriage to the woman he loved, and citizenship, Rhys would walk over hot coals if Thornton asked him.

At the moment, Vivian's uncle looked more like he wished to ask Rhys to throw himself off a cliff. "Now that you are no longer a prisoner, there's no need to linger in the dungeon." Aldric turned and waved an impatient hand at the stairwell. "Let us all go inside and have a brandy. Lord, how I wish I could drink more than a little dram."

Still dazed, Rhys rose to his feet and clung to Vivian's hand as they followed the Lord Vampire into the manor. The sight of the bright lanterns, plush carpets, and luxurious furnishings took Rhys aback. For a moment, he felt a twinge of the old hostility at the sight of such wealth. One of those silver candlesticks could have fed Emily and the children for nearly a year.

But Emily and the children would be comfortable now. He could hardly believe it. Rhys would at last be able to make sure of it. He didn't know if Aldric would be generous enough to grant Vivian money as well as land for her dowry, but he did know that as a legitimate citizen of Blackpool, Lord Thornton would grant him some sort of employment.

Thornton settled them in a large sitting room full of plush sofas and overstuffed chairs. When they were seated, he rang for a servant.

"Tea, wine, or whisky?" he asked Vivian and her companion.

"Wine," Vivian said, while Rhys and Madame Renarde opted for whisky.

When the footman arrived, Thornton entranced him with his eyes and led him to Rhys's side. "Normally, my servants are not to be dined upon, however, you need to feed, and I do not want you to bite my niece."

"My control is better than that, but I thank you for your generosity." Rhys inclined his head with gratitude and carefully fed from the footman's wrist. It was so much better than the pig and last night's rat. Still, out of consideration, he drank as little as possible, and was careful to heal the man's wounds with his blood. When he finished, Lord Thornton released the man and ordered their requested beverages.

While they waited, Thornton turned to Madame Renarde. "How in the name of heaven did you manage to deceive me into thinking I'd successfully banished your memories, break into my study, and discover where I was holding Rhys?"

Madame Renarde shrugged. "Old habits. I was a spy, after all, trained by *Le Chevalier* herself."

"Picking the lock on your study was my idea," Vivian said defensively. "I wanted to know if Rhys's niece had received the money and paid the mortgage."

Her uncle regarded her with a chiding expression. "Believe me, I know when mischief occurs in this house, and whose idea it was. I was merely curious as to how your unique companion carried off such impressive feats, rather than wishing to punish her for aiding you."

Madame Renarde spoke. "Thank you for your mercy, my lord. But I still suppose that I am now consigned to join the fold of your kind."

"By law, you should," Thornton said. "However, as you were able to fool me, I think it likely that you will fool other vampires. If you do wish to be Changed, you have that choice."

"Not unless the only other choice is death," Renarde answered. "I have transitioned from living as a man to living as a woman. I do not want to transition into a vampire as well. One double life is enough for me."

The footman returned with the wine for Vivian and whisky for the rest.

"Thank you, Jeffries. You may retire for the remainder of the night." When they were alone, Thornton sipped his whisky and turned to Vivian. "Before we discuss this abominable marriage, you must make a choice. Do you wish for me to Change you, or for him?" His thumb jerked back to point at Rhys as if Thornton couldn't bear to look at him.

Vivian glanced between the two vampires before taking a sip of wine and turning back to her uncle. "I would be more powerful if you did the deed, yes?"

Rhys stiffened with hurt. He'd thought Vivian would choose him.

"Yes. I am two hundred years his senior, so that means more power." Thornton remained expressionless.

"While I do like the idea of having power after being powerless for so long, I will opt with Rhys." Vivian threaded her fingers through his. "I want to share a life with him, his name, and his blood."

"So be it." Though it could have been Rhys's imagination, for a moment it seemed there was a glimmer of hurt in Thornton's steely grey eyes. But when he turned to Rhys, his expression was glacial as ever. "I suppose I had better legitimize you now. Kneel before me."

Rhys slid off the couch to his knees and faced the vampire who would be his new lord.

Thornton stood and placed his hand on Rhys's shoulder. "I, Aldric Cadell, Viscount of Thornton and Lord Vampire of Blackpool accept you, Rhys Berwyn as one of my citizens. Do you solemnly swear to keep my secrets, and obey me for as long as you live?"

"I do so swear," Rhys said.

Aldric bit his finger and held the bleeding digit toward him. "With my blood, your oath is sealed."

Rhys felt a jolt of power as he tasted the Lord Vampire's blood. Power Vivian had rejected in favor of her bond with Rhys.

With the blood oath complete, Aldric bade him to rise. "You are now a citizen of Blackpool and under my protection." Rhys opened his mouth to give thanks, but Lord Thornton's sinister smile gave him pause. "However, just because I've legitimized you and permitted you to marry and Change my niece does not mean I will not make you pay for the havoc you've caused."

"My lord?" Rhys asked with foreboding.

"First, you will not be permitted to be alone with Vivian until after you're married," Aldric said. "Just because you've preempted your wedding night does not mean we shouldn't maintain propriety."

Madame Renarde nodded with approval as Vivian and Rhys exchanged mournful glances.

"That is reasonable." Though he prayed the wedding would be soon. Besides, after days and nights locked in a dungeon, Rhys was content to merely be able to see Vivian and be near her.

"Second," Lord Thornton continued, "You will remain under constant supervision as long as I deem necessary."

Another logical decision, though Rhys knew he'd bristle at having someone breathing down his neck all the time. "With all due respect, my lord, for legitimacy, the security of my family, and having the woman I love by my side, I will endure anything."

"I will hold you to that," Aldric said in an ominous tone. "Now I must give you a tour of the boundaries of the territory as well as have a few more words with you in private before I show you your sleeping quarters. You may bid my niece goodnight before we depart."

Rhys pulled Vivian into his arms. He didn't care if Thornton objected to such intimacy. Right now, he needed the contact with her more than anything.

"I love you," he whispered as he felt her heart beat against his. "I never imagined I could ever be so happy."

"I love you too." She rose up on her toes and kissed him.

As his lips melded with hers, Rhys ignored her uncle's muffled curse. No matter what Lord Thornton put him through, Vivian was worth it.

Epilogue

Six months later

Vivian suppressed a groan as she watched Rhys straining to hold the massive beam in place for the barn. It was mere hours before dawn and her husband had just finished a long shift laboring for her Uncle, repairing a ship that he hardly ever chartered. Uncle Aldric had kept to his word to make Rhys pay for his crimes. He worked Vivian's new husband like a dog.

However, no matter what menial or laborious tasks Aldric put him through, Rhys constantly smiled as if each chore was a reward. His cheer drove her uncle mad, a constant reminder that no matter what he did, Rhys had gotten everything he wanted after all, the return of his family's farm, safety for Emily and the children, legitimacy, and marriage to the woman he loved.

The only times her uncle had abandoned his hostility towards Rhys was for the night he Changed Vivian, and her wedding night.

Rhys had held her tenderly as he'd plunged his fangs into her neck, with uncle standing near, watching the proceedings with visible worry. Vivian had felt pure bliss at Rhys's bite, then ecstasy when he'd brought his bleeding wrist to her mouth and she drank of his rich power.

She ran her tongue along her new fangs and shivered, remembering how painful it was when they'd grown. Both her uncle and Rhys had held her hands and whispered comforting words as she'd writhed in agony. After the pain had come the thirst, which was thankfully assuaged by an unknown man that Uncle brought in.

Her first taste of human blood had been nearly as heavenly as Rhys's. Thank God that her uncle had stopped her before she took too much and killed the poor man. And oh, how fierce her hunger had been for the first few nights. If not for Rhys and Aldric at her side, she may not have been able to avoid the temptation to sink her teeth into every human who came near her. The first days had been awkward as well, joining Rhys and her uncle for the daysleep in the very dungeon in which uncle imprisoned Rhys. He wouldn't even let them share a cell.

She knew that wasn't where uncle normally slept. He'd just wanted to further torture Rhys before the wedding, making the three of them bed down in the same chamber so she and Rhys couldn't make love.

Thankfully, that torment was brief. Uncle Aldric had sent for a special license, which arrived three nights after her transformation, and he immediately summoned a vicar. They'd been wed in a small ceremony at Thornton Manor with only Madame Renarde, Lord Thornton, and his second in command, Bonnie, as witnesses.

Aldric then let the servants spread the word that Vivian's disappearance had been a trip to Gretna Green. The gossip spread throughout Blackpool and now no one ever called on them.

True to Uncle Aldric's prediction, Vivian's father had disowned her after receiving word that she'd eloped with a penniless commoner.

Vivian was quite happy with that outcome, for it gave her more time with Rhys, and to adjust to her new life as a vampire. Once married, Aldric allowed them to move to a house he owned that was only a few miles from Berwyn Farm.

Rhys hadn't been given an official position of employment yet, as Aldric seemed to be enjoying himself with assigning any and every grueling job he could think of. Vivian had a feeling that it would be a few years before Uncle forgave Rhys for abducting her and accepted him as family.

But no amount of icy glares and onerous tasks could dampen Rhys's happiness. Especially now that the farm was being restored, partially with Rhys's own hands. Vivian and Madame Renarde spent much time with Emily and the children, which was a blessing as well as a curse. Emily treated Vivian like a sister, something both women had longed for all their lives. And Vivian fell in love with Jacob and Alice. Playing and reading with the cheerful scamps made her sometimes wish she and Rhys could have children of their own.

Alas, that could never be. And in a few years, she and Rhys would have to leave the family, before it was seen that they did not age. Their only consolation was that when they returned, there would be a new generation to care for.

Leaving Madame Renarde would be difficult as well, but Vivian was comforted to see that her companion had taken to Emily quickly. While Vivian and Rhys slept during the day, Madame Renarde acted as a sort of nanny to Jacob and Alice, teaching them their letters as well as French. She spent more time at the farmhouse than at Vivian and Rhys's home these days.

Rhys broke off Vivian's reverie as the beam he'd lifted dropped into place with a ground-shaking thud.

"You'll wake your cousin and children!" she admonished.

Rhys jumped down from the scaffolding with a triumphant grin and landed on his feet beside her. "That was the last one for tonight." He scooped her up in his arms and kissed her as if they'd been apart for days instead of hours. "Now I wish to return to my honeymoon."

Vivian laughed. "I know it was cruel of Uncle not to give us a few nights in peace after the wedding, but that was months ago. You do not need to keep calling every moment we spend together a honeymoon."

"But it still feels like one," he said as he carried her home in a preternatural burst of speed. He adjusted his grip around her waist to open the door of their small house and carry her over the threshold like he did every night. "Does it not feel like a honeymoon to you anymore?"

Vivian entwined her fingers around his neck and pulled him down for another kiss. "It will if you take me to bed again."

He carried her downstairs and laid her on the bed that was much more comfortable than the cots they'd shared. "I love you, Vivian."

She reached up and caressed his silken hair. "I'll never tire of you saying that."

Rhys chuckled and kissed her neck. "Good, because I will say it for eternity."

Acknowledgements

Thank you to Shana Galen, who read my original outline years ago and gave excellent suggestions. Thank you to Brianna Cowles, for proofreading and Bonnie Paulson, for getting me through a writer's breakdown.

Thank you to Bad Movie Club, for giving me a place to let loose my insanity, and my newsletter readers for your support and kind emails.

Thank you to my friends and family.

Thank you to my son, Micah for being the best son a mom could have, and thank you to Kent for loving me.

Books by Brooklyn Ann

Series by Brooklyn Ann

Scandals With Bite

(Regency paranormal romance)

Bite Me, Your Grace

One Bite Per Night

Bite at First Sight

His Ruthless Bite

Wynter's Bite

The Highwayman's Bite

~~~~~~~~~~~~~~~~~~~~~~~~~~~~~~~~~~~~~~~

Brides of Prophecy

(Paranormal Romance/ Urban Fantasy)

Prequel: Tesemini

Wrenching Fate

Ironic Sacrifice

Conjuring Destiny

Unleashing Desire

Pleading Rapture

~~~~~~~~~~~~~~~~~~~~~~~~~~~~~~~~~~

Hearts of Metal

(Contemporary Romance)

Kissing Vicious

With Vengeance

Rock God

Metal and Mistletoe

Forbidden Song

For excerpts and special content,
visit BrooklynAnnAuthor.com

I love hearing from readers! If you have any questions or
comments, feel free to send me an email!

Contact@brooklynannauthor.com

Made in the USA
San Bernardino, CA
24 April 2018